THE NIGHT STOCKERS

KRISTOPHER TRIANA
&
RYAN HARDING

BAD DREAM BOOKS

ISBN: 978-1-961758-12-4

Cover Art, Design, and Interior Layout by C.V. Hunt

Devil's Food logo by Nick Justus

Edited by K. Trap Jones (first edition edits)

First published by The Evil Cookie Publishing (2021)

Bad Dream Books
P.O. Box 447
Hope, RI 02831

For signed Kristopher Triana books and merchandise, visit:
TRIANAHORROR.COM

"There is no love sincerer than the love of food."
—George Bernard Shaw, *Man and Superman*

"Say you love Satan!"
—Ricky Kasso (a.k.a The Acid King)

for Bryan Smith

metal health has driven us mad

ATTENTION SHOPPERS

AN INTRODUCTION BY KRISTOPHER TRIANA

I owe you an apology.

Well, sort of. It depends on what kind of reader you are. If you've picked up this book expecting something along the lines of my more conventional horror novels, such as *Gone to See the River Man* or *Shepherd of the Black Sheep*, you may be disappointed in your purchase. This is not like those books. Like, not at all. However, if you loved the ghastly, vile depravity of *Toxic Love* and *Body Art*, then you're in the right checkout line.

Still, I feel the strange need to apologize. This book is truly gross and twisted, but when you combine my sickest indulgences with those of fellow Splatterpunk Award-Winning author Ryan Harding, author of *Genital Grinder* and co-author of *Header 3* with the godfather of gore Edward Lee, you get depravity concentrated down to its purest form.

However, I wouldn't consider *The Night Stockers* an extreme horror novel. For me, extreme is all about the tone of the story, the cruelty that it drips. It has to be frightening as well as disturbing. Jack Ketchum's brilliant *The Girl Next Door* is extreme horror at its best, but there are no gallons of guts and bile. The book you hold in your hands is more of a splatterpunk horror novel than an extreme one, but it is also something readers may not expect from a Harding and Triana collaboration.

It's a comedy.

Sure, it's a black comedy. Coal black. Blacker than a crow's asshole. But a comedy nonetheless.

When we first set out to work on something together, we knew we'd be writing passages just to make each other giggle at the absurd grossness. Ryan and I have a shared love for fictional brutality, but it doesn't come from a sense of sadism, but more of a sense of humor for the absurdity of gore taken to ridiculous levels. We knew fans of splatterpunk fiction would see our names together on the cover of a book and would expect nothing less than the gruesome, revolting, and utterly offensive trash fiction we have delivered. But seeing as even the name of this book is a joke, ideally you'll understand what we were going for and won't take it too seriously. It's all in good fun, as long as you're utterly deranged, as Ryan and I hopelessly are.

Perhaps that is why we share an adoration for death metal, something this book highlights rather heavily. It is set in 1992, which was the time of the rise of death metal music, particularly in America. Bands like Cannibal Corpse, Deicide, Carcass, Morbid Angel, Carnage, Entombed, Napalm Death and many more played a big roll in destroying Ryan and I's young, impressionable minds, and we pay tribute to them in this odyssey. Any fan of this particular brand of music will appreciate all the little nods we placed throughout this book. As for you fans of grunge rock…well…we're sorry (but not really).

Some of you may be curious about the setting. We chose a grocery store for our gore bash because Ryan and I both have experience working for different grocery store chains. This shared vocation gave us a lot to work with based on all the insider information we'd gathered, such as the many tools used in these stores that could be made into weapons. We also got to vent a little, as retail jobs can be rather unpleasant (though thankfully not quite as unpleasant as what happens to the characters in this novel). The only obstacle we had to overcome was avoiding making the story reminiscent of Stephen King's *The Mist* or the 1989 slasher cult classic *Intruder*, which are both grocery store themed masterpieces of horror. If anything this book is more like the latter, but we feel we've strayed as far away from that plot as possible without taking things outside the store. Our novel is not a slasher but a siege story, kind of like *Assault on Precinct 13,* only with satanic cashiers, knife-wielding demo ladies, and whiny customers who really have it coming.

Ryan and I hope you'll enjoy your shopping experience. We have a lot of tasty treats at a reasonable price, and we're working on passing our next health inspection, honest! Just be careful if you hear a page for a cleanup on isle three, because that is *not* marinara on the floor.

Kristopher Triana
January 2021

THE
NIGHT
STOCKERS

PROLOGUE
REVOCATE THE AGITATOR

THE SERVICE IN THIS GROCERY store was simply the worst.

This was Becca's first time in Devil's Food but if the manager didn't make this right it would be her last. First the deli staff was too slow to help her. She had more important things to do than wait five whole minutes for them to get their butts in gear. Then, to make matters worse, the woman who served her screwed up an order so simple even a child could have gotten it right.

"This is as thin as I can get it without it falling apart," the peon said, holding up the slice of turkey she'd cut with the deli slicer.

The audacity to speak to Becca like that! She was the *customer*!

Becca glowered. "I'll be the one to tell you when it's thin enough."

So the woman cut it thinner. *Too thin*! It was practically falling apart. As a mother, she wouldn't have Conner and Sophia eating turkey so shaved it came off in clumps. It was simply unacceptable.

Becca maneuvered her cart to the front of the store. Of course it had a wobbly wheel. Yet another thing the manager would have to answer for. Becca's thick thighs jiggled beneath her slacks as she picked up the pace, anger-walking to the front end, her short-cropped hair lining a sour expression. At the first register was a cashier young enough to still be in high school. She wore all black clothes and a nose ring. Unbelievable. Becca glanced at the girl's nametag.

"Laila," Becca said. "You need to go get the manager for me, right away."

Laila gave Becca a look she didn't appreciate.

"Sure, ma'am, just one sec—"

"Do *not* call me, *ma'am*! I'm not an old lady!"

Laila fingered her necklace, a gaudy piece of trash—faux silver with some kind of star pendant. Childish. Stupid.

Becca's face pinched. "I said, *go get the manager.*"

The cashier rolled her eyes—actually *rolled her eyes*— and walked off toward an office near the customer service desk. Becca crossed her arms, not deigning to follow. The manager would have to come to her. Another cashier watched Becca but looked away when she stared back. It seemed everyone here needed an attitude adjustment.

A man came out of the office, better dressed in pressed slacks and a tie. Late thirties. Tall and broad-shouldered with a shaved head. Some men just couldn't bald gracefully, Becca thought. They had to turn it into some sort of macho thing. Pathetic.

"Hello, miss," he said. "My name's Desmond Payne. I'm the store manager."

He held out his hand. Becca only glanced at it, leaving him hanging. She huffed and he withdrew.

She said, "I want you to know that you're doing a terrible job managing this store. You really ought to be fired."

Payne's smile didn't falter. "I'm sorry to hear you're displeased. What can I assist you with?"

"I don't have the time to list all the ways Devil's Food has disappointed me today, so I'll just keep it to the deli. First of all, they're too slow."

"I'm sorry, miss. It's just that it's five-thirty. This is when we get the evening rush, so they're a little busy over there."

"I don't want to hear any excuses!" Becca pointed her finger just inches from Payne's nose. "Now let me finish!"

The manager nodded, still all smiles as he raised both hands in a passive gesture.

"The woman behind the counter," Becca said. "Her name tag says *Eve* and she *claims* to be the deli manager. If that's the case she should be demoted if not fired. She couldn't even slice cold cuts correctly." Becca opened the bag and unfolded the wax paper, revealing the slivers of turkey flesh. "I told her I wanted it *thin*. She seems to only know how to cut it too thick or completely ruin it. I mean, how hard is her job? And how hard is yours for that matter? You're supposed to be running this store, aren't you?"

She pushed the bag of cold cuts into Payne's hands.

The large man nodded. "I understand your frustration, miss—"

"You need to make this right. Do your job."

"Oh, I intend to. Why don't you step into my office and let me prove to you how we value you as a customer?"

Becca sighed. "Fine, but you need to speed this up." She snapped her fingers thrice. "I haven't got all day. I'm meeting with my church group at six."

Leading her, the manager smiled with all of his teeth. They were somewhat yellow beneath his moustache. They stepped inside the office and Payne closed the door behind her. It was a tidy room with a wooden desk, swivel chair, and a Mac SE computer. Behind it was another smaller door like a closet, flanked by filing cabinets. Laila was standing by the desk, as was the deli manager, Eve. Becca's stomach rolled with the bile of hate.

"I don't want to speak to these two," she said.

Payne tossed the bag of cold cuts onto his desk and began cracking his knuckles.

Becca put her hands on her hips. "Look, are you going to give me a gift certificate or free goods or what?"

Payne and his lackeys shared a laugh.

"That's it," she said. "I want the number for Devil's Food's corporate office. I want the owner's name and number. I will have all of your jobs for this!"

Payne stepped forward—a little too close now. Becca retreated.

"Miss," he said, "there's really only one way to get in touch with the owner."

"Then give me—"

Payne silenced her with a punch to the gut. Her flabby belly swallowed his fist and Becca bent over, designer sunglasses flying off the top of her head. Had she not braced herself on the manager's desk, she would have collapsed to the floor.

"Still angry?" Payne asked.

But Becca couldn't reply. The blow had stolen all her wind.

Payne leaned over, face to face. "You're all so bold when you think you have immunity. You bitchy, entitled customers would never dream of talking this way to someone outside of their workplace. You're too cowardly for something like that. Instead you take out your anger on people in the service industry. You think your lousy dollar gives you the right to shit all over them."

When she tried to raise her arms, hoping to plead with him, the two women took her by the wrists and wrenched her arms behind her back like a pair of schoolyard bullies. Spasms of bright pain twitched up her spine.

"Hurts, doesn't it?" Payne asked. "You know what else hurts? That any cranky, privileged, miserable excuse for a human being can walk through the doors of a store or restaurant or hotel and make an innocent employee's life a nightmare. And it's almost always entitled, middle-aged white women like you. And the employee just has to take it because their bosses value the customer's money more than the dignity of the people who make that money for them. I used to have to tolerate that when I worked at Freshway." He reached into his pocket, bringing out a box cutter. "Well, you see... we do things a little differently here at Devil's Food."

The closet door came open, revealing a ghost-white, rail-thin young man with a Mohawk. He wore no shirt, only a covering of ferocious tattoos featuring skeletons, demons, carnage, and naked women behaving in sexually abhorrent ways. Etched into the center of his chest was a large inverted cross. Had she not been so frightened, Becca would have demanded he cover himself up. As the young man came forward, she realized this was not a closet at all, but a passageway of black concrete lined with flickering torches, like a crypt in an old mummy movie. He carried a box. The cardboard was streaked with something dark brown and runny, something liquid that had dried. He placed it on the desk, his smile growing wider, revealing teeth filed-down to points.

Becca almost got out a scream but Payne grabbed her by the ears and head-butted her. Her nose snapped like a toothpick, blood gushing from her nostrils and bubbling over thin lips as she muttered prayers and begged for mercy. Payne replied with the box cutter, opening both cheeks and leaving her entire mouth in ruin.

Laila giggled. "She looks like a Pez dispenser, boss!"

Eve said nothing, but dipped her fingers into one gash and snapped free a strand of Becca's dangling flesh. She sucked it between her lips as if it were a noodle of spaghetti.

The ghoul man held the cardboard box in place.

Payne reached inside. "Thank you, Gore."

The man named Gore did a half bow to his store manager.

"Here at Devil's Food," Payne told Becca, "we have our own core values. Serving our community isn't one of them, and neither is putting up with the unreasonable complaints of diseased cunts like you. Our core values are to make money, take care of our store's family, crush our competition, and please our owner." He removed the deli slicer from the box and placed it on the desk before her. "As I was saying, there's really only one way to reach him… and that's to die."

Becca tried to scream but could only gargle blood. The women slammed her against the desk, bending her over further, and Gore seized her by the neck, slamming her head into the deli slicer and screwing the plate on tight. The pointed teeth that held cold cut roasts in place bit into the side of her head. Despite thrashing, Becca couldn't escape. Sweat bubbled where her breasts met her belly. She found it hard to breathe.

Eve switched places with Gore and gripped the handle of the slider. She pressed the green button and the slicer blade began to spin, as close to Becca's left eye as her finger had been to Payne's nose when she'd first complained. Gore and Laila held her as Eve pushed Becca's head forward, the saw spinning into what was left of her cheek, smooth and sharp. Payne was still giving Becca his best customer service smile as Eve sliced away, circles of tissue sluicing through the machine until it began to grind against her skull.

Eve stopped. Payne reached beneath Becca's mutilated head and lifted up a perfectly circular sliver of her face for her to see.

"What do you think, miss?" he asked. "Is this fucking *thin* enough?"

Becca's tears salted her wounds, so she closed her eyes.

The staff of Devil's Food fell upon her, their box cutters held high.

SOME TOWN IN AMERICA
1992

CHAPTER ONE
HATING LIFE

MILA HAD A GREAT SET of tits.

Fenton snapped his gum, watching her unload a tray of fresh pies from the oven. He'd like a piece of *her* pie—that was for damned sure. Kyle in grocery had dated Mila for a while and it pissed Fenton off to no end. Dude had been an honor roll pussy in high school, hitting the books and kissing ass. He didn't deserve her. The thought of anyone planting their face between those magnificent mammary glands made Fenton want to kick throats, though. If he couldn't have them, nobody should. Word around the store was Mila was having breast reduction surgery next month, even though she was only twenty—such was the glory of those luscious hooters. He hoped she would reconsider.

There were also rumors she was a virgin. But that was the thing about working in a grocery store. Rumors and gossip spread like STDs. Freshway was no different.

There were no secrets here. It was one of the many reasons Fenton hated this fucking place. Sure, there were some fine pieces of ass (on top of Mila there was Stephanie the teen slut cashier, and

Darla in produce prep had been nice-looking before she'd gotten knocked up), but it hardly made up for having to deal with Todd. The store manager was a real Napoleon, both in ego and stature. His expectations were too high as it was; now he was demanding even more.

"Are you even listening?"

Fenton looked back to Todd. "Huh?"

The store manager's eyebrows drew together. "Spit out that gum."

Fenton sighed and spit the Big League Chew into his hand. Todd crossed his arms, trying to look more impressive with his new platform dress shoes. Despite the added height, Fenton could still see the bald spot at the crown of his boss's grayed head.

"Look, Mr. Brown," Fenton said, "I just don't think I can do it."

"And why is that?"

Fenton bit his lip, wishing he'd had advance notice of this. It would have given him more time to come up with an excuse.

Todd said, "Look, as a full-timer, you were hired with open availability. If I need you to do an overnight, then you have to do it. Otherwise, you know where the damned door is."

"But, Mr. Brown—"

"You're the janitor. I need my store to be spotless."

Fenton hated when Todd called it that. *My store.* It wasn't like Todd owned Freshway.

"I know I'm the janitor, but why can't I just keep cleaning during the day?"

"I want this place deep cleaned. I can't have our guests shopping while the floors are wet and everything is taken apart. I want my store to look like it's the grand opening—*every day*. It's one overnight, Fenton. Everyone else is on board. If you're not a part of our team, maybe this isn't the job for you."

A knot twisted in Fenton's chest. It sucked to both hate and need this job at the same time. "Sorry, Mr. Brown. I'm on team Freshway, for sure. Just let me know what time to be here."

Todd flashed a fake, condescending smile and patted Fenton's arm. "Atta boy. We'll be here at ten p.m. We'll head out at six in the morning when the bakers arrive for their morning shifts."

Todd walked off toward the deli, barking at them that he wanted another load of rotisserie chickens to go in the oven. Yesterday he'd barked at them for making too many; today there weren't enough.

Typical cocksucking Todd. He always had to find fault, always had to know better than anyone else. Fenton gave his boss the finger behind his back and snuck another glance at Mila as she stretched to reach an oven rack, her shirt tight against *her* rack. Fenton bit his bottom lip. Sure, Mila was a tad chubby, but in all the right places.

He hummed Biz Markie's "Just a Friend" and wheeled his mop and bucket to the front of the store, planning to attack the bathrooms. He passed by the display of Butterfingers he'd set up earlier, the cardboard standee of Bart Simpson on his skateboard with the catch phrase "Nobody better lay a finger on my Butterfinger" rising out of his mouth in a speech bubble. Fenton certainly liked it better than the life-sized Bob Saget standee over in the magazine isle, a promotion for *TV Guide*. That thing gave him the willies.

He passed by Bart by chance, but passed by Stephanie on purpose. The young blonde was twirling her hair around one finger, hip cocked inside stonewash jeans tighter than skin.

"Hey, Steph."

She glanced his way, the atomic wave of her bleached bangs a good four inches above her head. "Hey, Fenton. Nice mop bucket."

She always teased like this, and always winked too. Fenton noticed she was chewing gum, but Todd hadn't said anything about it. The store manager was in his fifties but let a high school girl manipulate him with doe eyes and perky titties.

"Nice necklace," Fenton said.

She fingered the ankh symbol pendant, some Egyptian trend that had caught on. If Fenton were still in high school he might have been wearing one himself, but his glory days were over. In the six years since he'd graduated, other punks had taken his place as the town bad boy.

"You doin' the overnight too?" he asked.

"Oh, you'd just love to spend the night with me, wouldn't you?" She raised an eyebrow. "Right, Fenton?"

He laughed. "You lousy, jailbait cock tease."

"Um, excuse me, but I turned eighteen last month, and I am *so* not a tease. Ask anybody."

"No shit? Eighteen?"

"Yup. I'm legal."

She winked to add emphasis.

"Shit." He leaned on the conveyor belt of the register between them. "That changes everything, baby."

"*Pfft.* In your dreams, toilet boy."

"Oh, I see. You don't want to date the lowly janitor?"

She smirked, still teasing. "Duh."

"Yeah, you'd rather have people in power. Guys like Todd."

"Ugh! That is so bogus. You're gross, Fenton!"

"*Me?* From what I hear *you're* the one who's nasty."

She took a rubber band from the box of pens and slingshot him with it. "Boys always say that when they want what they can't get." She put her hands on her hips, smacking gum with her tongue. "Anyway, what's this shit about an overnight?"

"Fuckin' Todd's making us do it. It's all 'cause of that new place across the street. Devil's Food. It's been hurting business—"

A voice behind him cut Fenton off. "And they took half our staff."

Fenton turned to see Booker. The man's face bore the exhaustion of working seven days a week now that he was the only assistant manager. Their second assistant, Desmond, had been one of the many staff members to desert Freshway for Devil's Food, taking a significant pay raise and moving up to a store manager position. Fenton wished he'd gone too, having heard of all the crazy perks they offered. Maybe he should have told Todd to cram it and walked across the street to greener pastures.

Primo gash over there, too.

"Being short staffed is the main reason we have to do the overnight," Booker said. "We have to catch up on things."

Fenton shrugged. "Todd says he wants to clean the store from top to bottom."

"That's right. Sales have been soft since Devil's Food opened up. We've gotta do whatever we can to compete."

Fenton nodded. He liked Booker okay. More than he liked Todd Brown, at least. The guy was the opposite from Todd in every way, being a tall black man who was easygoing and actually cared about the people he worked with. At least he was honest and upfront with them when it came to stuff like this.

"Todd says *we'll* be here at ten," Fenton said. "As if *he's* really going to be here at night. He never even does closing shifts, man. He makes you do them all."

Booker looked away, not arguing this fact but also not bad-mouthing the boss. "Look, nobody wants to work an overnight, but sometimes it's necessary. I'm sure Todd will be here for at least some of it."

Stephanie scoffed. "Yeah, right. He'll be here for like half an hour. I can do it though. I could use the extra cash. I know I just run a register but I can clean and price things and stock shelves 'n shit."

"Okay. We're taking whoever we can get. I appreciate it, Steph."

Stephanie flashed a warm smile at the assistant manager. It wasn't her usual flirty flash of cherry lips, the one she used to get whatever she wanted from men. This smile was genuine, inviting. That she wanted to fuck Booker was common knowledge throughout the store. He was in his early forties, but that didn't seem to deter her. She'd talk about her affinity for older men to anyone who would listen. It was all that gave Fenton hope he had a chance with her, being at least in his twenties. Of course, Booker ignored Stephanie's advances, always keeping his interaction with subordinates professional. That was one of the things Fenton didn't like about the guy. He was too much of a Captain America goodie-goodie. In Booker's place, Fenton would have crammed his dick in every hole he could fit.

A customer approached and Booker waved her over with his best customer service greeting. She bellied up to the register, looking like an escapee from the old folks home. Fenton despised the elderly. They were always asking for help finding things. *Milk is in the dairy cooler, you crone. Is this really your first time in a grocery store?*

"I can take of you right here," Stephanie said to the old bat.

Fenton wiggled his eyebrows at Stephanie's choice of words. She gave him a sly look and then returned her attention to the customer, ringing up prune juice and Tums. Fenton headed for the bathrooms, as if he hadn't put up with enough shit today already.

Fucking Todd.

~

Ruby had to use a pair of pliers to adjust the temperature on the hot plate. You'd think the company would invest in a new one, but apparently the tools needed to do her job were too much to ask. It was irritating, but she understood why the supply budget had shrunk. Business had been slow. As the "demo lady," she saw firsthand how Freshway's customer count dwindled. She found herself making too much food for sampling, having been used to a production that was no longer required. She could cut her samples in half and still have enough to make it through a Saturday afternoon.

THE NIGHT STOCKERS

As the stew beef sizzled in the pan, Ruby cut up the sourdough baguettes and laid out all the serving trays. She made sure the trash bin was in plain sight so the customers wouldn't leave the used sample cups all over the store. Just as she was looking for a box of napkins, Booker came over to her station with one. He was always sweet like that. Ruby figured he gave extra care to her because she was elderly, but she certainly didn't mind. Her back hurt a lot less since he'd thought to get her a comfort mat to stand on during her shifts.

"Smells good," he said.

"I just hope people come around to eat it. I hate to just stand here."

"It's been a slow week, but I think people will start coming back once the excitement of the new store fades."

"Well, let's hope so, Booker. Let's hope so."

He stepped in closer, his voice low. "Listen. I hate to tell you this, but Todd wants to cut back your hours."

The color left her cheeks. "What? No!"

"Ruby—"

"He can't do that! I need this job. You know I'm alone." She told the story so many times, but always felt the need to repeat it. "My Fred's been gone eleven years this December and we lost our son Jack in Vietnam. I don't have anybody else to take care of me."

"I know. But don't worry, okay? I'm looking out for you. He wants to cut back on demo hours because of the low customer turnout—"

"That little bast—"

"—but I don't know how he expects that to help bring customers back. People love free samples. I tried to convince him but... well..." Booker shrugged. "Anyway, I managed to get you some hours, but I wanted to ask how you felt about them first."

"I'll take whatever I can get. I need that money. My prescriptions alone..." She trailed off, feeling short of breath just thinking about it. "What can you give me?"

"It's night work. After we've closed."

"Demos at night? That doesn't make any sense."

"No, no. It'll be packing work. You'll be putting bulk nuts and candy into plastic tubs, and weighing and stickering them. We're doing an overnight tomorrow and I can use your help."

"Oh, goodness. An *overnight?*"

"I know it's not an ideal shift. But I'll get you a chair to sit in while you do it, and you can leave whenever you feel like you need to."

Ruby tossed the beef in the pan. "Oh, I'm sure Todd will just *love* that."

"Let me handle Todd. If you want the hours, I'll give them to you. I'm offering them to you first, Ruby, but if you don't want them, I understand."

She patted his hand. "Oh, Booker. You're too good to us, you know that? I'll take the hours. I don't like it, but I need them. Thanks for looking out for me."

"No, problem. Hang in there, Ruby. Things will turn around for us. I have a feeling we're all gonna be just fine."

~

Darla took a deep breath. She shifted where she sat, the wooden bench rather unkind to her hemorrhoids. It was one of the many things no one had warned her about getting pregnant. She hadn't even told Mark about them. Having this swollen belly, it was hard enough to feel sexy in her husband's eyes without telling him she had sores on her ass.

Todd's voice came over the intercom, shrill and annoying. "Darla, come to the office. Darla, office."

Christ, *of course* he would call her in while she was on break. If she were back in the cooler coring pineapples, he'd never pull her away from that and give her a moment off her feet in the office. These little meetings of his always had to be on *her time*. She struggled getting up. It was becoming harder to rise out of a sitting position on her own. She blew her hair away from her eyes and balanced herself against the wall, feeling older than she'd ever had before.

My second husband and my first child. What a difference a year can make.

Darla headed to the manager's office, waddling like Danny De-Vito in the movie she and Mark had gone to see last weekend, *Batman Returns*. Todd was punching numbers on the adding machine, glasses low on his pointy nose, his face vulture-like. Stacked on the desk was a pile of invoices and the hardboiled eggs he always ate for lunch. He didn't even acknowledge her as she sat across from him. Basic manners were too much to ask of this asshole.

"You wanted to see me, Mr. Brown?"

Todd continued to scowl at his adding machine. He finally spoke but without bothering to look at her. "Darla, I need you to do an overnight tomorrow."

She blinked. "A what?"

"Ten at night until five or six in the morning. We need to get caught up in produce. The wet wall needs to be cleaned out and the tables need to be culled. We can't have our fruits and vegetables getting soft and moldy."

"Okay, but—I mean, this is really last minute. And I can't work an overnight. I mean, look at me." She gestured to the beach ball of her belly. "I have to stay on a consistent sleep cycle. The baby—"

"Yeah," he said, cutting her off. "But you've missed a great deal of work already, due to your... *condition*."

Darla had to bite her tongue at that one.

"I've let a lot slide with you," Todd said, looking at her now. "You get away with far more than I'd allow any of my other employees."

"I took time off because I had complications with my pregnancy. It was for my health as well as the baby's. I had a doctor's note and—"

"And I abided by it. But now you've been cleared to work. This is *my* store, understand? And I need you to do an overnight. You're full time, which means you have to have open availability."

"Come on, Todd, I've done lots of early morning inventories as well as late night holiday prep. You should know me enough by now to know I'd never complain about doing an overnight if I wasn't pregnant. Besides, it's not like I can stock product or get down on my knees and clean shelves."

Todd leaned back in his chair and examined his fingernails. "There's other work you can do. I need people here, Darla. I need *bodies*. You know the produce department. It has to be presentable. Heck, the word *fresh* is in the name of the store. Produce is the first thing our guests see when they walk in. It needs to feel like a warm hug."

God, he could lay it on thick. Thick as vomit.

"I'm sorry, Todd, but I just can't do it."

He was silent, his eyes narrowed, drilling anxiety into Darla's heart.

"That's where you're wrong," he finally said. "You *can* do it, you just don't want to. But I don't care about that. This is your *job*, missy. I schedule according to the needs of my store. What you want is secondary. Now, your schedule for tomorrow has been changed to an overnight. Either you suck it up and come in, or I mark you down as an unexcused absence for refusing to work your shift. I think you know what'll come after that."

Darla's shoulders tightened. "You'd really fire me over this?"

"That's all up to you, isn't it? Either you want the job or you don't, missy."

"I've worked here almost five years—twice as long as you. I have a lot invested in this store."

"Well then, act like it." He checked his watch. "It's been half an hour. Your break's over. I want the veggie kits packed up before you leave today. Don't take off without asking me first."

The fax machine bleated, startling her. Todd's attention fell to the paper feeding through, not offering to help Darla as she maneuvered out of the chair.

"Remember what I said about tomorrow," he called out.

Darla went back to work.

~

"We hope to see you here at Freshway again soon," Kyle told the frizzy-haired woman, slamming the hatch of her minivan and muting the ear-splitting antics of her two hellions in the backseat. One of the little bastards had ripped open a box in the cereal aisle, which Kyle cleaned up because of course it happened on Fenton's lunch break. Maybe they'd tear into the groceries he just stowed away and scatter shit everywhere on their ride home. He bet Mom would show a more animated reaction than the blank smile and shrug she gave him when he showed up with a broom to sweep the mine field of Cap'n Crunch.

Kyle perked up when he turned to find Frizzy staring into her open wallet. She'd never tipped him before, but there was a first time for everything.

She snapped the wallet closed and smiled. "Okay, just wanted to make sure she gave me the correct change. Bye now."

"Bye," he said with the requisite false cheer. He couldn't say Devil's Food dried up his tips because only one out of every ten people threw him a buck in the best of times. Todd didn't even want the staff accepting tips—a new rule.

He steered her cart over to the return rails where shoppers stowed their buggies in the lot—or where they were supposed to, anyway. Several stood abandoned in random spots because lazy customers wouldn't push their carts another five yards. Given the chance to self-govern for the good of society as a whole, people always showed their selfishness.

Kyle gathered the carts now, wondering how they added up like this with business being tortoise slow. Across the street, Devil's Food looked like a car dealership in comparison. No one orphaned their buggies, either. It made Kyle wish he didn't work at Freshway.

That wasn't anything new, though.

When he started this job part-time he was in college with a major in physical therapy. He'd expected to finish the undergraduate program by twenty-two. The last-minute heroics which served him so well in his high school classes failed to translate to college, however, and within two years he lost scholarships and a grant due to poor academic performance. He went full-time at Freshway, and his one-year break turned into four with an even faster proliferation than those shitty *Witchcraft* sequels showing up on the video shelf.

Even when everything went south with Mila, he put no serious effort into moving on. He'd resigned himself to making only seventy-eight cents more per hour than when first hired, in a job where he wasn't supposed to even think about taking a break or punching out for the night until he cleared the lot.

He adjusted his Freshway baseball cap and wrestled the line of carts through the automatic doors of the entryway, past the gumball machines and the stock car kiddie ride with an OUT OF ORDER sign. The metal clashed as he drove his payload into the waiting line.

"Thanks, Kyle," Booker said, on his way to the room past the time clock, where they counted down the tills. "Take your lunch whenever you're ready."

Kyle nodded, emerging from the entryway in time to spot Mila passing the checkout lanes in a huff. He verified no action at the registers—and, more importantly, no Todd—and hurried to catch her.

"Hey," he said to her back.

Mila stopped near a table with containers of cookies and cupcakes. A kaleidoscope of emotions played across her face when she saw him. He felt his own pangs of desire and frustration, a recap of the months of their relationship. One more unfulfilled dream.

"Something wrong?" he asked.

She looked flushed, her mouth drawn thin and brow furrowed, blue eyes reluctant to settle on him. She kept her blonde hair pulled back, and it bounced behind her as she glanced around the store, maybe seeking an escape. A gold cross necklace caught the fluorescents and seemed to glow against her chest.

A talisman against the sinful ways of the flesh, he thought bitterly.

"Todd wants us to work overnight tomorrow," she said, almost inaudible.

"Why? Does he need a whole team to sweep up all the tumbleweeds?"

Mila frowned, not understanding.

"Because it's like a ghost town in here," Kyle amended.

"Oh." She smiled weakly.

The past few weeks, they'd tried to keep their respective distance. The break-up added a new level to the misery of working at Freshway, with Kyle forced to think about it each time he saw Mila or heard her laugh through the white noise of every third customer telling him not to crush their bread or eggs.

"Todd really said an overnight?"

She nodded. "He said something about us needing to catch up."

There was no reason in the world why Todd would want him and Mila to catch up, but for a moment Kyle couldn't come up with any other interpretation to what she just said. "Wait, you and me?"

"No!" She sounded alarmed. The smile vanished. "A bunch of us have to help."

"Oh." Kyle gave his lame *courtesy clerk* vest an adjustment it didn't need. "That's weird. Did you have big plans tomorrow night or something?"

He didn't mean to suggest she had a date, but somehow it came off that way to his own ears. She heard it that way too, judging by the way she twitched.

"It's really not a good time," she said.

Kyle hoped she meant the overnight and not this conversation. He knew he should bail out now, but wanted to keep it going. God, he missed her.

"I thought maybe the Creep said something to you." The name from their prior shared language just came out. It didn't seem to resonate with her anyway.

"No," she said.

"Okay."

Fenton was "the Creep." Mila caught him ogling her countless times, as well as the other women of Freshway. She even caught him scoping Ruby's backside once with a contemplative expression, and they'd made jokes about Fenton wanting samples of the elderly lady herself. Kyle started noticing all the leering more and more after that.

Maybe it was the paranoia of raw emotion, but he could swear Fenton kept smirking at him since he and Mila broke up, relishing his failure. Kyle knew him from their high school days, where Fenton cultivated a personality like Judd Nelson in *The Breakfast Club,* minus any of the charisma. To have to work at the same place as that jack-off only underlined for Kyle the nadir of his twenty-four years. He should have run back to college the day Fenton showed up.

Kyle forced a smile. "Well, Todd didn't say anything to me about any overnight. I'm off tomorrow, so maybe he didn't mean me."

The intercom clinked and Todd said, "Kyle, come to the office. Kyle, office."

"Fuck me!" Kyle said.

Mila cocked an eyebrow at the choice of words, looking a bit sadder. "Well, thanks for checking on me. I'll see you."

"Okay. See ya." He watched her curvy shape float over to the bakery counter, jeans swishing.

No crucifix in the way on this side, at least.

He turned away when he realized he wasn't much better than Fenton right now, lusting from afar. Still wanting her, as much as when they were together—more now that she was gone.

Kyle sighed and headed for the front of the store to Todd's office. The full ramifications of an overnight sank in, particularly how he would also be expected to work the closing shift the day after. Devil's Food putting this store out of business might be the best thing for him. A fresh start from Freshway, and maybe the only way to save him from himself.

~

"Hey, Mila!"

Antonio offered her a big smile and wave as he walked toward the front to clock out for break. He didn't bother to take off his meat coat, a white smock like a doctor's or painter's. It was benefitting in its way. The guy was an artist with his meat cleaver. She'd cut off her fingers if she tried to use one as fast as he did. Though in the shadow of fifty, he might be the most physically fit employee at Freshway. He even played some sports in an adult league in town, including soccer (which he called "football"), baseball and tennis.

Mila liked his accent. It made everything he said sound flowery, charmed.

"Hey, Antonio."

He paused at the bakery counter where she stood. "I been hearing the boss man call others to the office, yeah? We are not closing, are we?"

"No. He's just telling everyone we have to help out tomorrow night, after hours."

Antonio ran both palms through his bushy black hair, a dismayed look on his face. "But I have to be here the morning after."

"Maybe Todd won't make you," she said, not believing it. Darla had given Mila an earful on her way back from Todd's office, and if he was making a pregnant woman help out, Antonio didn't stand a chance.

"*Ese chupa vergas,*" he muttered, shaking his head. She didn't know what that meant, and should probably keep it that way.. He reached for the coat pocket where he stuck his cleavers and knives, and frowned to find it empty. Break time regulations. "You are still taking classes, yes?"

"Yeah. Wish I had the summer off, but I can get my bachelor's next year if I go every semester."

"What was major again?"

"Education."

"Oh, yes. You want to teach."

"Yeah, in the early grades." She smiled. "Get them before they're lost."

"I think you will be good with that." He waved. "I am going for smoke. I will see you."

"Bye."

Mila verified Fenton wasn't lurking anywhere in sight, then arched her back with her hands on her hips and stretched. Working the bakery counter shouldn't result in so many aches and pains, but back problems plagued the women in her family. She planned to be the first one of them to do something about it with her breast reduction, having saved up for it.

She pressed the cross between her thumb and index finger, which always comforted her, centered her. She wanted to feel it with her skin before she sheathed her hands in plastic to handle the dough.

Todd and Kyle knocked her out of sorts with a 1-2 punch of the unexpected. The timing of the overnight couldn't be any worse. She'd planned to go on a comfort mission tomorrow evening at the home of Becca Foster, a member of her church group who hadn't returned home last night. She couldn't imagine what her family was going through, but praying together would help. Becca could be a tad abrasive—even downright obnoxious—and was always over-zealous at the prospect of damnation for any nonbelievers, but she and her family showed up every Sunday and loved the Lord.

It surprised Mila that Becca would go somewhere with *Devil* in the name, but Devil's Food offered lower prices and Becca liked to pinch pennies. The offering plate didn't get any heavier after making a pass on the Fosters' pew. That was between them and God, though.

Mila wanted to ask off early so she could accompany the church group to Becca's house, but not only would she have to work her full shift tomorrow, she'd have to stay all night long too. She'd be off too late tonight to drop by, and had to finish a research paper for Biology II—if she could even focus. Her conversation with Kyle didn't bode well for that. Lately her thoughts took her down such painful paths. Faith taught her life didn't magically become smooth sailing when you accepted God's plan, only that you could endure the trials in store. That must be what this was.

Mila loved Kyle and thought he loved her too, but he wasn't willing to prove it by waiting until they were married to have sex. She forgave Kyle his indifference to religion and lack of ambition, but he wouldn't meet her halfway. He couldn't understand the sanc-tity she placed on her purity, or why she thought satisfying him with her hand or mouth corrupted that too. He also didn't seem to grasp the burden it placed on her. Mila wasn't asexual—far from it. She was human, sorely tempted like anyone else, and not above keeping the showerhead between her legs until that wonderful heat erupted all through her. She tried not to give in to those urges, though, to save herself for all the pleasures which would reward her patience.

It was hard sometimes, though. She had the connection with Kyle, wanted to give herself to him some day, but he bailed on her when she was steadfast about their premarital abstinence. She wasn't going to change her mind after a few more months, no mat-ter how good his hands and lips felt on her breasts. He called her refusal "medieval" and said other hurtful things to her that last night. She should have found another job and spared them both the pain of seeing each other, but she was weak, and still hoped he might change his mind.

It wasn't doing either of them any good to stay here together, though. Mila might have to be strong for both their sakes and go. She just hoped she would be ready when the time came.

Fenton rolled the mop bucket over to her side of the store. He leered at her as he did so, and angled his head to where he could still watch her while he shoved the mop back and forth in front of him. She couldn't wait until he ran out of floor and vanished down another aisle. He could get back to that *Infinity War* comic book she caught him reading when he should have been working, and keep his eyes off her.

Mila sighed when she looked at the clock. She still had half her shift to go.

Please, God, get me through this day... through this whole week, for that matter.

~

Antonio sliced into the shoulder clod. It was nice and fresh. The ground chuck would be good today. Taking pride in his work, in the trade he'd mastered, Antonio was very particular about the meat he accepted from the warehouse. Todd often yelled at him for refusing shipment and leaving certain items out of stock, but Antonio would rather have holes in his meat case than product that would spoil the same night the customer brought it home, or red meat that wasn't marbled enough to make it worth the cost. If it were up to him, Freshway would only carry prime beef, but if the company could cut corners, it did.

At least he convinced Todd to let him carry some prime steaks. Sure enough, they became an immediate hit with customers. When regional management came by to congratulate their store on the wise move, Todd took all the credit, telling the higher-ups it was all his idea, saying it right in front of Antonio. If he didn't need the job so bad, he would have asked Todd to step outside.

But he did need the job. He had to take care of his wife, children and sick mother. At least Mamá could watch the children while he and his wife Nelly worked, saving them money on sitters.

He also liked the job—just not his boss. Being a butcher brought him satisfaction, even pride. He loved everything about meat and engaged the customers with genuine passion. A good team of meat cutters worked under him, and by and large his coworkers were friendly. He'd found some Americans less than welcoming when he'd first moved here from the Dominican Republic, but felt no such hostility among the staff at Freshway. Even Todd, prick though he was, didn't show any racial prejudice. If he were a bigot it would be hard to tell, seeing how he treated everyone like dog shit. Only their old assistant manager, Desmond, seemed to resent an immigrant managing the meat department, but he was gone now. Knowing he ran Devil's Food, Antonio would never defect to the place, despite the higher pay for certified meat cutters.

With Nelly working nights at the hospital, he would have to call Mamá, make sure she was well enough to watch the kids tomorrow night. His son Roberto was in his first year of college, but his daughters were eleven and nine. The oldest, Bella, kept pressing to be babysitter, but it would be a few more years at least, and even when she was old enough, her sister Emilia would have a fit about her being in charge.

He smiled just thinking about them all. His family was his everything.

To hell with Todd, he thought. The boss couldn't bring Antonio down. Not when he really had it all.

~

Stephanie caught him in the break room alone, upstairs where they stored the dry goods. You had to walk through metal shelves stacked with supply boxes to get to the table. Kyle sat with his chair titled back against the soda machine, listening to his Walkman. Stephanie recognized the muffled sound of "Smells Like Teen Spirit." In a year's time Nirvana's catchy tune had become the defining anthem of Generation X.

She hated it.

But she didn't hate Kyle. In fact, she lusted for him almost as much as she did Booker. He lacked the bad boy rudeness that often drew her to the worst possible guys, but he had a firm body, his manual labor as a stocker adding size to his arms, and being on the local softball team had put steel in his buns. He had the face of Jason Priestley and the ass of Luke Perry, and she wanted to nibble on both. Now that he and Mila were caput, that fanny was up for grabs—literally.

Stephanie came up behind him and ran her hand through his hair. He turned to face her and when he saw who it was he looked disappointed, then took his headphones off and gave her a smile out of politeness.

Probably was hoping for Tits McGee instead, she thought.

Clearly he carried a torch for his ex, but Stephanie was confident she could take his mind off of Mila. If the rumors were true, she only had to give the poor guy what his girlfriend had been denying him, something she was happy to provide.

"Hey, cutie," she said, sitting down next to him, her chair backwards. She leaned over so her v-neck shirt would offer him a glimpse of the goodies inside. "What's up?"

"Nothin' much."

"Jamming out to some tunes?"

"Yeah. Just waiting for the time to clock back in."

She raised an eyebrow. "Oughta get some Guns 'N Roses. Some Ratt and Skid Row, dude. Ditch that whiny Cobain crap and learn how to party."

He smirked. "Hey, I know how to party."

Now it was she who smirked. "Prove it."

She stared him down and slid her hand over his thigh, scratching gently at his jeans, making exciting little kitten noises with her nails. She pushed her tongue through her gum, giving it a little ghost costume, then snapped it at him and giggled. Kyle watched her, trying and failing to hide his arousal at the sight of her mouth's handiwork.

"Come on," she said. "Prove it."

"Prove what?"

"Prove you know how to party."

"How do you expect me to do that?"

Stephanie looked to the bathroom door. She wiggled her eyebrows. Kyle raised his.

"Come on," she said, taking his hand.

He got to his feet, chuckling. "What? You got a joint?"

She didn't answer. She just led him into the one-toilet bathroom and locked the door behind them. She reached to his crotch and found his cock semi-hard. His eyes went wide and she giggled again, a Lolita seductress.

"Looks like you're the one with the joint," she said, giving him a squeeze.

"Whoa... Steph..." He smiled nervously. "We can't just... I mean..."

She took the gum from her mouth, stuck it to the wall next to graffiti claiming *Todd Sux,* and shut up Kyle's hesitations with a

French kiss. Their tongues intertwined for a moment, but then he resisted.

"I shouldn't..." he said, "I mean, I can't."

"C'mon, Kyle. You know you want me as much as I want you. I'm legal now—it's open season on this pussycat."

She kissed him again, harder this time, pushing his back into the wall and rattling the mirror. The paper towel dispenser popped open and the roll unwound. Brushing her cheek against his, she felt the scratch of his five o' clock shadow and it just turned her on all the more. God, she dug guys who were older than her. They were men, not the mere boys Polk High School offered. She pulled at the button of his jeans, popping them open, and with her other hand she unzipped his fly. His body pulsed in response, all his blood rushing to one area, but still he tried to slither away like a doubtful worm.

"Steph... we can't do this."

She breathed into his ear. "We can do whatever we want. *You* can do whatever you want... *to me.*"

"It's just that... well, Mila..."

"She's your *ex*, Kyle. You've gotta over her, so why don't you let me get under you? C'mon. I'll do all the things she never would."

She slipped her hand beneath the band of his underwear and clutched the now fully hard penis. He was bigger than she'd expected. Her panties grew damp and she grazed one leg up, pushing against him, grinding.

"We can't bang at work!" Kyle said in a whisper-shout.

She licked his lips. "At least let me suck your dick."

Kyle sighed. "Ohhh boy... oh, jeez..."

Before he could object again she bent over and slipped the head of his cock into her mouth, putting her samurai tongue to good use. Already Kyle's legs were trembling. She took him in deeper and he throbbed between her cheeks like a bratwurst on the grill. His breaths came out in shudders, moans aflutter. She had him now. She was sure of it. Leaning back up, she pulled her top off, revealing the black, lacey bra (she'd filled out to a B-cup this past year) and undid her belt. The bathroom was tight, but he could bend her over the sink. They could watch themselves in the mirror! They'd just have to do it quietly, if possible. But in the time it took for her to roll down those extra-tight stonewash jeans, Kyle had zipped up his own.

"Sorry," he said. "It's just that I'm still with Mila… I mean, well, sort of."

She rolled her eyes. "So what? She doesn't have to know, right?"

He looked at the floor. "Yeah, but *I'll know.*"

Stephanie's eyebrows drew closer together. She wasn't used to this kind of faithfulness in a guy, having never seen it before—*not once*. She was sure every dude she'd ever dated had cheated on her, and she'd stolen more boyfriends than she'd had for herself. Her old man fucked around behind her mom's back so much she'd become a lush to numb away the sting of betrayal, avoiding having to mourn their marriage and dodging a divorce that would force her to go back to working again. Wasn't monogamy just a bunch of chick flick bullshit? Didn't all boys think with their little heads first, not their big ones, and certainly not their hearts?

Kyle checked his Swatch watch. "Shit. I gotta punch in. You know how Todd gets about lunch breaks. Such a douche."

Stephanie resigned to the lost cause and pulled up her jeans, taking a deep breath in order to squeeze back into them. She fumbled with her shirt but said nothing.

"Don't be bummed," Kyle said. "It's not you. You're super hot. Any guy would be lucky to be with you. I'm talking jackpot lucky."

As she got into her shirt she looked in the mirror to fluff the tidal wave of her metalhead hair.

"No shit, Einstein," she said. "Just don't come crying to me when Sandra Dee won't give you so much as a tug job."

"Steph…"

But she'd already pushed past him.

CHAPTER TWO
REVEL IN FLESH

ALARIC LOOKED LIKE MOST ANYONE in a regional managerial position—pallid skin, withering expression, appropriately soulless eyes. The black cowl might be uncharacteristic, but appropriate attire for him, and strangely formal with the nametag pinned to his breast. Despite dressing for an occult ceremony, the inspection proceeded efficiently, business-like, like a visit from the health department. He scratched notes on a clipboard as they walked.

"We've been pleased with your earnings," Alaric said. "Good numbers, though that's to be expected from a new chain."

Desmond tried to remain stoic. His "metal face," as he called it. He played up the glad hand for the customers, but Alaric was no fool and wouldn't appreciate it. They made their rounds in the store. Devil's Food had closed half an hour ago and only key staff remained.

"The real test will be when the honeymoon's over," Alaric continued.

In the deli, Eve busied herself in front of the service counter, wrapping items in cellophane beneath the glass shield. Normally she would have already attended to that and clocked out, but Desmond wanted his most trusted associates available after Alaric departed.

Eve kept her thick auburn hair brushed back into a coil that revealed a pale forehead. A convenient style for someone who worked in the food industry, but she said the inspiration came from a painting of Elizabeth Bathory, the seventeenth century Hungarian countess who bathed in virgin blood to preserve her youth. Eve looked a fairly youngish forty already, so slathering her face with Becca Foster's blood yesterday improved nothing. In Countess Bathory's defense, Becca was no virgin.

"This was where the unpleasantness began yesterday?" Alaric asked.

"Yes, through no fault of Eve's own."

"I'm sure. I saw the family on the local news. The husband almost looked relieved."

Alaric made notations on his clipboard. "And this Eve's part of your Inner Circle?"

"Yes. She didn't come from Freshway. She's already one of my most valued staff. Employee of the Month, too."

"And what are you doing to satanize the deli section?"

Desmond blinked. "You mean *sanitize?*"

"No, I mean *satanize.* This is Devil's Food. This here looks so… common."

"We were going to discuss that at our next team meeting," Desmond said. Since he had no idea what the hell Alaric was talking about, he asked, "Are they doing anything special in Molina?"

"They're using sacrificial goat blood and semen to season the deli meats," Alaric said. "A brilliant innovation."

"Uh, how are they getting the semen, exactly?"

Alaric shrugged. "I didn't ask. I don't need to know how the sausage is made, so to speak. But I saw the baster. In a word, *foul.*"

They wandered away from the deli, arriving in the produce section just as mist burst from the overhead nozzles of the wet wall. Alaric scribbled some more notes.

"Freshway is hurting." Desmond said, mindful of timing. "We have more cars outside the moment we open than they do at their busiest time."

"And does that satisfy you?" Alaric cocked an eyebrow. His lips twisted like dying earthworms. When Desmond first met him, it took him awhile to figure out why the manager's eyes seemed so intense, until the man himself explained it.

I wanted to see the light of Lucifer as close to me as I could. I burned off my lashes. Now I keep looking to see his wisdom.

"No," Desmond said, even though it did satisfy him—at least a little. "I won't be satisfied until we drive those dipshits into the ground and Todd's out on his ass."

Just thinking of his old boss made Desmond's bowels gurgle.

"I respect vengeance," Alaric said, "but be sure you do this foremost for the glory of Hell."

"Of course," Desmond said. "Hail Satan."

"Hail Satan."

Gore approached them from the adjacent bread aisle. Desmond assigned him the busy work of removing anything that expired in three days. Gore looked jubilant, but his filed teeth gave him the mouth of a shark with the dental decay of Henry Lee Lucas. Between that and his emaciated figure, Gore remained gaunt and unsettling despite his cheer.

"Hey, Mr. Payne, I meant to tell you, I ran into Fenton out on lunch. You know, from Freshway?"

Desmond nodded impatiently so he'd get to the point.

"Well, he said they're so behind that Todd's got him and a bunch of the others pulling an all-nighter tomorrow. Even that old bag Ruby! Anyway, just wanted to let you know that."

"Thank you, Gore."

"Pardon me, sir," Gore said to Alaric. He bowed and returned to the bread culling.

Desmond couldn't restrain his smile. He had Freshway on the ropes, and their collapse would greatly boost his numbers even further over projection. Good news, since apparently those who followed the left hand path cared about more numbers than just 666.

"That's interesting," Alaric said. "Let's hope those efforts aren't rewarded."

Payne had hoped for more enthusiasm. He'd plotted with Gore earlier to repeat his news for Alaric's benefit, but Todd Brown's gradual decline still offered him some solace.

A few months ago, Desmond himself was one of those underappreciated slaves across the street, obeying Todd's narcissistic whims in an assistant manager role. Suicide would have been a quicker and more painless transition. Wherever Todd didn't want to be, he pushed Desmond. Appeasing irate customers and vendors;

resolving discrepancies in the tills; closing regularly (often opening the mornings after too—the dreaded *clopen*); firing employees who needed the job while Todd teed up on the ones who couldn't care less; dealing with fallout from schedules where Todd disregarded employee requests. All while Todd made no mention of retiring anytime soon, which would allow Desmond to take his place as manager. In other words, a steady buffet of diarrhea where Desmond decided he'd had all he could eat.

Devil's Food put Desmond in the driver's seat immediately. They authorized him to do what he pleased, as long as he got results. No more eating shit, not from Todd or his higher-up (a real cunt of a zone director), and not from haughty customers either, like that fat bitch from yesterday.

Desmond finally liked his life, and all it took was the proper bow to Satan. As a metalhead who'd spent the 80s banging to the likes of Celtic Frost, Possessed, Slayer, Mercyful Fate, and Venom, as well as the harsher music of rising bands like Morbid Angel and Deicide nowadays, this seemed almost inevitable. These oft-satanic songs provided the soundtrack for the past several years of his life, thriving underground like the aggression and hatred simmering beneath his veneer of respectability. Lord Lucifer had given him not only the power to kill, but also the okay.

He would do everything it took to please those above him, and especially those below.

"Gore is also part of your Inner Circle." Alaric resumed scribbling on his clipboard. Desmond didn't know what he could be writing, but feared the worst. Their bananas somehow weren't evil enough? Overlapping cucumbers almost formed a cross?

"Yes, sir. He's one of the people I brought over from Freshway with the right… mentality."

"True sons and daughters of darkness."

"Absolutely. Gore keeps up morale. He likes to collect videos with real death footage, and he makes compilations of his favorite clips for everyone."

"Exceptional."

They found Laila as they rounded out of produce, stacking soft drinks on the end of an aisle. A pyramid of twelve-pack cases stood on a platform cart beside her.

Alaric brightened at the sight of her pentagram necklace, though seemed to admire the rest of her just as much. The black Devil's

Food shirt fit her snugly. Desmond stole her from Freshway too. Back then she wore her chestnut hair like something out of an 80s cock rock music video, but she'd since dyed it jet black and straightened it. Black fingernails and lipstick completed the ensemble.

Alaric's approval evaporated when he noted her progress. "Not like this."

Laila organized Coke and Sprite evenly on both sides of a cube currently at knee level. Standard grocery store practice, and nothing to criticize that Desmond could see.

Alaric said, "You want the Coke top to bottom in the middle. Stack the Sprite up on both sides for about four rows, then Coke for a couple rows, then back to Sprite. You can stick what's left of the Coke behind it until you use everything, but facing out you're going to have…"

"An inverted cross of Coke!" Laila said. "That's so cool." She began moving the cans, enthusiastic about the new craft project.

"High schooler?" Alaric said as they moved on, out of earshot.

"Graduated in the spring, sir. Eighteen, but responsible. She's a head satanic priestess already, very knowledgeable of the black arts. She cast spells of misfortune on Freshway— Todd specifically. We're, like, eighty percent sure he broke out in genital warts after one of those."

"Outstanding. I'm always encouraged when the young are adept with their infernal studies and servitude." Alaric nodded approvingly as Deicide's "Blasphererion" played over the store speakers. "Going forward, I want you to make a bigger effort with that subliminal symbolism I was showing her. I want this store to whisper damnation in every aisle."

"Consider it done."

"Be innovative. At the Molina store, they've painted subtle crosses on the ground so the people waiting in line have to step on them to check out. All the good little Christians profaning their holy symbol just to give their money to us."

They wound their way down the laundry aisle, past the regular stocking crew. These were the people who'd be at it until sunrise, moving row by row to replenish throughout the store, and help unload any morning trucks.

"Speaking of little Christians, you'll love this," Alaric continued. "Molina sketched tiny pentagrams on the bathroom light fixtures. Little kids are always turning those on and off, you know—being a nuisance. Now they're hailing Satan." Alaric imitated a child reaching up to flick a switch, barely any difference from a Hitler salute. He shook his head at the riotous amusement of it.

"Ha, I'm sure they're weeping in heaven," Desmond said, his chagrin growing. The Molina store had operated longer, but only by a few months. It sounded like that manager was kicking his ass, a man who stepped into his role with a lot more experience, particularly in the field of serving the dark lord. The Freshway store still hung around in contention out there, though, so if Desmond vanquished his competition first, no amount of clandestine blasphemies perpetrated in the Molina store would matter.

Desperate for a little more positive feedback, Desmond directed Alaric past the frozen section on the rear wall and through swinging doors into the back. They found Marcel presiding over the cadaver of Becca Foster. She lay prone on the platform cart, an ugly divot in her back from where they stuck her on a hook in the meat locker after yesterday's blissful blood shower. Red droplets spattered the ground, dribbling off the side of the cart.

Marcel grinned as he stuck a meat thermometer in the divot. Nearly thirty years old, he stood over six feet with a blond mullet right out of *The Lost Boys*. He seemed quite personable in his assistant manager role, but the temperature of his smile dropped several degrees behind closed doors to a demeanor comparable to the doctor described in Slayer's "Angel of Death."

"Almost room temperature," Marcel reported.

Alaric examined the handiwork, nonplussed by the abundance of wounds carved into her flesh. He lifted her head up by the hair. The special, extra-strength slicer had done a gruesome number on her face, opened the skull and ocular bone. An impatient poke with Eve's box cutter had burst the eyeball itself. Her forehead thumped on the cart as Alaric relinquished her hair.

Alaric said only, "You were visited by the police?"

"We confirmed she was here, even ran her credit card to make a paper trail. Gore and Marcel figured out which car was hers and ditched it halfway to Molina."

"I wasn't worried. You shouldn't be either. *He'll* protect you."

Desmond nodded, but recalled the book he read about Richard Ramirez last year. The devil-worshipping serial killer was beaten within an inch of his life by a mob until the intervention of police who were presumably not dispatched by Satan for his rescue. What kind of fucking protection was that? There was having faith, and then there was being a moron.

"We'll be using her corpse in ritual," Desmond said, since Alaric didn't seem inclined to ask why they'd kept the body around. Seizing inspiration from tales of Molina, he added, "We're going to package up the choice cuts and sell those so our customers are eating human flesh." Another burst of inspiration. "Human flesh used in *a satanic ritual*. We'll call some of it pork butt. No one really knows what that is anyway."

"It's the shoulder," Alaric said automatically. "You don't think he would prefer something actually killed in his name? Something you didn't have to thaw out first?"

Marcel spoke up, Lucifer bless him. "We're watching out for people who won't be missed—bums, train-hoppers, junkies. They've come through now and again."

"Interesting, because I'm told you had a vagrant type in here last week. Someone who might have shoplifted. Stealing from Devil's Food is like stealing from Lucifer himself."

Desmond and Marcel shared a stunned look. "How did you…"

"We're everywhere," Alaric said. "An army in every city, the Faceless Ones."

"Okay, well, it was fifty-fifty he was a bum or just into that grunge music."

Alaric's brow furrowed. "Grunge?"

Marcel said, "Alternative rock. Fuck, does it suck and—"

"You should have killed him either way."

Marcel glanced at Desmond, mouthing *I told you.*

"We didn't see anyone steal from us," Desmond said.

Alaric sighed. "Payne, this has the potential to be a premiere Devil's Food location and a credit to our dark lord. I need to see more initiative, though. A month from now, I can't confidently say—"

"We're hitting Freshway tomorrow night," Desmond heard himself say. The words may have surprised him more than anyone, but they felt right as soon as he got them out.

This was the answer, the initiative. His boss's eyes brightened, yellow and blistered.

"*Hitting*, you say?"

"I've decided that taking their customers isn't enough. I want our store to kill the competition—literally. They'll be begging for mercy at our feet. We're going to cross the street and slit their fucking throats. All in Satan's glorious name."

For the first time, Alaric's teeth formed a smile within the shadow cast by his cowl. Desmond released a long breath, suddenly validated in his dual role—manager, master of ceremonies.

Hail Satan.

~

Gore wished he could film this. Slicing that woman up yesterday had been a supreme thrill, but how much cooler would it have been to record it for one of his compilations? He'd like to see himself mutilate, watch flesh separate beneath the stroke of his own blade. Relive the screams and the power of taking someone's life, then rewind. They raped that holy bitch's soul until she saw the Devil clear.

Now this.

They hung the flabby bitch from a hook, glittering in the torch-lit chamber. Her hands and feet were nailed to beams with roofing nails, turning her into an inverted crucifix of flesh, her body hung upside down like the wretched Saint Peter. Gore could barely take his eyes off her tits, dangling on her chest toward her face. Big pink nipples. Thick bush between her cellulite-riddled thighs. Amber light played across her punctured skin, creating moving shadows that almost made her seem alive.

In a fashion, she looked like the girl strung up at the end of *Deranged,* if older, larger, and less nubile. In the Freshway days, Gore sought lesser known horror films like that Canadian offering through bootleg catalogs he scored from ads in the back of *Fangoria.* He loaned them out to Fenton and sometimes Kyle, sharing the gospels of Dario Argento, Lucio Fulci, Mario Bava, Jean Rollin, Joe D'Amato, Jorg Buttgereit. There was Nazisploitation, nunsploitation, Charles-Bronsonsplitation. Shot-on-video cannibal films, discount slashers, giallo splatter and bonerjam sleaze. He had little time for that these days, though. Now his film fanaticism was focused on scouring for shockumentaries packed with real death scenes from recorded accidents and executions. Man, did he get off on that. Fenton and Kyle were pretty much dead to him now, though Fenton did at least seem interested in joining Devil's Food. *Put in a good word for me, dude, I'm pretty sure I want to leave fuckin' Freshway.* But Gore had no use for good words and was skeptical of Fenton's commitment. Here, you had to be prepared to kill at a moment's notice, much like yesterday. Fenton had been a bit of a local bad boy in his youth, but he'd softened into the stoner slacker life, more prone to daughters and Sega than slaughters and Satan.

They'd transported Becca's body through a concealed doorway in the chamber (behind a banner of the Goat of Mendes framed in a pentagram), away from customer eyes, to stash her in the back in deep freeze. Now gravity exsanguinated her of the blood left inside. It formed a Rorschach blot of crimson beneath her, spattering on the ash of a pentagram. Laila crouched under the body with a black chalice, wherever the thickest deposits of blood threatened to drip off, her nude body nubile in her writhings.

Gore had crafted the pentagram earlier while Desmond finished up with Alaric. It wasn't his best work, admittedly. Angles were off, the circle uneven, but he figured the thought was what counted. No one would look at it and not know what it was. The ash came from crematory remains filched from a funeral home run by Eve's uncle. It was she who lit the black candles around its perimeter.

Everything felt primal here. Ancient. The way evil spirits in the forest seemed possible in the black of night, so did this ceremony in darkness manifest the potential of Hell. In this place, it was easy to believe a rift opened for Lucifer to hear their petitions and prayers, and bestow his wicked blessings.

Gore, Eve, and Desmond knelt naked around the circle. Marcel stood beside Becca's body, the only one of them adorned with any-thing—a saber-toothed tiger mask, which looked like a genuine hol-lowed-out animal head but with proper dimensions for his eyes to see through. He also held a butcher knife in hand, his erection puls-ing uncomfortably close to the blade.

Laila stood and took her place at the top of the circle. She held the chalice aloft and recited, *"In nomine Dei nostri Satanas Luciferi excel-si,"* before bringing the cup to her lips.

Gore focused on her naked body—in particular the Baphomet tattoo along her thigh and the *Necronomicon* symbol on her mons pubis. He licked his cleft lip. Laila shaved *down there*, something that still blew his mind and inspired him in a roundabout way to consid-er splicing porno footage into his *Snuff World* death compilations. It would be artistically profound to cut something together like the scene where Bud Dwyer blew his brains out on live TV, then show a dude nutting on Traci Lord's underage face. Something about it spoke to him, even if he wasn't exactly sure what the fuck it was saying.

As if the shaved pubis wasn't exotic enough, Laila also had piercings in both nipples. Gore thought she was cute even before their Freshway days, when he still went by the boring Christian name Gordon. They attended the same school, with him two years ahead of her. He and Fenton killed a lot of boring hours at the store talking about Laila and Mila and Stephanie and the bad, bad things they'd like to do to their bodies. Somehow it didn't lead to Gore actually asking Laila out, but what a difference Devil's Food made, a place where such wanton carnality was practically part of the job description. Fenton would be banging on the door right now if he knew about that, but the third key of black magic was to keep silent, so Gore never blabbed of his escapades. It also precluded recording this ritual on home video.

Laila passed the chalice to Desmond next, her chin smeared with blood.

She resumed her invocation.

Marcel stuck his butcher knife below Becca's sternal notch and ripped upward to open her belly nearly to the point of the pubic hair. The wound only bled slightly. Gore's eyes watered as her intestinal gases wafted through the room. Beside him, Eve accepted the chalice and took her own sip, then handed it to him next.

He expected dead blood to somehow taste different and it did, though maybe it was only psychological. It seemed heavier, bitter, but he managed to swallow down Becca's juices and extend the chalice to Marcel.

Laila's hands vanished into the corpse's belly and reappeared with a clump of organs in her palms. She pressed them to her face, smearing it with blood, pus and gastric juices.

Beside Gore, Eve looked upon the scene with horny rapture. Her knees parted slightly and she slipped a hand to work between her legs in the patch of naturally auburn hair, something that transfixed Gore nearly as much as Laila's bareness. The deli manager was older than him, but he had no problem with that when mature bitches looked this good. She started breathing through her mouth, quicker and quicker before shuddering with a long exhale. Gore's skinny cock hardened, slickened with pre-cum. He could and would take Eve and Laila both. It was allowed, even encouraged.

He couldn't fathom someone denying himself these pleasures and aligning with people who wore their Sunday best and pledged *not* to do anything that might actually feel good (like that prissy bitch, Mila, from what he'd heard). What kind of sickness was that?

The ratio here usually favored the men 3-2, but tonight they had even numbers...if you counted the cadaver.

~

Little shockwaves of pleasure radiated through Eve in the aftermath of her orgasm. Watching Laila caress and nuzzle the entrails required a release. She couldn't help it.

She loved blood—drinking it, lathering herself with it. She would climax if she saw someone bleed enough. It was wave after wave of pleasure as they stabbed the Foster woman again and again. Good thing Eve was nude. If she tossed her panties at the wall afterward, they might have stuck, rolling down like one of those jelly octopuses in the little plastic capsules in the quarter machines.

It thrilled her now to still see some blood left to leak out, like the body was freshly dead. Enough to get Eve wet in all the important ways. To someday bathe in the crimson rivers of a virgin like Countess Bathory would fill her with unholy light, something she trusted her lord and master would see fit to provide her if she continued her devotion to the store.

Laila's invocation had commenced at some point in Eve's delirious haze. Wet viscera dripped through the girl's fingers, fondling the coils of Becca's farting intestines. A bundle of them hung in the groove Marcel fashioned with the knife.

"Father," Laila said, "accept this ruined flesh we offer thee, and bless me with the gift of prophecy." She caressed the greasy sausage-like links. "Reveal to me our future, make these entrails as the very strands of fate."

Desmond watched expectantly from the ground. He'd made a bold promise to the regional manager, and they all felt the electricity in the air. Tomorrow, they would eradicate their competition and establish their rightful dominion. Death to the weak, wealth to the strong.

Laila's glassy expression cleared. She let the ribbons of guts slip through her fingers to pile on Becca's chins.

She smiled at her boss. "Satanic victory is assured, and evil will prevail!"

A blissful expression curled behind Desmond's moustache. To Marcel, he said, "Cut her down."

The sabre-toothed mask nodded, and Marcel claimed a meat

cleaver from the floor. He whipped the blade through the air to separate the corpse's hands at the wrists, then her feet at the ankles. He and Laila helped maneuver the body to the stone floor with a delicacy they'd shown it at no other point.

Eve crawled to the supine body to seize the nearest stump—one of the ankles. She squeezed the calf with one hand while stroking it with the other, like a gigantic penis. Her ministrations coaxed a delicious spattering of blood over her pale breasts. Had she not come moments ago, it might have been enough to trigger an orgasm. She needed a little more.

Beside her, Marcel entered Laila from behind, both of them crouched on the ground. Chalice and internal blood smeared her face. Eve bent forward and licked Laila's mouth and chin like a mother cat. The pressure of another orgasm rocketed inside her from the coppery taste as Laila exhaled at her, gasping and shuddering as Marcel pounded her little pussy.

Desmond's hands folded over Eve's breasts, his erection pressing between the cleft of her buttocks. She twisted away, murmuring for him to hold on so she could guide one of Becca's wrist stumps against her ass and let the blood lubricate her anus. Once satisfied it had, she offered her backside to him while still remaining upright. The girth of his dick impaled her asshole slowly, sweetly.

Between Becca Foster's dead legs, Gore lapped away at her cold vagina, chewing the graying meat of her curtains.

Eve took hold of some loops of Becca's small intestine and mashed them together to large intestine dimensions. She pushed the entrails against her clit, eyes rolling back in her head as she rubbed them back and forth, the stickiness of the blood merging with her wetness. She gasped, fancying she could feel the slickness of the blood on Desmond's cock inside her. Eve stuffed the entrails into her dripping cunt, thick enough to stretch the membrane and push back against Desmond's length. She fucked herself until the orgasm struck her like lightning. Desmond came too, pulling out and cock-decorating her. His semen rolled down her back like hot wax.

Momentarily quenched, she let the innards slide out of her like a detumescent cock. Seeing that Gore at last immersed himself within Becca, pumping wildly against her immobile form, Eve strung a single coil of the intestine over to him, sliding it into his rectum. The young man squeaked, his hairless butt cheeks aquiver.

"Keep fucking her!" she demanded.

THE NIGHT STOCKERS

The boy rocked into the oozing wound and Eve pushed the guts deeper inside him, pulling his Mohawk, his head now snapped back. She tongued his ear for wax, his nostril for mucus—any taste of human excretions. Sucking on his neck, she could feel her favorite fluid of all pulsing in his veins. She was tempted to bite and relive the "vampire" days of her teen years, during the whole satanic panic of the 1980s. She and her girlfriends had formed a coven of sorts, but instead of witchcraft they were obsessed with vampire films like *Fright Night* and *Near Dark*, and fancied themselves as brides of Dracula. Of course they weren't really the undead, but that hadn't stopped them from drinking human blood, taking razors to boys willing to spill a few drops just to be touched by these gorgeous goth babes. In Eve's case, some of the blood she'd drunk had been from victims who weren't so willing—mostly children from the neighborhood when their mommies weren't looking.

Small hands came around her and cupped her breasts. Eve turned back to see Laila. The girl's face was covered with more than blood now, Marcel's seed dripping from her forehead to her chin. The women smiled and once again Eve lapped at her, slurping the first strains of a child who would never be born deep into her mouth—savored, swallowed, damned.

CHAPTER THREE
FOR THEY SHALL BE SLAIN

BOOKER COULD'VE KILLED THE LITTLE prick.

Todd stood with his hands on his hips, head back to look at the ceiling. "Yep. Best to clean both sides."

The vents of their air ducts were black with dust and grime. Booker couldn't imagine them having ever been cleaned in all the years the place had been open. But it looked like it was his job now, quite a respectable task for the second in command of the entire store.

"I'd have to unscrew them to get both sides," Booker said. "I don't know if I can reach them even with the ladder. The duster is at least long enough to clean off their exteriors."

Todd glowered with his vulture face—nose hooked, mouth tight. He was rarely reasonable, and when he was it was only because it suited his other needs. But in this store, no ideas were good ideas unless Todd came up with them himself.

"If you can't unscrew them, then they can't get clean," the boss said. "And I want my store clean. Figure it out."

The manager walked off, turning his back on Booker. He

watched Todd approach the bakery, giving Mila directions for the night. But Booker knew Todd for the dirty old man he really was. Todd was just talking to Mila to get a glimpse of her ample cleavage. She'd grown hot moving crates around and had undone the first two buttons on her shirt. When she bent over to get more crates, even Booker had admired the view. Now he was too pissed to admire the young baker's generous curves.

Every time Todd said "figure it out" Booker wanted to punch the old man's teeth down his throat, especially when Todd knew damned well they lacked the resources to do whatever task he was insisting upon.

He was already pissed at Todd as it was. This overnight was his dipshitty idea, but while he talked up how he'd be here to supervise, now that the night had come he invented a horseshit excuse not to be here, claiming the zone director might visit in the morning. Therefore, Todd had to be there early just in case the director made an appearance, and so he needed to get to bed early and couldn't be at the store late tonight. It was an excuse Todd fell back on often to free himself from closing shifts, despite the fact that these surprise visits from regional leaders never actually happened. Such visits were always rigidly scheduled. That Todd expected Booker to believe the same empty lie again and again just added further insult.

The produce manager had been set to be tomorrow morning's key-holder and run the store until Booker came in later in the day. That was the plan; one Booker knew Prince Todd wouldn't follow through with. *To hell with it*, Booker thought. *At least I won't have to deal with the son of a bitch micromanaging me all night.* Booker would run this overnight better without Todd making everyone redo things *his way* just so he could feel superior. Maybe they could even get out at a more reasonable hour than six in the goddamned morning. This job disrupted Booker's sleep patterns often enough without this horseshit.

Lack of sleep, high stress, and a prick boss had led to the disintegration of any passion he'd once brought to his job. Worse still, it facilitated the already-in-progress implosion of his marriage. Jamena had been gone for almost two years now and he still rolled over in bed expecting to feel her there. He missed his wife. He missed the opportunity to start a family. He missed a lot of things.

Heading to the backroom, he noticed Fenton leaning on a U-boat picking his nose. When he spotted Booker he straightened up and pushed the boat full of milk crates, pretending like he'd been working. Booker let it slide for now. He didn't want to take out his anger against Todd on Fenton, even if the kid was a steaming turd. Kyle from grocery came out of the dairy cooler where he'd been organizing the back stock.

He took down the hood of his sweater. "All the boxes have been dated, boss."

"Nice job." Booker looked to Fenton. "Why don't you work with Kyle on aisle one and work your way from beer down to frozen. Check expirations, take all the product off the shelf and wipe it down, then front and face it all back."

The young men glanced at each other with sour smirks. Booker knew Kyle and Fenton weren't very fond of each other, but they were here to work, not make friends. Besides, having someone else working alongside Fenton would assure he kept busy and didn't just fart around. The young men walked off together, giving each other a good seven feet between them as they headed out to the sales floor.

Darla came out of the produce prep cooler, her round belly drawing the white butcher's smock tight. She looked beyond tired, exhausted by the dual weights of pregnancy and a job that kept her on her feet forty hours a week. Booker admired her; not in the way he admired Mila, but as any good man admires a strong woman. If she was single and he wasn't her boss, he might have made a move a long time ago, pregnant or not.

"You sure you're ready for tonight?" he asked.

She shrugged. "I don't have much of a choice."

"Todd?"

She sighed. "Todd."

"Well, I'll make things as easy as I can for you. I have a list of things that need to get done. Take a look and see what you think you can handle."

"Okay. Thanks, Booker. But I don't want to slow everyone else down. I don't want to keep you here later than you have to be."

He almost put his hand on her shoulder, but then decided against physical touch with an employee. They chose to pair her with Ruby to clean up the front end and windows. Keep it simple, light. Take caution and avoid liability.

Booker would bounce between bakery and meat tonight, assisting Mila and Antonio with the deep cleans and inventories. He wasn't exactly sure where he'd put Stephanie, but he'd think of something. If paired with the wrong person, the teenage sexpot would probably just create more of a distraction than contribute much productivity. Best to keep her buried in solo work.

Booker yawned, a bad omen for things to come.

It's gonna be a long night.

Todd paged him to the front and Booker circled back to the sliding doors of the foyer where Todd stood, already in his coat.

"Make sure they don't half-ass this," Todd said.

Booker acted like he was scratching his lower back so he could hide the fact he was flipping Todd the bird. "Don't worry, I've got it under control."

Todd's eyes were like piss holes in the snow. "You'd better. If we don't step it up, Devil's Food is gonna kill us."

~

They watched the back of the store from Desmond's truck. In the passenger seat, Eve smoked a clove cigarette and the perfumed puffs made him long for something he couldn't name, something tender. He shook his mind free from it to focus on the task at hand.

"Sealing off the emergency exits will be easy," Desmond said. "The front doors will be tricky, as will the loading dock, but I've called in all our best employees for this, and I know this store inside and out."

"What about the roof?" she asked. "Is there a hatch?"

"Yes, but it's not accessible without the manager's key. And counting the upstairs storage, they'd be jumping two stories onto concrete."

"And the phones?"

"Gore's on top of it."

"Superb." She puffed the potpourri odor, lips like blood-plumped leeches. "So are we ready?"

Desmond cracked his knuckles. He'd hoped to see Todd's Cadillac here, even though he knew from experience the manager kept all the day shifts for himself. Working under that shitbird had been the single most miserable job of Desmond's life. One day he'd gut the old man and hang him by the ballsack from the Freshway sign out front. But not tonight. He had more important business than mere revenge, no matter how gratifying it could be. Alaric would be judging his leadership and it would be a large factor in his review. If Desmond were ever to climb up the corporate ladder to the glorious gates of hell, he'd have to prove he could handle killings far more significant than eliminating the insufferable Beccas of the world. Tonight, Freshway would have to bleed and burn.

Eve's hand slid across his thigh, the blood countess already frisky at the thought of all the sticky red she'd soon be slathered in.

"It's a lovely evening," she said, gazing at a waning moon. "Such a wonderful night for a slaughter."

Desmond grinned as the rush began to build. He no longer needed the ecstasy or acid or coke of his youth. The high bestowed upon him by hell's fiery serpent was all the buzz he needed. Murder toppled narcotics every time. To get them further pumped, he popped a cassette into the tape deck. Carcass's *Peel Sessions* filled the speakers with the first song, "Crepitating Bowel Erosion". Jeff Walker roared, Bill Steer grumbled, the guitars and drums and bass creating a ferocious cacophony. Desmond nodded his head in rhythm. Once it'd been mosh pits that helped him get out his aggression. Now that he was a slasher for Satan, such a thing would seem sophomoric, like comparing a comic book to one of the great Russian novels.

As Eve undid his zipper and her head lowered into his lap, Desmond whispered an incantation and began carving it into his forearm with his box cutter. The ancient Latin made his skin shiver.

Let it begin…

Arm dripping with blood, he pushed Eve's head down, forcing her to deepthroat him, and raised his other hand out the window and gave the signal. The five cars lined up the street came back to life and the rumble of motorcycles rose from the woods like the battle cry of jungle beasts. The vehicles stalked forward, taking the store on all sides.

Desmond grabbed Eve's hair and pulled her head up.

"That's enough for now," he said. "Let's focus."

He hadn't come yet, but that was okay. He'd have someone suck his dick later.

~

"Something's going on out there," Ruby said.

Darla lowered the glass cleaner and put her hand to the window to get a better look. Something was definitely moving around the parking lot, and moving *fast*. Clouds had moved across the sliver of the moon, muting the glow, and the black shapes zipped through the shadows, shimmering like wet vinyl.

"It sounds like engines but I don't see any headlights," Darla said.

The noise grew louder, the machines getting closer to the store. As the clouds passed, the moonlight made the chrome flicker blue and shined off the leather-clad bodies in the parking lot.

Ruby put a hand to her bosom. "Holy shit."

At any other time, Darla would have been shocked to hear the elderly woman swear, but right now she couldn't think of a more appropriate response. It seemed a gang of bikers were using their parking lot as racetrack, driving in circles like a bunch of dirtbag NASCAR rednecks. That they kept their headlights off made it all the more sinister.

"Better get Booker," Darla said.

But Ruby was ahead of her, already heading for the pager. She called their manager to the foyer, the tremble in her voice expressing the urgency. When they heard his keys jangling at his hip, Ruby went to him and pointed out the window. Booker's face went slack, then hard. He shut off the lights in the foyer and Darla instantly wished she'd thought of that sooner. He checked the locks and ushered the women back.

"Get away from the windows," he said.

They came into the front end and Booker locked up both sides, securing the entrance and exit doors with their simple tumblers. It made Darla feel a little better, but not much.

"What's going on, Booker?"

"I dunno, but I sure don't like the looks of it."

Ruby said, "You think they're robbers? Maybe they want what's in the safe?"

"If so, they're making a big show of it."

Darla shook her head. "Somehow I don't think money is their main objective here."

"Well then, what is?" Ruby asked.

But Darla didn't have an answer to that; at least, not one she wanted to say aloud. It would make it seem all the more true, all the more horribly real.

Booker took charge, but his nervous eyes betrayed his strong appearance.

"Ruby, call 911," he said. "I'll gather the others."

The elder woman went to the phone by register one, then clicked the button repeatedly, and when her face went pale so did

Darla's. She knew the line was dead before Ruby even said it.

Darla placed her hands over her belly.

Booker paged everyone to the front of aisle four, where another phone hung on a load-bearing pole. It too was dead.

"The lines are down," he said.

But Darla knew—hell, they all knew—they'd been cut. They just didn't know why and were too scared to ask each other.

Ruby put her hand on Booker's shoulder. "We should turn down the lights so we're not sitting ducks in here. They can see us but we can't see them."

"We can't," he said. "The lights in the foyer are on a switch, but the store lights are on a timer."

"What about the circuit breakers?"

"That'll cut off more than just the lights. We might need electricity."

Kyle approached with Fenton loping behind him, hands in his pockets, slacking off even in an emergency. The others followed after, each walking slower when they saw the faces of their coworkers and the tornado of steel and leather outside, a howling cyclone of menace closing in.

And then there was flame.

~

Mila stepped closer to Kyle; a simple reflex. Her ex-boyfriend had his faults, but cowardice was not one of them. She'd always felt so safe around him, the polar opposite of how she felt around most males. They always looked at her as if she were a pork chop and they'd been starving on an island for forty years, their eyes locked with hunger, their mouths glistening as they licked their lips. Kyle stared down those types of guys; not out of any kind of jealousy, but because he demanded people treat Mila with respect and decency. Even when he'd pressured her for sex, he never made her feel like a mere object. He hadn't liked it when she said no, but he always followed her rules, however begrudgingly.

Somehow she doubted the men outside were as gentlemanly.

They had poured lines of gasoline upon the asphalt, then surrounded it with a circle, and one of the thugs flicked a cigarette butt into the fumes. The gas lit up, forming the shape of a star, and then the ring flickered too, revealing their artwork as a flaming pentagram.

Mila clutched the cross at her bosom.

She and her coworkers stood behind the row of registers, a barrier between them and the biker gang that merely gave the illusion of safety.

"We gotta get outta here," Kyle said.

Ruby turned to him. "Now just hold on."

"Hold on, my ass! If we can't get through to the cops we've gotta get outta here, right?"

"I can't run as fast as you, sonny." She pointed to Darla. "And neither can she."

Kyle deflated. It seemed he hadn't thought of that. "Well, okay, but I can run pretty fast 'cause I play ball. I can go get help."

Stephanie said, "I ain't fuckin' staying here. If you get to split so do I."

Suddenly everyone was talking over each other. Booker put up a hand to quiet the panic. "Everybody take it easy. We don't know what these people are up to. They may just be using the parking lot for some kind of partying or drag-racing. Or maybe they just want to hassle us, ya know? Spook us."

Ruby shook her head. "We can't take that gamble. Let's just pull the fire alarm."

Darla said, "No! We do that and they'll hear it. That'll just piss them off, right? Who knows what will happen before the cops and firemen get here. At least right now these people are staying outside."

The group fell silent then. Mila watched Booker. They all did. It was a natural reaction to turn to him for leadership. He was their boss, and unlike the boss above him, he actually cared about his crew. She hoped he was up to the task at hand. It's not like biker gangs and bonfires in the mark of the beast were in the employee handbook.

"Okay," Booker said. "Looks like they're sticking to the front of the store. Everyone follow me to produce to the emergency exit."

Mila shivered. "Won't that sound the alarm? They'll hear us sneaking out."

"But the door triggers a signal to the security company. They'll send the police if they can't get through to us on the phone. I'll just open the door, then close and lock it again. We'll hide in here until the police arrive. Those bikers hear that alarm and it just might scare them off."

"Or piss them off," Kyle said, "like Darla was saying."

When Kyle stepped forward Mila took his arm, surprising both of them. He looked at her and she held his gaze longer than she would have yesterday. Still, she let him go.

Antonio rolled his shoulders, an athlete prepping for action. His dark eyes had gone hard and tight.

"We need to arm up," he said. "Just in case. I have a cleaver and some knives. And there are lots of box cutters."

Ruby hung her head. "Oh my god…"

Stephanie clutched her hair in both hands like a security blanket, and Mila was suddenly reminded how young the girl was. Mila was only a few years older but those few years made a great deal of difference. She went to Stephanie and when she put her arms around her Stephanie leaned in for a hug. Before now, they'd hardly ever spoken, being two very different girls from two very different worlds. Funny how fear unifies.

"Antonio's right," Darla said. "I have knives in produce too, big ones to cut melons."

"Okay," Booker said. "We'll arm ourselves and then we'll trigger the door alarm. But for Christ's sake be careful. The last thing we need is any accidents."

The group followed Antonio to the meat department, which had more sharp objects than any other, and they picked up additional knives from the produce cooler. Mila had one with a long blade. In her small hands it might as well have been a machete. Antonio was double fisting, a cleaver in one hand and a butcher knife in the other. His white smock, already stained with meat juice, added a menacing edge to his muscles. Even Ruby looked ready to slice and dice anyone who pressed her.

Fenton sneered. "Think these things will stab through leather?"

Mila turned away from him. Even at a time like this he had to be a sarcastic pessimist. And yet he wondered why she was always avoiding him and wouldn't give him her number. She'd sooner date an eel. It'd be less slimy.

Following Booker to the emergency exit, the group stayed close to one another, huddled as they marched, soldiers on D-Day. Booker grabbed the security bar, took a deep breath, and pushed. The door opened only an inch. There was no alarm, but there was a clank as metal hit metal.

"What the…?"

Mila leaned in, her heart falling into her stomach when she saw.

A car had parked in front of the door, making it impossible to swing it open. Booker could only open it enough to maybe pass a hand through.

He closed the door. "They're trapping us."

"What do these people want?" Darla asked no one in particular.

Mila held her knife a little tighter. "And what happened to the alarm?"

"I don't know," Booker said. "It should've gone off."

Kyle said, "They must have deactivated it too, just like the phones."

"What about the other emergency exits?" Mila asked. "Let's try them."

The others agreed but Booker shook his head. "The alarms are all fed through the same line. If one phone line is down, they're all down. They would have blocked those too. The only thing left to try is the fire alarm."

There was one of the boxes with the pulley on the wall nearby. Darla whimpered when Booker went to it.

"We have to call for help," he told her. "The fire station is just a few blocks away. They'll be here fast."

He pulled the alarm and the store howled with the deafening bell.

~

Desmond grinned. Everything was going to plan, the Freshway crew behaving just as he'd predicted, as if this were all some cheap horror novel he and a friend were writing just for shits and giggles.

The fire alarm was not run through the phone line like the security alarms were. They were hardwired and more sturdily based, incapable of severing, especially from the outside of the building. It was inevitable that the Freshway fools would try it. They had no reason to think their old assistant manager was leading this siege.

He lifted his car phone and dialed the fire station. When the line was answered, he gave them Booker's name and told them the pulley had been banged into on accident and that all was well inside the store. The alarm could be canceled. He gave them the store's security code and told the fireman to have a pleasant evening, thanking him for his assistance.

A moment later, the alarm went silent.

Beside him, Eve giggled, girlish in her excitement.

~

"What the fuck?" Fenton said.

Mila looked up, looked all around, just as confused as he was, as they all were. The alarm had simply *stopped*. She didn't know they could even do that. Something cold moved through her chest.

She swallowed hard. "No one's going to come are they?"

Booker opened his mouth as if to object, but seemed to think better of it. He put his hands on his hips in concentration.

"No sense waiting to see if the fire department got our distress signal or not," he said. "I say we try to find another way out."

"The loading dock!" Kyle said. "That door's too big to block with a car. We can go out that—"

Mila gasped. "No! What if they're waiting for us out there? What if they have guns?"

"Well, we have to do something. Confronting them may be our only way out."

"Kyle, that's crazy!" Mila had always admired Kyle's courage. Now she wondered if it was more like carelessness, a testosterone-fueled bravado that could get them all killed. "We have to take precautions for everyone's sake. That door is for unloading tractor-trailers. The opening must be, like, fifteen feet tall and twelve feet wide. You'll be letting them all in at once."

The group fell silent. Antonio broke it by saying, "Then there's only one thing we can do."

"What's that?" Booker asked.

"We wait. See if they make the first move. They have boxed us in, but maybe we can box them out, use pallets and U-boats and whatever else to block the front foyer."

"Yeah. It's all glass doors. It's the most vulnerable spot in the store."

"Of course they'll see us doing it, even with the lights off. Unless…"

The group waited. Mila asked, "Unless what?"

Antonio's eyes went tight. "We create a diversion."

CHAPTER FOUR
BLEED FOR THE DEVIL

MARCEL NEVER WORE A HELMET. HIS blonde mullet whipped in the wind with absolute freedom, his cycle roaring between his thighs, much as he had roared between Laila's before shooting his dick milk across her pretty, cherub face.

What a job. Fucking jailbait, worshipping the devil, killing motherfuckers—all while on the clock. It sure as shit beat McDonald's.

People had the nerve to call grocery store employees low-skill workers, but Marcel had learned a trade. Being a professional meat cutter took skill, training, and certification. Now he was going to enhance those skills to new levels of excellence. Tonight his slaughterhouse was an entire store full of his competitors. Human meat. The chops and steaks of his fellow man. He was going to enjoy this.

Pushing his Harley to its limits, he made figure eights in the open lot, Lou Gramm's "Lost in the Shadows" stuck in his head, Marcel liking it there. Though not a vampire, he'd always been what you'd call a lost boy. Now a man, he'd found his place, his purpose, and that was to pay tribute to the goddamned glory of Lucifer, the fallen angel who had brought a little piece of heaven down with him, offering the sweetest delights for those wise enough to serve.

The cacophony of the motorcycles was loud enough to cloak the sound of the tractor-trailer as it pulled around the back of the store so Big Delbert could block the loading dock. Gore had finished cutting Freshway's phone and alarm lines. The punk was a good solider and a devout Satanist, one of their better hires. With the back exits sealed, the little Freshway fairies would be stuck, and then the Devil's Food army could strike like lightning. Desmond's plow truck hummed in the lot behind the bikes, idling, ready.

Marcel smirked as he gazed up at the glowing, green Freshway sign on the front of the building. It might as well have said DEAD MEAT. That's when he noticed movement in the second floor window.

Someone's up there.

Marcel brought his hog to a stop.

Were they panicking, looking for a place to hide? It was futile. Marcel would search every shelf, every cooler, every shitter. Search and destroy. Or were the Freshway staff up to something, maybe planning to strike first?

The window shattered, glass falling like sleet onto the front walkway. The other motorcycles slowed when Marcel raised his hand.

Laila pulled up beside him. "What is it?"

He pointed to the window just as something long and black poked through it. It was an elongated shape, slender and pointed like a—

No fucking way.

The shape in the window moved back and forth, as if scanning the lot.

Laila gasped. "Dude, is that a rifle?"

"Retreat!" Marcel shouted.

The motorcycles revved and rolled out just as a loud cracking sound came from above. Marcel hunched up his shoulders as if he could hide his head like a turtle, peeling away from Freshway, sweat bubbling in his mullet despite the chill of the night.

Why the hell would they have a rifle in a grocery store?

He raced towards his boss's truck and pulled up alongside the driver's door.

Desmond leaned out the window. "What the fuck are you doing? Why'd you pull back?"

"They've got a gun up there, boss—some kind of rifle. They're going all Charles Whitman on us."

"There's no way someone has a goddamn gun in a Freshway. It's against store policy, an offense that leads to immediate termination."

"But I heard the shot."

"I saw the window break, but there was no muzzle flash. You sure you heard shots?"

Marcel looked away. "Well, I heard at least one, then got the bikes going again."

"Christ whipped on the fucking cross! The noise could be anything. Maybe one of the bikes backfired. Whatever you see up there, I swear on a hellion's burned-up ballsack it isn't a rifle. And even if it was, that doesn't mean we start shaking like Frenchmen in a thunderstorm and run away."

Eve leaned across Desmond. "Yeah, Marcel. Grow a ballsack of your own and get back there."

Marcel pointed at her. "Watch it, bitch. I'm your supervisor."

"I serve only one."

Desmond shoved her back into her seat. "Both of you shut up. Focus! I don't need any of you fucking this up." He ran his hand over his shaved head. "Tell the others to fall in on either sides of the truck. I'm through fucking around."

~

Mila pulled the broomstick back from the window. Behind her, Stephanie stepped over the large chalkboard she'd pushed to the floor to replicate the sound of a rifle shot, puffing the cigarette she'd used to replicate gun smoke by blowing it upward at the windowsill. A few months ago the board had fallen on the hard floor and was so loud everyone jumped. Mila remembered how it made her nearly leap right out of her shoes. Now, upstairs in the break room, the sound had been amplified by the concrete walls.

"They've backed up," Mila said.

Stephanie pumped her fist in triumph. "Fuck yeah! That actually worked."

"Hopefully it bought the guys some time."

Downstairs, the men of the group had dragged whatever they could find to the front end, planning to haul it out into the foyer to barricade the sliding doors if the bikers retreated.

"C'mon," Mila said. "We've got to help them."

Stephanie leapt ahead, taking the stairs two at a time on her way down. The girl's burst of energy surprised Mila. She seemed excited now, as if they were winning at some cruel sport. Mila knew better than to celebrate just yet, though she took it as a good sign that no one returned fire. Maybe they didn't have any guns either. Mumbling a prayer just between God and herself, she hurried down the steps.

When they finally reached the foyer Booker was using the pallet jack to wheel a second stack of wooden pallets in front of the doors. Kyle and Antonio were moving a display shelf while Fenton rolled in a U-boat stacked with twenty-four packs of beer.

"This'll never work," Fenton said.

Mila steamed in silence. It was as if the jerk wanted them to fail.

"Shut up and keep stacking," Booker said, going for the last stack of pallets.

"It's just not enough stuff. There's too many of them out there for this to do jack shit."

Kyle turned to Fenton. "He said *shut up*! If you're not part of the solution, you're part of the problem, dickweed."

Fenton's face became a Sid Viscous sneer. His beady eyes flashed like razors catching firelight. Mila had never liked what she saw in Fenton. Now she almost feared it.

"Let me help," Kyle said to Stephanie as she scooted a metro shelf.

Mila joined them, feeling Kyle's warmth beside her. Thank God for him. Kyle was so much more mature than Fenton, so much more adult than child. He wasn't the typical twenty-something guy, playing flip cup until he puked and wasting all his money on strip clubs and Sega. He was something so much more, so much better than a jerk like Fenton could ever be.

She thought of Proverbs.

A friend loves at all times, and a brother is born for a time of adversity.

Kyle was that kind of friend and brother to others, and he was proving it right now. In a time of crisis, he'd stepped up. Soon as they got out of this, she had to tell Kyle how she really felt. Christ forgives. So should she.

Mila looked to the doors as the roar of engines returned. They seemed to grow louder by the second. Mila shivered to think they weren't just going in circles anymore.

Stephanie cried out when the truck's floodlights came on. The group retreated, Booker urging them away from the windows, but they had only seconds left to run. Having just pushed the shelves to the front, Mila, Kyle and Stephanie were closest to the doors when they exploded, the plow decimating the glass and doorframes, making a mockery of their barricade by knocking the pallets over, creating an avalanche of the heavy wood. Stephanie jumped and rolled, dodging them just in time. Kyle's reflexes were equally good and he only took one blow to the arm. As a pallet flew toward her face, Mila saw him out of the corner of her eye, reaching for her.

The last thing she ever heard was the boy she loved crying her name.

~

Kyle screamed as Mila's neck snapped. The pallet made her face implode, the bones of her skull crushing inward, her head crumpling like a wad of paper. Her eyes and nose holes became one, the connective tissue and cartilage pushing deep, popping and fizzing. The plow shoved its way forward and the other pallets were forced into Mila's body. Her ribs snapped and spiked out of her back in a burgundy mist, her splintered skeleton going through flesh and clothing like chucked spears. Mila's body opened and gassed, her hot insides spewing out of holes both old and new. Blood left her in a detonation.

Mila was pulverized.

Kyle wanted to go to her, to cradle what was left of her in his arms, but there was no time to grieve. The truck was backing up for another go. He knew he should run, knew Mila was dead, but couldn't bear to leave her there. Tears clouding his vision, he went for her, but something tugged at the back of his shirt, pulling him away. He turned to see Booker.

"Move your ass!"

His boss was stronger than he looked. He yanked Kyle away from the body and as they ran toward the front of the store Kyle saw Fenton sprinting through the entryway, knocking Ruby aside. She fell into Darla, both women spilling to the floor. Booker and Antonio dragged the women out of the doorway and behind the concrete wall to relative safety. Kyle was the last one out of the foyer, getting inside just as the truck was pulling out. The bikers were dismounting their cycles, silhouetted by the floodlights, looking like a scene from *The Warriors* or *Mad Max* with their chains and baseball bats and sledgehammers. The one at the front sported a bleached mullet and a leather trench coat. From the holster at his hip, he pulled out a large hunting knife. The handleformed brass knuckles that slid over his fist, lined with a row of metal spikes. He used it tear open one of the twenty-four packs and took out a can of Schlitz. He punched it open with the spikes and held it above him, titling his head back with his mouth open for the beer waterfall.

Kyle went behind the wall with the others. Ruby had gotten up but Booker and Antonio were still helping Darla back to her feet. Kyle seethed. If not for the bigger problem chugging beer behind them, he would have knocked Fenton's dick in the dirt.

Booker looked to the group. "Run! I'll take care of Darla. You all run!"

Fenton didn't argue, swiftly heading toward aisle three. Stephanie was next. Antonio looked to Booker and the manger nodded, so Antonio took Ruby by the hand and they followed Stephanie's lead. Kyle started to go, but when he saw the strained look on Darla's face and the way she clutched her swollen belly, he found he couldn't leave them.

Booker said, "Get out of here, Kyle!"

"No way."

"I am *your boss*."

"So write me up then, but I'm staying with you two."

He took Darla's arm and Booker took the other so they could carry her out like a wounded marine. She groaned as they retreated to the produce department where they might stand a better chance of hiding behind the sturdy display tables. Darla breathed heavy, her brow wet. Her eyes were tight, nearly closed. The fall had clearly hurt her, and perhaps her unborn child too.

If these lunatics didn't kill Fenton, Kyle would kick his ass straight to hell.

"Let's get her to the apple table," Booker said.

Kyle grit his teeth. "We have to get out of this store."

"I can't go that far," Darla said. "Please, don't leave me."

"No way," Booker told her. "No one's going to leave you. I promise."

"My baby…"

"You and your baby are going to be fine."

"You can't know that for sure." Tears rolled down her cheeks. "They just killed Mila! They killed her, Booker! My God, they just freaking *murdered* her."

Kyle's jaw tensed. The woman was right. They knew now what they were up against. These weren't robbers. They weren't drag racers. These people were maniacs.

Darla said, "What do they want? Why are they doing this to us?"

"I don't know," Booker said. "I wish I did. Maybe then we could reason with them."

"Reason with them?" Kyle said. "Are you nuts? They're killers, Booker. Cold-blooded psychos. There's no reasoning with people who want your blood. All you can do is fight back." He drew the produce knife from his belt. "Fight with everything you've got."

~

When they reached the end of the aisle, Stephanie looked back and forth, unsure where she was even running to. She was faster than the others, so they tailed behind her through the detergents and paper towels. This would give her time to do something that had become important to her. She tucked behind the soda display and waited for Fenton to appear. When he did, she sprung out and caught the bastard with a punch to the face. He fell backward and landed on his ass. Stephanie's hand stung, but it was worth it. When Antonio and Ruby came out of the aisle, Ruby was smiling at the sight of this justice.

Fenton glowered. "What the fuck, Steph?"

Ruby looked down at him. "Serves you right, you little pecker! Pushing an old woman into a pregnant one to save your own skinny ass. Shame on you!"

Fenton started to get to his feet. No one helped him. He grumbled at Stephanie, calling her a bitch under his breath. She rolled her eyes. To think that just hours ago she'd still entertained the idea of fucking this guy. Stephanie liked bad boys, not cowards. Had she been in his way, he would have knocked her to the floor too. Wimp.

"What now?" she asked the others.

Stephanie wasn't sure whom to turn to for guidance now that Booker wasn't nearby. Antonio was the strongest, but Ruby seemed wiser, perhaps solely because of her age.

"There's a lot of them," Antonio said. "Looked like maybe twenty, yeah?"

"So fight or flight?"

Ruby shook a fist. "I say we kick 'em where the sun don't shine!"

"How do we do that?"

Antonio said, "We're outnumbered and not as well armed. If we hide it'll buy us some time, but not much."

"Well," Ruby said. "I say we hide and pounce. My husband killed Nazis in World War II—the big one—and my son fought the commies in Nam till he could fight no more. I'm from a family of soldiers and I won't let them down by just waiting around to die." She raised her knife, teeth bared. "These punks just fucked with the wrong old lady."

Stephanie smiled. She knew who her leader was now.

~

Gore stepped carefully through the ruins of the Freshway barricade, following Marcel's lead. Desmond's truck had obliterated the storefront like a Pete Sandoval blastbeat, "Ripped to Shreds" level.

Doors slammed shut behind him as Desmond and Eve exited the truck. The other Devil's Food faithful trailed Gore, weapons brandished in case their quarry seized the offensive. This would have been the best opportunity for Freshway, with entrance mobility limited by the precarious state of the ground—pallet pieces, metal, glass, capsized carts, even fucking gumballs blown out of cracked machines, ready to roll under someone's feet.

Gore entered with no fear, though, because he knew better. The "gunshot" earlier was bullshit. His former coworkers had no defense. These pussies were fodder for the beast.

He ran his tongue across the points of his teeth, relishing the sharpness. He was no longer human, just a vessel for the wrath of Lucifer. It gave him such a chubby. Gore carried a machete, but he'd also strapped on a tool belt stolen from his old man's work shed this afternoon. He had no use for dear old Dad these days (or his fat ass mother for that matter) but their tools would come in handy tonight. The loaded belt was unwieldy, but using the same weapon on everyone would be boring, aside from maybe a chainsaw. He gave himself a few options, inspired by some of his favorite films—a hammer (*Hellraiser*), a screwdriver (*Dawn of the Dead*), and the most exciting find, a portable drill (*Bloodsucking Freaks* and *Driller Killer*). All of it uncomfortably heavy around his waist, but he enjoyed feeling like some satanic Batman.

Gore caught up to Marcel beyond the landfill of obstructions scattered through the entrance. He found his supervisor standing over a body. It took Gore a minute to even identify Mila, barely recognizable after getting bulldozed to that bakery counter in the sky.

"Damn," Gore said.

Marcel's mouth curled. "You gonna cry or something?"

"No, we just blew a killer opportunity. She was a virgin."

"What? Bullshit!"

"No, she was," Laila said, appearing at Gore's side in skintight maroon jeans, a leather corset and a black choker. "I sense her purity with the eye of Satan."

She fingered an orange pendant hanging around her neck from a leather band. An ominous eye hovered like a burning sun above the sigil of Lucifer, which was comprised of an inverted isosceles triangle. Lines branched out from both base angles and crossed to create an X. The lateral sides surpassed the triangle tip until they ended in curls, intersecting with the arms of a V at the bottom of the pendant.

"Told you," Gore said to Marcel. "She always said she was saving herself for God."

Marcel glared at her crushed body in the growing pool of blood. "I guess the wait is over."

"Don't worry, Gore," Laila said. "Shedding virgin blood first thing is a good omen. Lucifer shall be pleased."

He nodded.

Lucifer might be pleased, but Gore wasn't. It had fuck-all to do with failing to properly sacrifice a virgin, because they were butchering enough pigs tonight for a whole year of black masses. He just hated to miss the chance to break Mila in himself, deflower the holy hole before he sent her to her maker, maybe christen those bodacious boobs with his dick snot. Bad enough they wouldn't get to torture Todd, but now Mila's hot, tight twat would be like cold pizza by the time they wrapped up the massacre. Cold pizza had its charms, but still. Definite bummer.

Desmond and Eve emerged with the rest of the Devil's Food crew. Eve smiled at Gore wickedly, obviously replaying last night's orgy in her mind with the weird intestinal butt play. He was still working out his feelings over that one, trying to assure himself it wasn't somehow gay since a woman did it to him and the intruding entrails also came from a female body. It had felt amazing and his cock spurted like a Super Soaker, but he wasn't sure he wanted her prospecting for anatomical butt plugs at every whim.

They stood before the line of cash registers, twenty-three disciples of Satan in all. Outside of the Inner Circle, that also added up to eighteen warriors for Hell, or 6+6+6. These were the peons, the part-timers and new-hires and illegals in Devil's Food's employ, here to prove their allegiance to the dark masters of retail.

Desmond stepped in front of the others, regarding them with an intense expression. He had to like what he saw, this army of killers. Some of them looked like they'd raided Rob Halford's wardrobe. A lot of studded leather, spikes, and a few BDSM masks making employees who bagged groceries and arrange bouquets in the floral department look like conquerors of Armageddon. They carried hammers, blades, ball bats full of nails, cleavers, meat tenderizer mallets.

Freshway didn't stand a chance in hell.

"You know why we're here," Desmond said. "Kill for Satan. Take your time, make them suffer." He pointed to a trio of motorcyclists on the end. Nails covered his arm on a homemade gauntlet, pounded through the leather. "You three set up shop here. This is the only way out. Anyone makes a break for it, cut 'em down. Keep watch outside, too, be ready to deal with it if anyone else shows up."

They nodded, choking up on their weapons. The biggest of the riders wore one of the S&M masks, but Gore was pretty sure he was one of the guys who stocked the frozen goods. A brass figurine of an inverted Jesus Christ hung from his neck. The other two wore death metal shirts with the cover designs of Obituary's *Cause of Death* and Malevolent Creation's *The Ten Commandments,* the latter reading THOU SHALL KILL! on the back.

Gore himself opted for his Immolation *Dawn of Possession* long sleeve, where demons tore angels from the sky. It reminded him how back when he worked here, he let Fenton borrow his Immolation tape. The alleged metal fan gave up after one side and made fun of the vocals.

Fucking poser.

Fenton would die tonight by Gore's hand if it was Satan's will, probably with Metallica's "black album" in Fenton's tape deck. A fitting epitaph for such a dicksucking wuss.

"They're all hiding in here somewhere, praying to their false prophet and pissing their pants," Desmond said. "Spread out and send them to the god below! *Ave Satanas!*"

His legion shouted in return, "*Ave Satanas!*"

The hunt began.

CHAPTER FIVE
BUTCHERED AT BIRTH

THEY HEARD THE *AVE SATANAS!* chant from the back of the store

"What the hell does that mean?" Stephanie said.

Fenton whispered, "It means they're crazy!"

Antonio crept around the end of an aisle several rows down from them. He ran in a crouch behind a line of other open freezers until he made it to their sanctuary.

"It means they're devil-worshipping pieces of shit, sweetie," Ruby said, patting Stephanie's shoulder. "They mean to kill us all."

Antonio held up a roll of tape. Ruby nodded and tiptoed from behind the open freezer to a swinging door. Satisfied they wouldn't be seen up front, she waved them over. Fenton learned nothing from getting popped by Stephanie and beat everyone there. After they'd all slipped into the backroom, he braced the door so it wouldn't shift back and forth behind them, a belated show of chivalry.

Stephanie frowned. *You freaking dick.*

Antonio brushed Fenton aside and peered at the sales floor

through the port window, ducking to keep most of his head out of sight as he looked left and right.

"You really think they're a cult?" he asked.

"No doubt," Ruby said. "They're all over the country, sacrificing animals and raping little boys and girls in daycares, putting rat poison and razor blades in Halloween candy. Evil S.O.Bs. Fenton, can you run and get the mops and brooms at the maintenance bay?"

"I'll go," Antonio said. Without waiting, he bolted down the corridor formed by the wall to one side and a mountain of boxes on the other—cleaning supplies, toilet paper, paper towels, diapers, canned and bottled drinks.

Fenton held his hands up as if to say, *What the hell?*

"We'd all be dead by the time you got back," Stephanie said.

"Whatever."

She thought of something. "Ruby, didn't they say nothing happened at that daycare a few years ago? That it was all made up? And wasn't it always someone close to the kids, like a parent, who poisoned their Halloween candy?"

"Go ask Mila if she thinks it's all a hoax," Fenton said.

Anger exploded through Stephanie to hear that chicken shit use Mila's tragic death in a debate against her. "Go ask Darla how softly she hit the fucking floor."

"Enough, you two." Ruby handed Fenton the role of tape. "Will you open that for me? Stephanie, can you keep an eye on the door?"

She nodded and turned away from Fenton before she could kick him in the nuts. It would probably make her feel better, but all his screaming would just give away their position, and then those psychos would head back here to slaughter them all like hogs.

The portal glass offered only a full view of one aisle and half of another. Neither had any intruders, though a group passed by the far end in the direction of the produce section. Nobody emerged from the peripheral aisles.

"No one from the cult is over here," she reported. "They're up in the front."

She tried to remember the feel of Mila's comforting hug earlier. It calmed her a little, or at least tempered some of the fury with sadness. She hated to leave Mila out there with those animals, uncovered. Frightened as she was, she almost looked forward to paying those bastards back.

"No sign of Kyle, Booker, or Darla," she added.

"Lord, I hope they're okay," Ruby said.

As she watched the aisles, Stephanie tried to process the enormity of the situation, the reality that these people came here tonight to kill them. Her mom watched those assholes on *The 700 Club* speak of devil worshippers like they were hiding under everyone's beds at night. They also claimed kids were going to hell if they played Dungeons and Dragons, though, so Stephanie wrote their warnings off as superstitious bullshit. An *Unsolved Mysteries* episode freaked her out once, though, where an arsonist narrated his allegiance to Satan as he filmed a burning house. It wasn't fear-mongering speculation but belief in action, and even that paled in comparison to this.

Antonio returned with two mops and a broom. He sounded light on his feet despite arriving at a sprint, but he might have been covered by the sounds of boots hitting the stairs to the break room in rapid succession at the other end. Maybe Stephanie's group should have holed up there, where only one or two of the maniacs could attack at once on the stairs. The strategy would backfire in more ways than one if someone tossed a Molotov cocktail, though. These people were crazy enough to do that.

Antonio set the stuff down. "This was all I found."

"Great," Ruby said. "See if you can pull those handles away and snap them in half. We'll have enough for all of us."

He stood on the brush cap of the broom and wrenched the handle away from it. He tipped the handle over, stepped on it at the halfway point, and pulled. The wood snapped apart in two pieces.

To be so much older, Antonio offered the kind of strength and resolve sorely missing from a wiener like Fenton. Stephanie didn't expect him to protect her, she just felt better about their chances with someone like him on their side. She'd flirted with him in the break room a few times. If they got out of this together, she might do a lot more than that.

Ruby turned to Fenton. "Start cutting off strips of tape. Make them about as long as your forearm."

He looked dismayed to be assigned another task. "What's all this for?"

"My husband told me if his regiment was overrun, they were ordered to 'fasten bayonets.' When you can't shoot 'em, you pig-stick the sons-of-bitches. That's what we're going to do with this tape and our knives…fasten bayonets."

Duct tape peeled off the roll, alarmingly loud.

Stephanie turned away from the discussion for another status check. Both aisles remained empty, but someone appeared around an end-cap of laundry detergent farther down—a dark-haired woman with a machete. Stephanie's skin went to goose pimples. Two men accompanied the machete lady close behind, a circus strongman-looking type with a sledgehammer and a long-haired blond with a butcher's cleaver.

Stephanie held her breath, willing them to turn to their left and walk away from her.

They didn't.

She ducked away from the window.

"We're not going to have enough time," she said. "Three of them are coming this way."

~

Kyle thought Darla must have fainted because her head dropped and her toes dragged without taking any steps, but she suddenly gasped and reared her head back. The arms thrown around his and Booker's necks clenched tightly. She moaned in pain, her face streaked with tears.

"God, it hurts," she said. A mild variation of her mantra since they'd retreated from the front of the store, alternating between her level of pain and fear for the life of her unborn child.

With Darla glued to his right side, Kyle carried the butcher knife in his left hand. Everything seemed like a contradiction, unfolding in slow motion but somehow also happening way too fast. No time to think, to breathe, to strategize.

To mourn.

He saw through a mist of tears, the store transformed to blurry colors. In his mind, they coalesced into the scene of Mila dying in front of him. It wasn't right. He was supposed to have the time to reconcile with her, and they were meant to have long lives ahead of them. None of this should have happened.

Those crazy fuckers destroyed her, but guilt weighed him down all the same, like a body anchored around his other shoulder. Somehow he felt like he'd brought this fate on Mila. If he'd never kissed Stephanie back, never let her slurp his knob for even a second, never entertained the thought of spreading her legs and sheathing his sex-starved cock in her nubile, teenage body, Mila would still be alive. It was an irrational guilt, but burdensome all the same. Maybe he would have acted quicker, pulled her to safety. It felt like some message from the universe, even though he understood the only ones to truly blame were the invading killers... and Fenton. He just couldn't feel it right now.

Kyle glanced over Darla's head at Booker, spotting a hint of uncertainty that disappeared so quickly he might have imagined it. Booker's control reasserted itself.

"Clear off the table and we'll set her down."

They'd reached the produce wet wall and angled their way toward the maze of table displays bearing various other fruits and vegetables some of which he couldn't have identified before he started running price checks. Plastic bags of Granny Smith apples were stacked like sandbags on a flat table near a spindle of plastic bags and a hanging scale. A sign proclaimed RED DELICIOUS APPLES 99 CENTS A POUND.

Kyle dropped his knife in an adjacent section of bananas on the display stand beside the apple table. The compartments on both sides sloped up to a flat juncture, with wax fruit artfully arranged across the top. This structure hid the table if you weren't right on top of it. Across from the table were standing coolers and the emergency door they'd unsuccessfully tried to flee through earlier.

Kyle slid out from Darla's arm and swept off as many bags as he could with both arms until he cleared the surface. He cringed at the noise of apples thumping on the tile, but it seemed like the intruders were still lingering near the entrance.

Near Mila.

He helped Booker set Darla down on her backside. They eased her back, Kyle picking up her legs to place them on the table. Her hands instantly went to her belly, face pinched in anguish.

Kyle reclaimed his knife, glad to have it in his dominant hand now.

Booker leaned in close to whisper to Darla. "Did you fall on...your face?"

Darla shook her head. "Kind of on my side. There's a lot of pain, though. Too much. I'm scared, Booker...my baby—"

"Are you having contractions?"

She shook her head again. Sweat glistened on her brow.

Kyle remembered to breathe out, as if he were the one who'd been taking Lamaze classes instead of her. Blood pounded in his head. This was enough of a nightmare situation without the complication of a woman in premature labor.

"You said you're having a girl, right?" Booker asked.

Darla nodded.

"You have a name picked out?"

She smiled faintly. "Abby. That's my mom's name…Abigail."

"That's a great name for a baby girl. Now, tell me, do you feel like you're bleeding?"

Kyle felt weird about staring at Darla's crotch, but she wore blue jeans too dark to easily see any patches of wetness.

"I don't…I don't think so. But God, it hurts so much—"

Kyle checked the front and back ends of the aisle flanking produce. Empty so far.

Where did Ruby and the others go? And what were he and Booker going to do now? Helping Darla seemed like not only the right thing to do at the time, but the only thing. Now he had a moment to consider there were just the three of them, one in no shape to defend herself, and they were badly outnumbered by the psycho scum upfront. Who the hell were those guys? Some kind of biker gang looting stores like in that old zombie movie, not bothering to wait for the zombie apocalypse?

"What about Abby?" Booker asked. "Can you feel her moving?"

Darla concentrated, as if trying to establish a telepathic link with her womb. "Yes! She is, she's moving...she just kicked." Her face brightened, a ray of hope through the cloud of despair.

"Okay," Booker said, "just hang on. We'll get you to a hospital, and Abby's going to make it. I promise you."

Kyle thought it a brash vow for Booker to make, but if he was wrong, he probably wouldn't be alive to answer for it anyway. Darla looked reassured. She stopped writhing on the table, almost peaceful in her repose. She cradled her belly, which seemed larger now with her back slightly arched. Kyle noted the empty hands. She'd lost her weapon.

Kyle said, "Booker, please tell me you still have your knife."

Booker nodded. He lifted his shirt to show the knife handle sticking through his belt loop.

"What do we do?" Kyle asked.

"Let's try to cover her up." Booker picked up two of the Granny Smith apple bags and draped them across Darla's feet and ankles.

Kyle bent down to grab some more. Between the two of them hey hid her quickly, being very delicate about covering her midsection and not stacking too much weight in any one place. They stashed the remainder under the table. It wouldn't fool anyone standing right up on her, but someone passing by might overlook it.

"I can barely breathe," Darla wheezed.

"I know, I'm sorr—"

From the front of the store, several voices at once: *Ave Satanas!*

Kyle and Booker shared concerned looks. Kyle barely knew any Latin, but he'd seen enough horror movies to get the gist of it. An already scary situation took on a heavier aspect of doom. These people were insane.

Booker crouched over the table. "Darla, be as quiet as you can and *don't move*." He pointed to the next station of fruits and vegetables toward the back of the store. "Kyle, hide over there. I'm hoping we'll get a chance to go out the front while they're looking for us. They're probably expecting us to hole up in the backroom."

"All right." Kyle crouched down beside a display with several bags of Idaho and Russet potatoes in purple netted and clear bags. Booker crab-walked to the pyramid table in front of Darla's.

He heard movement throughout the store. Whoops of delight and falsettos farther off. Someone's impression of vocals from one of those death metal bands: *I vomit on God's child!* Footsteps raced across the tiles while others struck at a more deliberate pace. A boot kicked open one of the swinging doors on the other side of the store. Cans collapsed and rolled down an aisle, probably the crate display of baked beans.

Darla groaned quietly and shifted on the table. One of the bags looked in danger of sliding off. Kyle scurried over to reorient it.

"Careful, Darla," he whispered and returned to his hiding spot

Booker nodded gratefully at Kyle's effort from two displays up. He tilted his head to see around the side of his station. He would have a partial view of the front aisles. Trying to get Darla back over to the exit would be dangerous, especially if they had to take time to uncover her first, and Kyle wasn't sure he could handle seeing Mila again. They also couldn't just leave behind the others, but if they made it to one of their cars, they'd at least be able to call 911 from a payphone and get Darla to a hospital.

Booker yanked his head out of sight and put his back to the station. Boot clomps echoed around the side of the aisle, more than one set. A scraping sound followed, something metal dragging across the tile. Maybe a lead pipe or axe head.

Kyle stared at his butcher knife. These monsters killed Mila. His blade would drink its fill of blood. Being found would almost be worth it. His violent urges surprised him. He'd never been the kind of guy who harbored those kinds of thoughts. Apparently seeing the girl you loved turned into blood pudding before your very eyes was enough to make an average Joe into Sylvester Stallone.

"Check the other side, make sure no one's back there," one of the intruders said. Not the rugged voice Kyle expected from some road warrior. Instead the voice was disturbingly familiar.

Booker stood up slowly. He made a "stay" motion at Kyle behind the cover of the display. "Okay, I'm—" he started to say, but someone cut him off.

"Booker! You're working late tonight."

For a moment Booker did not reply. Kyle saw the recognition come over his boss's face, followed by confusion.

"*Desmond?*" Booker said, identifying the voice. "What are…why?"

Kyle almost stood up, disbelief so profound he wanted to see this with his own eyes. Desmond left months ago to manage Devil's Food, taking Gordon and Laila with him. Kyle hadn't seen either of them since, other than their dim figures in the opposite parking lot. He wouldn't have left Freshway for Devil's Food because things were then heating up with Mila, but Desmond never asked him aboard in the first place.

Why the hell would Desmond be here? Had he come to help? Surely he must've seen Mila in the foyer. Why would he be so cavalier?

"We're here on behalf of Lord Lucifer," Desmond said.

Kyle froze, inside and out. His sphincter sealed up tight.

A female voice added, "Satan is our master, we live only to serve him, and we kill only to serve him!"

Another, younger female voice: "*Nam gloria satanas!*"

Jesus, is that…Laila?

Booker walked around the table with his knife held below waist level. He maintained an angle where the display would shield his weapon from Desmond and friends.

Kyle chanced a look around the side of his hiding place. He saw the arm and leg of a man in black leather pants with studs across the knee cap and thigh. More studs lined the length of his boot and the toe to mid instep. The blade of an axe rested upside down beside him, likely the source of the dragging sound a moment ago.

Kyle drew back into hiding. Booker had told him to stay, but

Kyle couldn't let the assistant manager sacrifice himself. Kyle would have the element of surprise on the axe man. That left at least Desmond and two women, maybe more.

Darla moaned on the table just as Booker told Desmond, "You killed that poor girl."

Kyle hoped no one heard her. He maneuvered around the other side of his display station, now out of sight from Booker.

"No one blocks the highway to hell," Desmond said.

"You should get Fenton to come clean her up, Booker," another voice said. "Virgin spill in the lobby." A cruel giggle. "I've heard of popping a cherry, but that was ridiculous!"

Kyle clenched the knife hard enough to hurt.

Damn it, at least five of them...wait, is that—

"Gordon?" Booker asked.

Desmond, Laila, and Gordon? Were all of the attackers from Devil's Food?

"It's *Gore,* you fuck!" the punk yelled back. "I don't answer to a Christian name."

Two or three of them spat on the ground at once.

"Go get Fenton to clean that up too," Desmond said. "Where is that slacker, anyway?"

"Why are you doing this?" Booker asked.

"Devil's Food aims to be the most powerful grocery chain in the world. We've slashed prices—now we're slashing souls."

"You're out of your mind, man! It's just a goddamned grocery store. Jesus, and I thought Todd took this shit too seriously! You've taken competition way too far. You have to stop this!"

Desmond laughed. "No. You need your god to stop it, but he won't...he can't."

The unknown woman said, "You're all going to die tonight."

And Laila's words were a moan of pleasure. "It is written."

"What'd you do with Darla, Booker?" Gore asked, stepping closer. "We saw you take her away."

Darla gasped to hear herself mentioned by name. It sounded megaphone loud to Kyle, but apparently no one else had heard.

Gore added, "She was looking ready to drop, but so are the rest of you cunts."

Booker lied. "We've called the police!"

Desmond only smiled at this. "Then I guess we'd better hurry."

Kyle came around the corner in a crouch. Desmond's group

numbered five—him, Gore, Laila, some redhead woman, and the biker type with the axe. He might not have recognized Desmond had he not known in advance, nor Gore for that matter. Desmond had shaved his head since Kyle last saw him and Gore had not only a Mohawk these days, but the body of someone just liberated from a concentration camp. His shirt draped from him like a sail, emphasized by a tool belt strapped to his waist like some home improvement gunslinger.

Kyle didn't recognize the redheaded woman. She and Laila both seemed unlikely allies for this invasion, but the axe-wielder had the studs and leather, a sleeve of tattoos on his arm and a collar with two rows of spikes. He'd since picked the axe up to rest on his shoulder. He seemed exactly the right type for all of this. Kyle inched toward him with the knife, ready to stick it in his throat and twist.

Laila glanced toward the back of the store, not focused on Booker, and spotted Kyle in his crouch mere feet from the biker. "Look out!"

The biker turned and swung the axe wildly, without full strength. Kyle dodged it and jabbed with the knife. The biker flinched, and the stab meant for his throat cleaved his nose instead. The bone resisted slightly, but a slight twist on the handle changed the angle and the knife cut through the cartilage like a wedge of cheese, leaving behind gaping caverns in his nose like a living skull. Blood dribbled down his mouth and chin as he screamed. He dropped the axe.

"Kill them!" Desmond roared.

Booker raced around his display, knife high. Both of the women moved to intercept him, Laila with some kind of dagger, the redhead with a meat hook. Kyle wouldn't get any help from the boss right away.

Gore was gangly, but quick, a spider boy. He darted to the axe ahead of Desmond and stepped on it before Kyle could snatch it up.

The biker seized Kyle's knife hand and twisted it, still screaming. The blade clattered on the floor. Kyle drove his other fist into the mess of the biker's nose. The punch lacked the strength of his dominant hand, but it sent the biker sprawling and shrieking, colliding with Desmond. They crushed a cardboard stand-up of hot dog rolls on their way down.

Gore reared back with his machete, ready to cut Kyle down.

Kyle threw his shoulder and blasted him linebacker-style, just like he had in his football days. Gore's scrawny frame hit the hard tile floor, machete skidding away. The axe was Kyle's now.

Booker screamed. The redhead's meat hook caught him from behind, stuck in the muscle between his neck and left shoulder. Blood rippled from the puncture. Kyle caught a glimpse of the woman hovering over Booker's shoulder with her tongue out, a look of warped ecstasy on her face.

Is that sick bitch trying to drink his blood?

Booker threw an elbow that clocked Laila in the chin. The redhead ripped the hook through his flesh and pulled away, lips glistening crimson.

Desmond and the biker were getting to their feet. They were the bigger threats right now.

Kyle charged them with the axe. "You murdering fucks!"

The biker dropped on his ass and held up a hand to ward off the blow. Too late. The axe struck the top of his skull like a tree stump. It collapsed with a wet crunch, and a mist of blood, bone, and minced brain tissue exploded from the cleft. Kyle planted a foot in the biker's face and wrenched the axe out, spattering his own face with red droplets. He blinked away something chunkier. The biker pitched over flat, where another layer of cranial contents burst across the ground like a shattered jar of pasta sauce. Head stuff farted out of his ears, gore gushing from his annihilated nostrils.

Booker lurched past Desmond to join Kyle, clutching his wounded shoulder, the blood sluicing through his fingers.

Darla cried out.

Gore turned his head. He'd heard her this time.

"Hey, over here shitbirds,"! he said.. "Your girl Mila's about to have a C-section."

Kyle whispered. "Oh, no…"

Gore and the redhead stood over Darla now. They'd dragged the table away from the station so everyone had a clear view, tossing aside apple bags that didn't slip off during the move. Grinning like an alligator, Gore held down Darla's arms. The redhead held the meat hook to Darla's throat, her mouth a bloody leer, eyes like Rasputin.

Booker held up his knife. "Get away from her!"

"Go ahead, try it," Gore chuckled. "Tell me something, Booker. Are you pro-life or pro-choice?"

Booker gulped, sweat forming on his brow.

Gore laughed again. "I think in this case, the woman doesn't have the right to choose."

Booker moved forward but Gore hissed him back.

"You'll get here just in time for the abortion, Booker boy!"

Laila found her dagger on the floor and walked over to the table, rubbing her jaw. She took over the responsibility of holding Darla's arms to the table, freeing Gore to do whatever evil shit.

Desmond's foot slid in the biker's blood as he examined the body but, wearing the mandatory slip-proof shoes, he righted himself with ease. He shook his head, disgusted, and pointed at Kyle and Booker, no longer the arrogant conqueror. A gauntlet full of gutter nails formed a quill around his forearm, probably his own creation judging by their lack of symmetry.

The baldy wasn't just dressed like Billy Idol. He sneered like him too.

"You motherfuckers are going to burn for this," Desmond said.

"Fuck you!" Kyle said. "You killed my girl!"

Desmond shrugged. "So?"

Kyle took a step toward him.

"Better not," the redhead warned.

Darla gasped as the meat hook slid down to yank her shirt up over her belly. The point rested in her belly button, turning lightly like a corkscrew ready to celebrate a new year.

Gore cackled then, animal like. Kyle winced, seeing now that his teeth were sharp and pointy, filed down in some grotesque self-dentistry. Kyle wished he'd hit him with the axe instead.

Gore said, "If someone told me I was going to gut a pregnant bitch at Freshway, I never woulda left."

Darla sobbed. "No! *Please!*"

"Don't hurt her!" Booker said. "We'll do whatever you want."

Or at least act like it until we can hit you with this axe, Kyle thought.

But then four more of Desmond's legion jogged around the front of the aisle. Another two came around the back end. Kyle's lip trembled. There was no way of knowing how many of them there were. Already there were too many. A feeling of doom draped over him in a black pall.

"Get your asses to the first aisle!" Desmond shouted at his foot soldiers, loud enough for others in the store to hear him at the opposite end.

73

There were so many just right here. Three on Darla, five in front of Kyle and Booker, two closing in behind them. No one came empty-handed. All brought something sharp or blunt, instigators of various degrees of pain.

"Just tell us," Booker said. "What do you want us to do?"

Gore picked up one of the 5-pound bags of red delicious apples. "Watch."

Frail as he looked, he had no problem swinging the bag overhead, round and round in a tornado, until it slammed down upon Darla's swollen stomach. The sickening thud seemed to rumble like thunder. As the wind exploded from Darla's lungs in an agonized gasp, the redhead raked the meat hook across the underside of her chin.

"No!" Kyle lunged at the table, but Booker seized his arm and dragged him toward the back in a stumbling run, still plenty of strength left on his unwounded side.

"There's too many of them," the manager said with despair. "We have to run."

But the two late arrivals barred the way. One carried a gardening sickle and wore a shirt with a green Broken Hope logo. His cohort dressed in a leather vest with a strange red and black mask Kyle would expect to see in a wrestling ring. He carried a club tipped with a black metal ball full of spikes, like he'd just stepped off the set of *Willow* or something.

Footsteps followed behind Kyle and Booker, though someone apparently skidded in blood, judging by a sudden cry and slap of flesh on tile. Booker grunted as he pulled over a standie of oranges, which thumped and rolled across the aisle in their wake. Kyle saw some black forms in the corner of his eye veer right to detour around the scattering fruit.

"We have to go through them," Booker said. "Don't stop. I'll take the left."

"Got it."

Kyle would have the wrestler, who stood with his morning star club held out in front of him like a sword. Kyle angled his axe to lead with the flat end. He rammed it forward like a giant pool cue as the wrestler pulled back on the club. The axe drove the club back in his face, the quiver of spikes nesting in the eyehole of the mask.

The wrestler shrieked and there was a wet pop like a suction cup coming free. Deep red exploded around the club. Punctured shreds of his eyeball oozed between the spikes like albumen through a boiled egg. Kyle struck him, knocking him around in a full spin. The wrestler planted his palms to keep from hitting the floor on his face, still screaming and dribbling. Kyle stepped on the back of his head, adding a hundred and ninety pounds of weight on the man's skull until he tasted the floor. Braced by the ground, the morning star burrowed deeper into the eye socket until facial and ocular bones crunched. Kyle felt the skull giving way under him like trash with more room at the bottom of the liner.

The screaming stopped.

Beside him, Booker slid between the open stance of the Broken Hope cultist. He jammed the knife between the man's legs as he passed through the arch. The silver tip jutted through the crotch of the cultist's pants, crimson spurting in jets across the floor with the beat of his heart. His hand flew to his decimated genitalia so swiftly that he cut off the tips of two fingers on the protruding blade.

Booker almost regained his feet before the cultist began screeching in earnest. Kyle grabbed his arm to tug him along. They turned the corner in a sprint, and Kyle knew Booker hated himself for leaving Darla behind just as much as he did.

~

Spasms of pain rolled through Darla.

I'm in Hell.

All her strength departed after the apples struck her belly. She felt like a pinned mouse on a glue trap, body stuck to a surface while its legs twitched uselessly. Her pants clung to her thighs, damp and sticky. She wouldn't be able to confirm it was blood without sitting up because she couldn't see around the dome of her belly. Since Darla's bladder failed her a few times during the last pregnancy, she could cling to the hope that was all it was, as long as she didn't check with her fingers; just the trauma of an injury to a sensitive area. She hadn't lost Abby, no matter the implications of the agony racking her body. She hadn't lost her baby. It wasn't possible, wasn't feasible.

Abby...

Darla's throat burned, but the hook had just opened the skin below her chin. It wasn't deep enough to sever arteries or veins, but Kyle and Booker must have thought so. She heard screaming now somewhere toward the back, maybe one of them, maybe not. Either way they'd left her alone with the beasts, alone but for the company of her unborn daughter.

The redheaded woman (her nametag read *Eve*) and Gordon stood above her, though he wanted to be called Gore now. His deformed teeth were better suited to someone named Gore, or maybe to some demon with poor health insurance. A few months ago he'd been someone else. This was a mere scarecrow of the young man who'd been perfectly nice to her before, if a bit awkward. They weren't necessarily friends, but people making the best of an imperfect situation together with the occasional joke and break room conversation when his shyness allowed it. She'd been closer to Laila despite the age difference, but that was nowhere in evidence now. Laila smirked at her as if she couldn't believe how pathetic Darla was. Her eyes were dead as Lincoln's.

"Whuh…*why*?" Darla said.

Gore met her stare, unashamed. Amused even, like someone pretending to throw a tennis ball and waiting to see how a dog would react.

He shrugged. "Why? You came to work."

She thought of Todd, how he'd threatened to fire her if she didn't come in tonight. Her pride had told her to flip off her boss and tell him to take this job and shove it, as the old song says. Instead she'd folded. Now she folded her hands across her stomach, trying to still the turbulent pain. It burst throughout her like magma, pure and blinding and unforgiving.

Eve licked the curved metal of the meat hook, sucking it clean between her lips. She set her forearm on Darla's forehead and bent down, closer still. A warm tongue slipped across Darla's throat, zigzagging along the incision, lapping up the bubbling brew of blood. Darla strained to raise her head and bite the bitch, but couldn't even lift it an inch off the table. She tried to pull her arms free from Laila again but was too weak. When the redhead stood back up, she had the curve of the meat hook pressed between her own legs, shuddering visibly as she licked her lips, eyes rolling over white.

Desmond appeared on the opposite side of the table. When Desmond left Freshway, she'd been a lot more discouraged about his departure than Gordon's. He did his best to insulate them all from Todd, and she'd had a good rapport with him. She didn't recognize this man now, and this would be true even if he hadn't shaved his head. There was no expression on his face, as stoic as a frozen sheet of steel, and if the eyes were the window to the soul these windows had been painted black like a crack house's. There was no soul behind them, no soul and no heart, and where there was no heart Darla knew there would be no mercy. Still, she had to try.

"Please," she started to say, not sure what would follow.

Desmond spoke over her. "Laila, what the fuck was that?"

The younger girl flinched slightly. "What?"

"*What?* Cory's got no fucking face, Ben's bleeding out from his ball sack, and Trevor has a morning star lodged in his brain. We didn't even mean to kill Mila, she just got in the way. Sure, we were going to kill her eventually anyway, but it only happened right then as a goof. Shit, if that's *Satanic victory*, I'd sure fucking hate to see defeat."

"It's what the entrails told me!"

Desmond shook his head. "Just tell me what we can do. What have the stars foretold this fucking time."

"The child," Laila said simply.

The redhead glowed at this response. "Such young, fresh blood."

"My baby," Darla said. The words always offered some talismanic power to her before, but this sounded despairing, a resignation to loss.

Desmond patted her head, pushing the hair back as gently as her father had when she woke from bad dreams. But there would be no waking up from this nightmare.

"The baby is not yours anymore," Desmond said. "It belongs to Satan now. It's his offering."

"No! Please, my…" She fought against the weakness of her body. "My family."

"Family?" Gore echoed. "You want go home to them?"

"I…love them."

He grinned. "Say you love Satan. Say you'll give your child to him."

"N-No."

"No?"

"*No.*"

Gore laughed with the smile of a piranha. He tugged something from a belt strapped around him which dwarfed his lithe frame, like a boy in Daddy's clothes. He now held what looked like a massive, yellow gun.

A drill.

He revved it for a couple of seconds before sticking it into the side of her pregnant stomach. She screamed. The drill bit met no resistance, slipped neatly through her skin until the barrel nudged her. Finally she pulled one hand free and gripped the top of the drill, but Gore pulled it away, held her at the wrist, and drilled her hand once, twice, burrowing holes through her palm. When she yanked her hand back, he poked her belly with the spinning bit once again. Laila snatched her wrist and pinned her again, and Darla squirmed, wanting only to cradle her stomach with both arms. Gore played, drilling into her elbow, her forearm, her wrist.

He depressed the trigger. The whirring ceased, leaving only her cries.

"How about now, Darla? Do you love Satan? Are you ready to give him your child?"

She didn't believe in Satan, but was this not the true face of evil? They tortured her and killed Mila. Strangers and former acquaintances laughing at her pain, threatening to sacrifice her child. The drill wounds burned her belly and arm, so hot she expected to see steam rise from them.

"All right, stop fucking with her," Desmond said, hands on his hips. "If a mother wouldn't want some baby with more holes than a sponge, why would Satan?"

Gore holstered the drill again, face now dotted in red.

The baby didn't move inside her. She thought Abby had moved after the blow from the apples, but it may have only been wishful thinking. If the drill infiltrated any unformed part of Abby, Darla might already be dead inside in the most unthinkable way.

She prayed for divine intervention. She didn't always believe in that either, but if it meant she could go home, she would try. She would pray to everyone and everything, to God and her mother and her husband. Mark would already be asleep himself now, unaware of this horror thrown into their lives, a horror that would have been unfathomable to her just hours ago.

~

Eve scraped the inverted cross into the pregnant bitch's gut with the meat hook. "Hold still, I don't want it crooked."

The sow's nametag said DARLA but that meant nothing. Maybe the fetus had a nametag too. They were less than human to Eve, just bags of worthless skin concealing the sweetest nectar. Actual human status wouldn't have meant much to her anyway. She had no use for it. Eve aspired to demonhood and the defilement and blasphemy of any "gift" of light.

There was certainly no bond with the writhing cunt on the table. No shared call of motherhood, of nurturing. Not even the feminist sisterhood of being women. Screw all that with a big rubber dick, forever and ever, Hail Satan. Life was an illusion, a dream dreamt by a meat machine to convince itself it had meaning and significance when it lacked both. Only death was true. Death was the great equalizer, the one certainty, the only promise that could never be broken. That was its beauty. That was its power—the power of being undeniably real.

Things were about to get pretty fucking real for DARLA.

Laila held up the medallion with its fiery eye and sigil of Lucifer. "Father Satan, we offer you this mother and child. Hail Abbadon, Baal, and Astaroth! May the lords of Hell grant us their infernal powers, and bless us with the wrath of evil."

She spoke with conviction, though Eve wondered about her. At that age, Eve too had thought she had everything figured out, but barely five years later she felt like a completely different person, embarrassed and disgusted by that high school graduate. Laila held power and prestige in the group, promising smooth sailing for the Freshway massacre, but here they were, down two soldiers and one dick in the first few minutes. Eve suspected Laila knew as much about the occult as a virgin did about sex—someone with a lot of reading, but precious little practice.

Marcel was among those who answered Desmond's clarion call. He stayed behind despite the pursuit for those who'd ran away. Eve felt better with the Inner Circle intact, even if it meant Marcel would probably perform the carving now. The Freshway swine were no match for his skill. In the land of the pig, the butcher is king.

On the other end of the spectrum, Trevor sat slumped against the bread rows with a bag of dinner rolls over his skewered crotch and a growing pool of blood spreading beneath him as he came out in chunks. Eve wished she could have abandoned her post to suckle at his spurting penile vessels. She'd already deepthroated one man tonight, but hadn't received that lesser but still valuable bodily fluid for her efforts. Trevor's bloody genitals would be a joy to gulp down. Desmond didn't dispatch anyone to the first aid aisle for the poor fuck. They all knew he was a goner. His face looked like wax paper as he clutched the rolls to his ruined manhood, a soggy gauze.

Laila turned in all directions as she continued her incantation. "Lucifer, protect your humble servants! We spill this blood in your name!"

"Hail Satan!" Desmond shouted. Gore, Marcel, and Eve echoed him.

DARLA begged through all of this. Eve blocked it out. It might as well have been baby talk, ironically enough.

Marcel stepped forward with his knife, fingers curled through the brass knuckle slots, spikes glimmering like glass shards. The shirt had slid back down over the woman's belly at some point, so he slit open the fabric as well as her jeans to reveal the full globular mass. A network of puffy stretch marks traversed the fleshy orb.

The woman renewed her struggles.

"Hold her down," Desmond said.

Gore pinned her legs. Eve took her wrists and pulled them into a stretching motion past her head. She kept her view of the bitch's eyes. The terror and hopelessness thrilled her, moistening her panties and making her salivate.

Marcel sliced with confident strokes around the circumference of her belly. He flicked his wrist and another arc of flesh split open, releasing a blanket of streaming blood. It pattered on the floor off the side of the table, each drop making a satisfying *splat* sound that echoed off the wet wall. White onions stared down like dislodged eyes watching the show, the bright fluorescents overhead lighting up the scene like a porno shoot.

DARLA's screams were vibrant, exciting. Such despair and anguish, watching what amounted to her own cesarean section and autopsy in the same surgical theater. So much blood.

Marcel completed the full circuit in counter-clockwise fashion. They saw the skin loosen as his blade met the 12 o'clock referent, like the skin oval abruptly shrank. He peeled away the disc of stomach and abdomen like an enormous scalp. Inner layers of pink skin tore with it. Marcel's swift knife worked through the intact abdominal muscle wall and amniotic sac, spikes poking holes through errant sinew, peeling it all aside to at last reveal Satan's sacrifice.

By this point DARLA became as immobile as the infant inside her on the table. Maybe dead, maybe only passed out from blood loss, perhaps crippled by shock. Eve hoped she was still alive to see this, to watch what they were about to do.

Laila chanted. "Father, we offer you the life of the mother."

Marcel brought his knife to DARLA's throat, its blade as wide across as the length of Eve's little finger. He used a punching motion to sink the knuckle-spikes into the mother's skin. Crimson erupted around the metal with enough buoyancy to indicate she'd still been alive after all. Marcel tore the pokers free, still pressing down hard as he did. They all heard the loud scraping as it sheared off chips of vertebral bone, her throat slashed all the way to the spine.

Laila scooped the child out of the womb.

Nope, no nametag.

"It's a girl child," she announced.

Gore hadn't totally missed with his drill. There was at least one burrow in the tiny head. Little cracks ran through it like a flicked eggshell.

The umbilical cord uncoiled as Laila picked her up. Eve was cheated of the opportunity to cut the sow open, but she wouldn't lose out here. She relinquished the woman's arms and snatched the cord with both hands. Satan could have the body and soul, but Eve would have the blood. She'd fucking earned it. She sank her teeth into the umbilical cord, biting predatorily between her hands. She tore through it like a sausage length, but there was only a meager spill. She smacked her lips into a frown of disappointment.

"Wait," Gore said, "let me see it a second."

He slid his hands under the baby and lifted it from Laila. He turned to the produce display they'd dragged the mother away from and set the child on the hanging scale. A tendril of the remaining cord draped over its side like a wet shoelace.

"A little over six and a half pounds," he said. "Oh shit, I bet she'd cost six dollars and sixty-six cents!"

Eve followed the umbilical to the placenta. Yes, this would be much better. She plucked it from the fleshy cavity. It looked like a dripping raw steak, but with prominent trails of arteries coursing across. She chewed into it, wrenching her head to pull free the tantalizing morsel. Coppery juices filled her mouth as she savored the glorious saltiness, an orgasm for her tongue. It dribbled off her chin, but Eve didn't care. As she gnawed, she dunked the placenta in the blood spooling beneath DARLA, letting it soak up additional sanguinary sauces like gravy on bread.

"The child has been consecrated in Satan's name," Laila said. "We will taste its unholiness and receive our lord's blessing."

THE NIGHT STOCKERS

A muted humming sound began during Eve's rapture, which she assumed to be a pleasure explosion in her brain, but when she opened her eyes she found Gore pushing his drill between the mother's legs. It was the sound of its attachment spearing through dead cunt meat. He popped the back of the grip with a hammer from his utility belt, cramming it deeper inside her. His hand sank into her, dead lips swallowing him up to the wrist. The rhythmic whirring abruptly grew in volume as the drill bit exited the cervix.

Gore whooped, head craned almost into the cavity for a bird's eye view of the anatomy he was despoiling. His smile turned crooked when he tried to pull the drill back out. "Damn, that fucker's locked tight in there. Where's that meat hook?"

Marcel had it, prodding into the sacrificial offering. Its soft, buttery flesh parted with ease. Eve felt nothing over this beyond pleasure at the sight of blood. Virtually no different from the semen she lapped up regularly, just a little more connective tissue. Damned and dead, soon to be swallowed.

Marcel handed over the hook and Gore worked with grim determination as he split the mother's torso open, taking care to leave some of the organs intact, unveiling something like a dropped Jell-O mold.

He neatly slipped the meat hook inside and held it aloft like an angler with a fish. Something like a red tulip bulb sat pierced on the end.

Gore's grin expanded around rows of needle teeth. "Help yourself to a slice."

CHAPTER SIX
SICK BIZARRE DEFACED CREATION

"HOW MANY?" RUBY SAID.

Stephanie slunk away from the door to stand with the rest of them. "Three."

"We can take 'em," Antonio said. "We have more."

Fenton balked to himself. *We're four but one's a granny and the other's just a girl. Hardly gives us an edge.*

He nestled into the tight cluster the rest of them formed around Antonio, as if to draw strength from one another. He felt none of that himself, only their continued disapproval since he'd pushed Ruby into Darla. Excuse him for wanting to live. Maybe if Ruby didn't run like she was trying not to slip on ball bearings, they all could have gotten away unharmed. The irony was he'd probably saved both their lives with his quick hands and quicker feet; otherwise they would have been smashed to shit like Mila. It wasn't like he wanted Darla to lose the kid, but hey, she could make another. Shit, he'd gladly help her out himself if she needed the hot beef injection. *No problemo.*

He couldn't believe any of this. This never would have happened if he'd just switched over to Devil's Food, or at least not to him personally.

"Everyone get ready," Ruby said.

Why the hell were they taking orders from one of The Golden Girls? Everyone was acting like she was Colin Powell because some *men* in her family fought a couple wars. She barely had a real job at the store—she just passed out samples all day. That wasn't to say Fenton wouldn't rip off her Depends and split her old, gray gash like a fire log, because she still had a pretty good body for a social security recipient, and he'd enjoy sticking it to a octogenarian just for the story alone—but he wasn't counting on her leadership in a satanic siege. He could talk tough too. That didn't mean they should put him in charge.

Fenton held his produce-prep knife out. It seemed the least impressive of the whole arsenal, which admittedly would have worked better as a bayonet taped to a broken mop handle. Too late now, and no better options. Nothing but a wall farther down to their left, and on the right, the search and destroy mission would be around the corner any minute now, with chains and swords and fire and whatever the fuck else—Tech 9s, cannons, a fucking tank. Who knew? All Fenton did know was they were prepared for combat, whereas the Freshway posse might as well have been shooting marbles.

He strategically positioned himself in the back row, not only to provide a buffer in the assault but because Stephanie was directly in front of him. He stood close enough to brush against her ass. She was too tense to notice. Fenton let the granny take the point position. Seemed only fair to let Ruby join the front line since she'd had time to tape her knife to one of the broken handles and "fasten a bayonet."

A fat goon with a buzz cut appeared in the port window of the right side swinging door. He had a ring through his septum and lightning bolts tattooed on his cheeks. Antonio sprang and kicked and the door crashed open on the interior side, colliding with the first in line. The buzz cut guy grunted and shot back like a pinball.

Two more took his place. A spindly woman with a machete and a short man with a hatchet slipped through on the other side, swiping at Antonio with their blades. Antonio stepped out wide to engage the man, cleaver in one hand and butcher knife in the other. The woman swung her machete at Stephanie, upward like a golf club. Ruby stuck her broom handle out and parried the blade, jabbing and pivoting like an old western Comanche with an atlatl. Two ladies against one.

Fenton would have chosen the female goon for himself as the weakest of the biker trio, but Buzz Cut burst through the door like the Kool-Aid man, nose bloodied, snorting bull-like, sledgehammer in hand. To Fenton's dismay, Buzz Cut took his lack of engagement as an invitation and charged with the sledge aimed at Fenton's head. Fenton jumped back until the man ran into the column of boxes stacked up against the back wall. He threw himself aside before the sledge demolished containers of dishwashing detergent that exploded soap throughout the receiving bay.

Fenton scrambled toward Antonio, whose cleaver flashed by in a blur as it chopped right the fuck through the short man's wrist. Shorty's mouth twisted in agony as he brought the gushing stump to his face, as though to verify it really happened. The hand lay on the floor like some dead sea creature, lifeless fingers unspooling from the hatchet they once clutched.

Fenton knelt to pick up the dropped weapon for himself as Antonio swung his cleaver into the side of Shorty's neck. It *thunked* like a side of raw beef, splitting open more than three-quarters of the way. The blade still in, Antonio pushed on the little man's head with his slick-proof shoe, pulled the cleaver back, and the head spilled off the neck, connected by a tendril of flesh like a wilting flower. Crimson jets exploded from the severed arteries on both sides in a shower-nozzle spray straight out of *Shogun Assassin*. Blood mixed with the detergent like some morbid water park ride. Fenton slipped around in it, hands and feet going every which way, and the decapitated body collapsed on top of him as he tried to stand up, bright red gouts splattering his face, detergent stinging eyes wide with fright.

Buzz Cut's second charge was interrupted as Ruby speared him in the side with her bayonet, calling him a goddamned Nazi. He stopped in his tracks with a grunt. Past her, Fenton saw the female goon racing down the corridor in the direction of the other search party, no longer in possession of her machete. Stephanie somehow had it now, and was burying it in Buzz Cut's piggy face with an overhead swing. He fumbled the sledgehammer, arms pinwheeling, dropping hard on his ass.

Fenton clawed himself out from under Shorty, letting Antonio help him to his feet. He wiped his face with his shirt tail. They joined Ruby and Stephanie over the fallen foot soldiers. Buzz Cut lay on his back, eyes still moving, face twitching uncontrollably, jangling his warthog nose ring. The spine of the machete jutted slightly.

Ruby looked to the young girl, her eyes like glaciers. "Make sure."

Stephanie nodded. Though she hesitated, an angry smile came across her face when she finally stomped on the blade. Over and over. She didn't know her own strength. The blade cleaved through his head in a series of cracks and crunches and the half-moon of one side flopped away like a split melon. Dark blood spritzed from severed cranial arteries, a profile view of skull and muscle layers Fenton could have done without. He turned away, gagging.

Stephanie huffed from exertion, but seemed calm and collected considering what she'd just done. Sweat sprinkled her brow. She bent down to retrieve the machete and Fenton nearly forgot to stare at her ass—that's how crazy shit was getting.

"Come on, we can't stay here," Ruby said.

Stephanie pointed with her eyes at the loading dock door. Antonio nodded in agreement. Ruby took a deep breath, hands still shaky. Fenton wasn't sure if it was her nerves from having stabbed someone, or just a case of the Parkinson's. Either way it didn't matter. He was going ditch these douchebags as soon as he could. He could sneak around easier on his own. Find his own way out of here.

Antonio approached the lever on the receiving bay wall and the group stepped closer to the platform. Looking at the loading dock's massive, rolling door, Ruby clutched her bayonet tighter.

"Hit it," she said.

Antonio pulled the lever, the chain rolled on its wheel, and the door began to inch up. There was a rumbling sound then, like a mechanical demon rising out of the earth, and as the door came up halfway, Fenton realized what it was.

Stephanie gasped. "Oh no…"

~

Desmond raised his walkie-talkie to his mouth. "Cut the power."

A static-filled voice said, "Right, boss."

One of his foot soldiers—a retired power company employee named Buck—had climbed up the telephone pole nearest the store, tools at the ready. Desmond preferred to hunt in darkness, for the realm of shadows was the right dimension for underworld creatures.

It made him feel vampiric, more demon than man. It would also hinder anyone passing down the road from easily noticing the truck lodged in the front of the building.

He called his posse away from the eviscerated mother on the table, where Eve licked Gore's drill-bit clean of blood and skin like the cake mix off a baking beater They'd had enough fun.

"Lunch break's over. You're on the clock. Let's get to work."

Eve slinked toward him, her eyes bright with desire now that she'd had her fill of fetal blood, the most virginal blood of all. He knew she'd be hornier than a toad right now, but he wasn't about to throw it in her with the competition still fierce, so when she pushed her breasts together he slapped her in the face. Her eyes went wide and she touched the red spot on her cheek.

"You brute!" she said.

"You love it."

She smiled devilishly. "True."

"I'll fuck you face-down in a pile of bodies later. Dry your panties and follow me."

As they walked out of produce and towards the seafood case, Eve snatched up the blood-sodden bag of rolls Cory used to staunch his hemorrhaging crotch. She crammed the crimson dough in her mouth without a look back. Marcel and Laila followed, faces so slick with blood they looked like busted tomatoes. Gore frolicked, a leprechaun swinging power tools. Goofy bastard. The other soldiers of the produce war lay dead. They would be cremated in the end when Desmond had Freshway burned down. He vowed to put all of their pictures up in his store under the *employee of the month* banner.

The lights went out, leaving only the moonlight through the foyer and the faint glow of a few cases via the backup generator, soft gold in the blackness of the rear of the store. The operating screen of the bakery oven still burned red, linked to an alternate power source, as was most of the heavy equipment. Apparently Buck had been unable to sever it.

Someone skinny sprinted through the shadows. Desmond flicked on his flashlight, spotting his front end manager, Dizzy Q. A retinue of soldiers fell in behind her. The woman's bird-like body and face were splashed with blood. He noticed she'd lost her trusty machete.

"They got 'em," she said, lips aquiver. "They done killed Fat

Freddy and li'l Jay too!"

Desmond grimaced. "This is getting ridiculous." He turned to his immediate crew. "Marcel, Eve and Gore, go to the backroom and take those other assholes down. Laila and Dizzy Q, come with me. We're gonna find Booker and his little boyfriend."

He considered sending the auxiliary soldiers with the Inner Circle, but without Marcel, Eve, and Gore, he might be the vulnerable one if Freshway thought they could stop the attack by cutting off the head of the snake. Better to fortify his own defenses. The Inner Circle could handle the Christian pests in the back.

He'd heard the rumble of the loading dock door, just before Buck cut the power. But it too was on the secondary power source, much like the rest of the receiving bay's machines, including the cardboard baler, the ice machine, and the trash compactor. Desmond could shut it all down if he accessed the motor room upstairs, but right now there were more pressing issues.

He lifted his walkie-talkie.

This time he called Big Delbert, the driver.

~

Ruby's heart sank into her stomach acid and boiled there.

Once the loading dock door was up, it revealed not the back parking lot, but another set of doors. They were locked together and dotted with bird shit, the big black frame reading *Devil's Food* with the cherry red cartoon characters of the grocery store's logo, little Red Hots devils in diapers. A steel bumper spanned the base of the doors, and rows of taillights ran all the way up and down both sides, their glow filling the now dark receiving bay with haunted, crimson light like a photo-developing room.

The rumbling they'd heard had been this tractor-trailer delivery truck backing up to the loading dock, blocking the doorway so they couldn't get out.

Antonio let out a roar of frustration and ran at the truck, hoping to squeeze between it and the loading dock, but there was simply no room in the gap. Even Stephanie wouldn't fit through a space that small. He swung his cleaver at the lock and Ruby called him back.

"You're just going to dull the blade, hon."

"But maybe we can get inside…"

"And so what if we did? You know all refrigerated trucks end in a steel wall. We can't get to the driver's cab from inside the shaft. It'd just be another box."

Fenton snorted. "*Shaft...box.*"

Antonio turned to the little twerp, fire in his eyes now. When he stepped forward Fenton scampered back.

"You ought to learn some manners," Antonio said. "Talking that way around ladies. What's wrong with you, *tonto*? You ought to be ashamed."

Fenton smirked. "And you ought to go back to Puerto Rico. *Andale Arriba,* Speedy Gonzalez."

Ruby had to get between them before Antonio socked the bastard. She felt no desire to protect Fenton, but there was strength in numbers. The S.O.B had proven useless so far, but he could at least be counted on to swing a knife at the bad guys, right?

"Simmer down, Antonio," she said. "You can tan his hide when this is all over."

Antonio glared once more at Fenton, then resigned. "Okay, Miss Ruby. I do it for you."

She patted his shoulder. "You're a good man. We get out of this and I'll bake you some of my famous chocolate cream biscuits." She looked to Stephanie. "You too, hon."

The blonde girl smiled. Until tonight, Ruby had disliked Stephanie, believing her to be too tawdry, a floozy. But maybe she was a misguided latchkey kid. Things just weren't the same in this country now that both parents worked. In Ruby's day the man stayed home and the women raised the children. She was no anti-feminist; she believed a woman had a right to want a career. But at least one parent should stay home to raise their children. Otherwise America churned out more wayward youths who hopped into bed with each other at the drop of a dime, their heads poisoned by the marijuana. Ruby vowed if they both got out of here alive, she'd make an effort to get involved in Stephanie's life. Maybe they'd find she not only needed her, but that Ruby needed Stephanie just as much.

But that was a thought for another day; one she hoped she'd live to see.

"So what now?" Fenton asked.

Ruby took a deep breath.

"You're our fearless leader, right?" Fenton said. "So come on, Mrs. General Patton, what are we supposed to do?"

"Hush, sonny! I'm thinking."

But there wasn't time to do so. Footsteps approached down the hallway of the backroom. The Freshway four turned to face them, weapons at the ready, knowing now what they were truly capable of when pushed too far.

Ruby grit her teeth, humming the old Pearl Harbor memorial tune *Praise the Lord and Pass the Ammunition*.

CHAPTER SEVEN
BLIND BLEEDING THE BLIND

THEY GOT LOW, HIDING BEHIND the meat counter as Desmond and his posse walked by. With the lights out, Booker hoped he and Kyle could remain out of sight until they felt ready to strike back. He wondered if he ever would be, after what happened to Darla. He'd only seen the beginning of the sacrificial slaughter, but it was enough to let him know what they were in for if the Devil's Food clan go a hold of them.

He heard Desmond say, "What's your 20, Big Delbert?"

A voice replied as if through a ham radio. "I'm out back here, good buddy. This diesel-drivin' daddy's boxin' 'em in."

"Just back up the truck, Delbert."

"Ten-four, good buddy. I got 'em."

Booker leaned in to Kyle, whispering. "They must be blocking the loading dock."

Kyle nodded but said nothing, a bead of sweat rolling down his nose. The young man looked the way Booker felt—scared and angry. They'd both been more violent than they'd ever been in their lives. They'd committed murder here tonight. Sure, it was self-defense, but taking a life was still taking a life. It rattled a decent man. Somehow Booker doubted it made Desmond so much as blink.

The man's hostility dumbfounded Booker. They'd never been the best of friends while working together, Desmond seeing their dual positions as a competition, but they'd gotten along well enough. The last time Booker had seen him, they shook hands and smiled when Desmond moved on to his Devil's Food job, promising each other they'd go out for a beer sometime, the way people often do whether they intend to or not. There was no animosity, no more rivalry. What had driven Desmond to want to kill him and everyone else in the store?

The Devil's Food clan marched past, flashlights scanning over the meat counter but not hitting him and Kyle with their beams. The soldiers headed toward the bakery and he and Kyle sighed with relief.

"We need new weapons," Kyle said. "I lost mine."

"Me too." It sickened Booker to remember the ease with which his knife went through that man's groin back in the produce aisle, but he also knew if he hadn't done it, he'd either be dead now or wishing he was. "Let's get over to the seafood prep room. There are more knives back there—filet knives."

The meat and seafood departments were connected. One long case housed the red meat, chicken, fish, and shellfish, all separated by glass dividers to avoid cross contamination. Both sections had their own refrigerated rooms where employees could prepare steaks, grind fresh chuck, filet fish, and access their walk-in coolers and freezers. Booker and Kyle crouched as they ran behind the case and slipped through the swinging door to the seafood room. The salmon filet knives were drying by the sanitation sink.

"Not as heavy duty as the butcher knives," Booker said, "but they'll do."

"There's got to be another way out," Kyle said.

Booker tucked his knife beneath his belt. The keys clipped to his hip jangled, giving him an idea.

~

Marcel ran his hand through his mullet. The blonde had turned pink with blood. In his other hand, the spikes of his knife were caked in baby bowels. Gore practically skipped through the darkness, the power drill whirring in his hand. Beside them, Eve breathed heavily, her loins so stirred Marcel could almost smell them. She'd already grabbed his ass and asked for a quickie, but he was too focused on the killing. He was putting that butcher's certification to great use tonight and it excited him even more than Eve's tight snatch. He promised he'd eat her out later if he let her fuck her in the ass, and she gave his package a little squeeze in agreement. The fuck would be a nice victory celebration.

Eve held no weapon but still had her favorite knife at her side, the one she used to chop celery for chicken salad. Once, she had caught a staff member taking a container of it to the break room without paying for it. Marcel brought the thief into the office, but instead of firing him he bashed in his face with an ashtray. Before the employee fell unconscious, Marcel had shouted, "I hate unexplained product loss! I'm going to reduce shrink by reducing you to pulp!" Then Eve appeared out of the hidden chamber, wearing her apron and wielding that very knife, slathered in mayonnaise from preparing the chicken salad. Since the man stole from her department, it was her responsibility (and great pleasure) to inflict the final blow.

With Marcel's help, they hoisted the thief up, bent him over the desk, and undid his jeans. He wore no underwear and there were a few nuggets of toilet paper stuck in the hair of his ass crack. His balls dangled low and Eve pawed at them like a kitten with a Christmas ornament. Pubic lice scurried into the cavern of his ass and Eve reared back and sent the blade between those dirty buttocks, widening the asshole in a jet of brownish blood. The thief awoke shrieking like an infant and Marcel held him down, hammering his skull, and Eve sodomized him with the deli knife until she sawed right through his taint and up into his scrotum, driving the blade into the wrinkly sack, impaling one testicle and then another, making a shish kabob of his quivering nuts.

Later Eve told Marcel she'd brought home and grilled the testicles, adding green peppers, onion and chunks of marinated chicken, making a true kabob out of them, and ate it while fingering herself to a new episode of *Family Matters*. Before the store opened the next morning, they skinned the thief's carcass and brought it to the meat team to be deboned and ground up for a buy-one-pound-get-one-pound-free chuck deal that sold out by closing time. As for the skin, Eve baked it in her chicken roaster, tanning it like leather, and made herself a holster from it in which to hold the esteemed asshole-skewering blade

She drew it from that holster now as they entered Freshway's backroom.

~

There was an old lady with a goddamned spear of some kind. It was hard to tell in all this darkness. Eve squinted. Next to the elderly woman stood a big man in a meat coat covered in more than just steak juice. They were flanked by a younger man and an even younger girl. Eve eyed her, liking what she saw in the faint, red light.

"Dibs on the teeny-bopper," she said.

Gore groaned in disappointment, causing Eve to roll her eyes. He was just like all the other teenage boys who joined their cult; nothing excited him more than rape. Their brand of Satanism attracted the kids who'd been jilted and denied by girls so much their lusts had turned violent. Rape was fine enough. Eve certainly partook of her fair share. But it was far from the most thrilling part of their job. One day Gore would learn that, even if she had to drive it into him slowly, just like the intestines she'd shoved up his ass, one bit at a time. If he was ever going to make grocery department manager, he had to learn the importance of rotation, organization, variety. Change things up. Keep things exciting. Even raping hot little bitches got old.

Approaching their prey, Gore held out his drill like a pistol, whirring the bit, small pieces of mommy-belly turning upon it. Its built-in light shined a path for them to see. Eve heard the leather of Marcel's glove as he tightened his grip on that replica of the knife from *Cobra* he was so crazy about. Eve understood how easy it was to grow attached to a killing tool. The knife in her hand prepped chicken salad, her top seller with the highest profit margin. It brought her luck in so many other ways too.

The old lady raised her spear as the Devil's Food trio approached, looking like Betty White playing a Ninja Turtle.

Eve saw her fallen comrades lying in pools of their own gore and felt nothing for them, nothing for anyone. She'd long ago detached from humanity. She was a demoness now. Eve's only emotions were lust and fury. Satan was the only one she loved.

"Stay back!" the old lady said.

"What're you gonna do about it, Nana?" Gore provoked, drilling the air, laughing. "Whatcha think you gonna do with that spear, huh? Knit me a sweater?"

Eve took a more serious approach. "You can't win. We have the store surrounded. You can die a lonely death, or you can give yourself to Satan as a human sacrifice. At least then you'll die with purpose. You might be lucky enough to serve him in the glory of Hades."

The old woman's eyes flashed behind her glasses. "You must be off your rockers. I'm not going to hell. I'm a good Christian woman and I'll be one even when I'm in my grave."

"That may come sooner than you thought."

"I've lived a long life, lady. And I've seen worse than the likes of you. Lost my husband of forty-one years and my only child died in the jungles of Vietnam fighting the men in the black pajamas! Compared to that, you all are about as troubling as a cloudy day."

Eve smiled. The old biddy surprised her. It was always nice to see a woman taking charge. Granny here had earned her respect, and Eve preferred a challenge. The teenage girl could wait.

"I'm impressed," Eve told the old woman. "You're not as cowardly as your co-workers. They ran away, leaving a pregnant woman to die."

The old woman's face sank. "Darla?"

"*Formerly* Darla—now just a spill in the produce department. Better grab a mop."

The man in the meat coat rushed them, Eve's words clearly setting him off. Perhaps it was this spic who'd knocked DARLA up. He ran with his cleaver held high.

Marcel came beside Eve. "This one's mine."

He sheathed his *Cobra* knife and reached into his coat, retrieving his special cleaver, the one with the handle of pearl. The two butchers charged each other in a grocery store joust, storming down the row of back stock, blades gleaming red in the tractor-trailer's taillights. When they collided, the blades connected too, clinking as they swung and pivoted, close enough now that Eve could read the large man's nametag—ANTONIO, MEAT MANAGER.

I wouldn't mind managing his *meat*, she thought. From his size and ethnicity, Eve figured ANTONIO would have quite the sausage in stock. She laughed to herself. Here she'd been looking down on Gore for thinking of sex during the siege, and she was getting horny again. If she got to slurp down that teen girl's blood, she might have to masturbate at the very least.

Marcel swung high above his head, aiming for ANTONIO's shoulder, but the meat manager was quicker, slicing across Marcel's abdomen, ripping open his shirt and exposing the pale flesh beneath. Slowly, a line of red appeared. It wasn't a deep cut, but it was a long one. The sight of the blood wetted both sets of Eve's lips.

Marcel didn't even flinch. He hacked with the cleaver and sunk it where ANTONIO's shoulder met his neck. An arterial spray erupted, spattering Marcel's face. Eve pinched her nipple, then darted through like a little girl under sprinklers, letting the hot gore give her a facial. She skirted the battling men and charged the others cowering behind them.

The old lady's nametag read RUBY.

Eve's favorite color.

~

Gore's dick was hard as granite as he ran by the others, going right for Stephanie. He'd wanted to fuck her since day one on the job, but the stuck-up bitch seemed to flirt with every guy except him, even Booker, who was old enough to be her dad! Here was the hottest slut in Freshway, loose and easy and totally metal, and she wouldn't even make polite conversation with him. Now he didn't want to hear her say anything...other than begging for her life and asking how he wanted his dick sucked.

Fenton stood behind her, a pitiful knife in his hand that could barely spread butter. It seemed almost a shame to kill the guy. He was just rotten enough to join the Devil's Food team, but too much of a slacker to make the grade. If he wasn't willing to work, he was never going to get anywhere in life. But he wouldn't have to worry about living anymore, now would he? He was going to be exterminated. They all were. Gore didn't care how these others would go out. All he wanted was Stephanie to die, slow and screaming.

But the cunt had a machete.

It was dripping red, so she obviously wasn't hesitant to use it. She'd have the reach on him if he used the drill, so he holstered it for now, imagining whirring it through those lovely blue eyes of hers so she'd be blind when he raped her, making her easier to dominate. He pawed at his tool belt, drawing the hammer and the huge, industrial screwdriver he'd filed down. He bet she'd spread real easy for it, too. He rolled his shoulders, preparing for battle, but Stephanie came at him first.

"Oh, shit!"

~

He was hurt. Hurt *bad*. But he wasn't down yet.

Antonio never gave up the fight on the football field, no matter the score. He brought this attitude to everything in life. He wouldn't drop until all his strength was gone.

But he was bleeding out fast. If he didn't take this mullet maniac out soon, he would exsanguinate. And the blood loss was already making him weak. His shoulder was so destroyed he couldn't raise his arm. At least it hadn't been his dominant arm. He could still swing his cleaver. He turned sharply, flipped the blade, and jabbed at the mullet man's side. This time he sliced the stomach with a much deeper cut, the blade sinking into the flesh with a wet pop.

Antonio's enemy stumbled from the blow, giving him another chance to strike, and he sent the blade into the exact same spot, deepening the wound. He continued like a boxer going for the ribs. He felt his rival's cleaver striking back, but Antonio was always one to play through the pain. He ignored it, believing the best defense was a stronger offense. He hacked and chopped that same spot, sawing down a flesh tree, the sinew flying in steaming confetti, and with the final blow the man's kidney burst and he shit himself audibly. He fell limp against Antonio, but Antonio kept on hacking, gutting the mullet man now, the innards unfurling and spilling out as one congealed blob. Half mad from the violence, Antonio just kept on hacking, even when the cleaver just clinked off the spine.

~

Stephanie had never liked this turd.

What was his name? Gordo?

Whatever.

She might not remember his name but she sure remembered his zit-coated face. When he'd worked here, those beady, black eyes ogled her so often she could have charged him a viewing fee. It wasn't just his greasy face and scrawny body that made him ugly; it was his personality. He stared hard from a distance but whenever she approached he could barely get a word out, always adjusting his balls or picking his nose (she'd even caught him eating a booger once). Plus, he listened to that awful death metal crap in the break room all the time, and everyone knows that people who listen to that kill-your-mother, rape-your-dog shit are demented dickheads with no lives. No wonder he'd joined up with these devil-worshipping killers! Those Cannibal Corpse lyrics rot your brain, turning people into psychopaths who toss babies in the oven. Her parents and teachers called her Motley Crüe records satanic! If they only knew...

She raised the machete over Gordo's head, but instead of swinging she waited until he looked up at it and then kicked him square in the nuts. He folded into himself, mouth making an O, eyes rolling.

Stephanie grinned. "Bulls-eye!"

Now it was the machete's turn. She swung but Gordo fell backward into a stack of toilet paper and the whole thing came spilling down between them. When Stephanie stepped out of the way, she fell over someone's leg. She saw who had tripped her as Fenton fled from the back room, into darkness.

Stephanie shouted after him. "Cocksucker!"

The prick knocked her down on purpose! Throwing her to the wolves to give himself a chance to escape, like a chicken shit in a zombie movie.

Or maybe he had other motivations for tripping her. Maybe he wanted them to lose.

But why?

Still groaning, Gordo pulled himself to his feet, and judging by the way he bared those razors he called teeth, he was hell bent on making her suffer for popping him in his little raisin balls. He closed in on her with his *Home Improvement* weaponry, but she slashed at him and he jumped back, the blade just missing his face.

Ruby came around a stack of bakery baskets, jabbing at the advancing redhead woman. In the low, crimson light, Stephanie couldn't tell if either of them was injured yet. She hoped Ruby was okay. Deeper in the row, Antonio made shredded meat of the shithead with the mullet. Seeing her fellow employees putting up a good fight inspired her to keep pressing on too. Stephanie charged at Gordo with the handle of the machete in both hands, feeling like Red-Fucking-Sonja wielding a sword, and her adrenal glands worked overtime at the look of fear on her opponent's pus-packed face. She swiped and swiped, Gordo walking back, but then he dodged under her blade, swinging the hammer right into her leg, bashing the kneecap.

Stephanie fell, the machete spinning away, and before she could grab for it Gordo hammered her in the skull, dizzying her, and he grabbed her by the hair with both hands and started dragging her into the shadows where no one could see what he was about to do.

CHAPTER EIGHT
NO FORGIVENESS (WITHOUT BLOODSHED)

FENTON SPRINTED DOWN THE FROZEN aisle on the balls of his feet. He'd just barely missed being spotted by the rest of the soldiers who were out on the sales floor. If he could just make it to the front he could see if anyone remained in the parking lot or if they'd all come inside by now. Maybe he could walk right out the front door. The old bag, the slut, and the Mexican (or whatever) sure hadn't thought of that. Buncha dipshits. Leaving them was a smart move, and ditto tripping Stephanie to buy him some time. That's what she got for being a cock tease. He didn't necessarily hope she would get killed but, to paraphrase Ivan Drago, "If she dies, she dies."

When he reached the ice cream he peaked around the corner, scanning the shadows for movement. There was nothing, but still he waited. The assassins could very well have planted a sniper. He hadn't seen any guns yet, but who knew? If only he had one of his old man's pistols. Dear old Dad was an NRA nut job, but when Fenton asked for a gun of his own the old man told him he wasn't mature enough, despite being well into his twenties. Like everyone else in the world, Dad was always trying to screw him. Well, Fenton had had just about enough of being fucked over. People were shit and it was time to flush. The only person he wanted to save tonight was himself.

Convinced the coast was clear, he rounded the corner and headed toward the front end, a new attitude showing in his stride. He twirled the knife in his fingers like Tommy Lee with a drumstick and when he reached the service counter he went to steal lottery scratch-off tickets and a few packs of cigarettes before leaving. He stuffed his jeans like back in his teenage shoplifter days. Maybe it was time to go back to that, only steal bigger, better things, stuff he could sell on the street. It sure would beat mopping floors.

When he emerged from the service desk, a fist slammed against his jaw and he stumbled into the plastic wall, cracking it against his back. He slid down until he was on his butt. The shadow of a man stood over him, flanked by two women, his shaved head gleaming in the faint glow of the streetlights outside.

"Well if it isn't the slacker," Desmond said. "Having yourself a smoke break?"

Fenton put his hands up in a passive manner.

Between the service desk and aisles, more Devil's Food faithfuls took their places as sentries to ensure no one interfered. Freshway had already missed their best chance to rescue him. Fucking pieces of shit!

"Drop the blade," Desmond said.

Fenton immediately obeyed, all his cocky assurance having dribbled away like so much piss. His lower lip trembled, nostrils moistening.

He whimpered through his sobs. "Please… please, don't hurt me."

It shamed Fenton when Desmond laughed, but the laughter of the women stung even more. Goddamned bitches were all the same.

"Please… please, I'll do anything you want."

"All except work." Desmond spat in his face. "You're lazier than a house cat. And I *hate* house cats. I'm fucking allergic!"

"I'm s-s-sorry. I'm s-s-so, so sorry."

The older of the two women chuckled. "Desmond, you may be allergic to cats but this twerp must be allergic to pussy." She sneered at Fenton. "Cry some more, dipshit, I really find that attractive in a man."

The younger, more attractive girl snickered. He recognized her from when she'd worked here. "Oh, yeah," she said. "*So* hot."

Desmond squatted beside him, his breath like dog farts against Fenton's cheek.

"You abandoned your friends," Desmond said, poking him.

"No… they… they ain't m-m-my friends."

"But they're your coworkers."

"Not no more. I… q-q-quit."

He felt the snot dangling out of his nose but dared not wipe it away. He tasted salt as his tears ran over his lips. If Desmond got any closer, Fenton might just lose bladder control.

"So you've left Freshway, huh?" Desmond said. "That must be a huge relief…for them."

"Fuck 'em." Desperate, he gave the horns salute made popular by Ronnie James Dio. "Devil's Food rules."

Desmond raised an eyebrow, and in that simple expression Fenton saw his opening.

"I w-w-wanna join up with you," he said. "I can help you find them."

The younger girl stepped beside her boss. Her nametag said *Laila.*

"Desmond," Laila said, "he's a betrayer! The cards spoke of one. He can be an asset to assure our victory."

Desmond scoffed. "I don't need a scout to track someone down in a fucking store. We'll succeed with or without Li'l Dicked Arnold."

"Of course. Praise Hell. But it would please our dark lord all the more to bring a Judas into our midst."

The dark lord?

Fenton didn't understand but didn't have to. If it meant it would save his ass, he would swear to Satan and obey this bitch's cards, whatever in their deck.

Desmond ran his hand over his chin, considering.

"So," he said. "You want a job with our great company then, do you?"

Fenton nodded emphatically. "Yes, sir!"

"Alright. You're the janitor here, which means you have keys to the motor room and everything. That's helpful, but I could always just take them off your corpse."

Gulp.

"But," Desmond continued, "Laila is our high priestess and I trust her premonitions. So I'll let you live for now, pussy. But if you want me to hire you, you have to show me you have what it takes to be part of the Devil's Food family."

"Yes, sir!" Fenton dared a smile. "I'll do whatever you want."

Desmond chuckled and stood up straight. He unzipped his fly, a thick dick flopping out. Fenton was frozen in horror, his eyes stuck on the growing erection. He felt the heads of the sentries turning, not wanting to miss out on this degradation.

"First," Desmond said, "you're going to suck my dick. And you're going to do a good job of it too. You'll know you're doing it right when your nose hits my pubes. You must swallow every drop of my demon seed."

Fenton shivered. "Um…"

"Shut up, pussy. Your mouth is for sucking, not speaking. Once you've guzzled my jizz, you'll have proved your devotion to me as your manager, but you'll still need to prove your subservience to Lord Satan."

Laila smirked. "And there's only one way to do that."

"That's right," Desmond said. "The next Freshway employee dies by your hand."

The three of them cheered in unison. "Hail Satan!"

Desmond came closer, brushing the head of his cock against Fenton's cheek, smearing it with drops of pre-cum.

Fenton closed his eyes. He also opened his mouth.

~

Ruby yelled, actually thrilled when her jerry-rigged bayonet pierced her attacker's belly. The woman gasped and she dropped the knife to grab the bayonet with both hands. She didn't try to pull it free; she just tried to keep Ruby from pushing it in any deeper. And she was succeeding. Even wounded, the woman was younger, stronger. She was also *fast*. It winded Ruby just to hold the crazy bitch back. Had she not held the advantage of a better reach, she might be a little more than a memory right now.

She held tight as the woman turned, taking the bayonet and Ruby with her. The woman's teeth clenched through rising blood and her eyes had gone hard and black. Ruby saw no humanity in them, only the deep, punishing stare of madness. This was no woman. This was a beast.

The beast screamed. "I'm gonna kill you, you old cunt!"

"Go to hell!"

"Yes!" the beast said, grinning with menace. "And I will take you with me!"

They spun and spun and Ruby flashed back on the merry-go-round of a long, lost summer. The horses gleamed with fresh polish, it being the opening day of the county fair. Beside her was Fred—called Freddy then—young and handsome, hair slick with pomade, eyes blue as Sinatra's. He bought her cotton candy. Won her a stuffed bear by swinging a strongman hammer and ringing the bell. She'd let him kiss her cheek that night. Their first real date, July of 1948.

Dizziness shook the memory away like a dream stolen by an alarm clock. The backroom of the grocery store returned to her now with the haze of crimson light and Ruby grew nauseous, her arthritic hands struggling to hold onto her only weapon, the only thing keeping her alive. All the while the stabbed woman cackled like a Halloween witch. Maybe that's what she was.

Ruby lost her grip.

~

Pain quivered through Eve in rapturous ecstasy. She loved pain. It filled her with the white light of the fallen one. And this pain was the most intense she'd ever felt. While it excited her, it also weakened her. She was losing blood, losing steam, certain the bayonet in her belly was the only thing keeping her guts intact. The taste of copper rose in her throat and she could almost hear the chattering teeth of the reaper. She did not fear him, as the song advised. She welcomed his eternal embrace for his realm was but the anteroom to Hades. There she would worship at the throne of Satan, be his mattress kitten and earn a place as one of the many brides of Hell. She knew this just as surely as she knew she would take this Golden Girl with her.

Bayonet still in her belly, Eve ran at Ruby as she struggled to get to her feet.

"You've fallen," Eve said, "and you can't get up!"

Eve spun her hips, cracking the old broad in the face with the wood of the other end of the bayonet. Ruby's lip split and Eve had the urge to tongue kiss her. She told herself to save her lust until the old lady was a dead lady. She spun her hips again, the wooden shaft flapping from her belly like some bizarre umbilical chord, battering Ruby about the head and shoulders. But Eve just couldn't build up enough momentum to really hurt the geezer.

"Fuck it."

She went to the icemaker, lodged the end of the bayonet between the machine's metal legs, and snapped it in half. The bladed end remained in her gut, but now the rest of the weapon formed a spear of jagged wood.

Eve charged just as Ruby got to her feet, the spear raised above her head, ready to stab the old bitch right in the back. Ruby turned her neck to see the pointed edge coming at her, her eyes going wide. Despite the woman's age she was totally unprepared to meet the reaper. It was sad, really. Pathetic.

Eve swung down.

The spear made it halfway through the lunge before Eve lost her grip on it, pain exploding through her lower back. She felt something sharp split the muscle, something hard clack against her vertebrae. Eve gasped. Tears flooded her eyes. She reached behind with one hand, feeling the cleaver wedged into her back, right where her tribal tramp stamp was. When she tried to take a step, her legs gave out. She fell on her knees, the concrete merciless against them. The Hispanic man came out from behind her, his meat coat tied tight around a shoulder wound. It was soused red, but he was still standing.

Eve shuffled toward him on her knees. She gently placed her palms upon his hips, as if she were about to give him head. But she wanted to suck something else. If she were going to die, she wanted to go out doing what she loved. The tail of the meat coat hung from the shoulder down to his waist. She put it in her mouth, slurping the blood the material had sponged up.

The meat man shook his head. "*Dios mío.*"

He pushed her to the ground and when she fell back she landed on the cleaver with all her weight and the blade entered her spine, severing it from her hips, paralyzing her. She closed her eyes and when she opened them again the meat man and the old bird were standing over her.

Ruby glowered down at her. "You know something? You're nuttier than a fruit cake."

Eve tried to make one last grab, get one more bite of flesh, but Ruby planted her foot on the bayonet in Eve's belly and pushed down, splitting her innards. Eve felt them ooze out of her like some Lovecraftian child, the intestines the unfurling tentacles, the fetid stink of her expunged bowels like the very breath of Yba'sokug as he devoured the world. The copper aftertaste in her throat became a surge of flavor, the salty brine of her own blood completely flooding her mouth. She began to choke on her own gore, and just before she released a final death rattle, Eve shuddered in one last orgasm.

~

"Are you okay?"

Antonio held Ruby by the shoulders, more concerned for her than himself, despite the severity of his wounds. He told himself he'd been through worse, knowing it was a lie, a lie he wanted desperately to believe. He thought of Nelly and the children. He thought of Mamá and how no mother should ever have to bury her own babies.

Antonio crossed himself, wondering if he were doing it right. It had been that long.

Ruby's eyes reflected the concern he should have had for himself.

"Oh, Antonio! We've got to get you to a hospital."

"Yes. But first we must get out."

He rolled the dead woman over, put one foot on her back, and pulled the cleaver free. He went to the man he had killed, took the dead bastard's spiked knife, and gave it to Ruby.

"Oh, my," she said, turning it over in her hand. "This is intense."

They took a moment to breathe and Ruby turned around, looking in all directions.

"Where's Stephanie?" she asked.

CHAPTER NINE
PRIME EVIL

SHE WAS ONLY OUT FOR a few seconds, but that was all the time Gordo needed to pull her into the produce prep cooler. Stephanie awoke to the smell of fresh vegetables, which Darla had cut earlier. Was she really dead? Stephanie always rolled her eyes at expecting mothers, never wanting children of her own. Babies were little screaming, shitting, money-sucking vampires that stole your life from you. But that made her no less appalled at the idea of Darla and her baby falling into the depraved hands of these human monsters. God only knew what they had done to them.

But now Stephanie had to worry what was going to be done to her.

Gordo straddled her, jagged nails tearing open her top.

"I'm gonna rape you," he said. "I'm gonna rape you and drill your eyes out of your head, and then I'm gonna drive away in your car while my load dries in your rotting cunt. Always wanted that Firebird, even if it is a rusted-out hand-me-down. I'm gonna be just like Burt Reynolds. But you? You're gonna be dead as disco."

She writhed against him but it just made her tits jiggle in her bra, exciting him all the more. The waves of dull, throbbing pain rolling through her left knee made her struggle all the more torturous. He punched her in the face and again she saw stars, and Gordo laughed and started to headbang, his stupid Mohawk flapping like a zebra's mane. He sang some lyrics she recognized. One of her boyfriends loved early doom metal bands like Pentagram and Trouble. She was pretty sure this was a Venom song.

Well, she had some venom of her own.

When Gordo leaned in to kiss her she spit into his eye, and in that split second of his blindness Stephanie rocked her hips, swung up her shins and clenched them around Gordo's neck, putting his throat in a leglock.

It pays to have older brothers who are obsessed with WWF.

Holy Christ did it hurt her knee, though, and tears of pain stung her eyes. Gordo pawed at her feet as Stephanie rolled backward, but the position put too much weight on her neck. She didn't have the leverage she needed to twist Gordo's head like a corkscrew, so she had to let him go, but she managed to sit up, knocking him back off her hips and onto her thighs, enabling her to punch him in the jaw. He let out a whine like a puppy with a stepped-on tail. She hit him again and this time he fell off of her completely.

But he drew the hammer. He was armed. All she had was her fists.

Well, that and her foot.

As she stood, she planted another kick into his already swollen nut sack, her leg nearly buckling. His eyes crossed and he caved inward, but didn't drop his weapon. Stephanie looked to the swinging doors.

She ran.

~

The cereal aisle stood empty.

There were a good amount of crate displays, so they went from one to the other, hiding behind them like cops in an action movie. Kyle clutched his filet knife so hard he feared he might break it, but his nerves wouldn't let up. He stood behind his boss. Booker breathed heavily. Kyle wanted to tell him to keep it down but was too terrified to speak.

Booker waved him forward and they sprinted to the next display, a stack of peanut butter and jelly jars in a series of wooden crates. It made Kyle think of his mom and dad, and how he'd been such a finicky eater as a kid, eating almost nothing but PB&J when he was seven. His dad gave him a hard time about it, but Mom always served up the sandwiches with a smile. Crusts cut off and slightly toasted. Some milk on the side, always served in his Garfield glass.

Something pinched in Kyle's chest when he thought of his mother now. To think he might never see her again. Hell, even thinking he may have eaten his last peanut butter and jelly sandwich upset him, despite having not eaten one in years. The finality of everything rattled him. If poor Mila could die, any of them could. She was the best of the crew, the sweetest, the kindest, the most pure of heart. A good Christian girl. What kind of horrible asshole would let her die first?

You're the asshole here, pal.

He thought again about how he'd let Stephanie put his dick in her mouth for a few seconds (his final blowjob?) and guilt made his stomach boil. Over and over he saw the pallets flying, Mila bursting like she was Gallagher's watermelon.

These Devil's Food monsters had taken his true love. Not just from him, but from a world made so much better by her presence. It already operated with a huge shortage of girls like her, a make and model the production line had discontinued. He didn't just mean those rockin' tits and rosy, cherub face. He meant her warm heart and giving nature, her book smarts and her faith and her near endless patience. If the God she worshipped had called on her, okay, but why did he have to let her go so violently? Mila deserved better than that. Unfortunately, Kyle could do nothing about the way she'd died. But there was one thing she deserved that he could still give her, and that was justice.

It wasn't fear that made him clutch the knife now.

It was wrath.

~

"Okay," Booker whispered as they reached the end of the aisle. "Follow me."

They had to go through one of the checkout lanes to make it to the front of the store and Todd's office. Beside that door was the emergency exit. Booker had no doubts the Devil's Food crew would have blocked it off, but there was also a stairwell there to the second floor storage room where they kept holiday decorations and old, broken shit Todd refused to get rid of, always saying they might need it someday. Booker doubted they would find anything substantial they could use as a weapon among the Christmas wreaths, but that didn't matter. What mattered was the roof hatch on the ceiling of that goddamned storage room.

He eased his head around the corner, his breath catching in his chest.

At the customer service counter, Fenton was on his knees, giving Desmond some customer service that really went above and beyond. The young man's head bobbed like he was trying to bite an apple for Halloween, Desmond's meaty shaft pumping in and out of Fenton's swollen lips as he grabbed his head in both hands, thrusting, pounding, fucking his face.

Booker was no homophobe. His own brother was gay and he loved him dearly. But the sight of this blowjob (and the grotesque nature of their particular performance of it) made him sick to his stomach. It was obvious that it was less about desires of the flesh and more about power, dominance. Desmond was proving a point here, and Booker didn't want to know what it was.

The only real question was should they try to rescue Fenton. Surely the stupid punk didn't want to do what he was doing, right? It was hard to tell. He gobbled that cock with the gusto of Linda Lovelace. But it was probably knob-slobbering or death. Why else would Fenton suddenly suck off the leader of the clan trying to murder them all? Especially with a rapt audience too engrossed by these oral antics to properly guard the front of the store.

Kyle peaked over Booker's shoulder and put a hand to his mouth.

"What the fuck?" he whispered.

Booker pulled him back into the aisle. "Okay. They're distracted. Now might be our best chance to get to the stairway. But we have to try and save Fenton first. I think we—"

"What? Fuck Fenton! After all he's done here tonight, why should we risk our butts to save him?"

"'Cause it's the right thing to do."

"He wouldn't lift a finger to save us, or anyone but himself."

"That doesn't matter. We have to do what's right."

Kyle peaked around the corner again, wincing at the pornographic scene. "I don't know, Booker. Doesn't look like Fenton's in much trouble to me. I think he's blowing Desmond for a reason."

"Yeah, to save his life."

"Nah, dude. I think he's like, being initiated."

"What?!" Booker whisper-shouted. "That's crazy."

"Seriously. I mean, what about fraternities that put their plebs through hazing. They put freshmen through hell."

"The frat brothers don't blow each other!"

Kyle shrugged. "Maybe not, but what about skinheads."

Booker furrowed his brow. "What about them?"

"They boot new members in."

"Boot?"

"They kick the shit out of their latest members as a rite of passage."

Booker shook his head. "Jesus, just when I thought skinheads had done the stupidest thing ever they come up with something even more idiotic."

Kyle glanced around the corner again. "Dude... Fenton is *chugging*. He's never worked this hard around here. I think I see cum coming out of his nose."

"Shut the fuck up, Kyle! I don't wanna hear a play-by-play. If they're almost finished with this, we have to make our move now. Desmond will probably waste him."

"There's too many of them. No way we ran out on Darla just to kill ourselves helping this worthless piece of shit."

Booker saw something in the young man's face then, something he'd not seen in Kyle before. He didn't like it.

"Fuck him," Kyle said. "He didn't help Mila. He pushed Darla and Ruby. He's been a snake all his life. But..."

"But what?"

"I don't want to head for the roof just yet."

Booker tensed. "What? Why?"

"I'm not leaving until I get revenge."

"Jesus, Kyle, you must be outta your goddamned mind. You just said yourself, there's too many of them."

Kyle raised his knife, wiggling his fingers around the handle. "I know. We can't take them all out. I just want Desmond. He's the one who drove the truck into those pallets. He's the one who killed Mila. I'm gonna make him pay for that."

Booker wanted to reason with the young man, wanted lay some wisdom down on him about the futility of revenge, of how hate hurts the hater more than his enemy. But there was no time. He peaked around the corner. Desmond was just zipping up and Fenton was rising out of the puddle of his own drool. The two women went to him and patted him on the back. The other onlookers filed over to him in a line, presumably to welcome him to the fold.

Shit. Maybe Kyle's right about this being an initiation.

"I'm going," Booker said. "If you've got any brains in your head, you'll come with me."

Kyle rolled his shoulders, popping his neck.

They sprinted toward register seven.

~

After redoing his belt buckle (a replica of the Danzig skull), Desmond took a black magic marker from the service desk and wrote on Fenton's head, branding him. The punk's eyes still watered, lips puffy and glistening. After cutting short Eve's pregame blowjob, Desmond's scrotum had been backed up with cum. He'd filled Fenton's head with enough jizz to drown a toddler in and the new employee chugged in obedience. Desmond still had his doubts about him, but this act of servitude certainly raised Fenton up a notch.

"Hail Satan," the women said, swiftly echoed by the soldiers.

Desmond stared at Fenton. The punk had a dumb, slack face, his eyes glossy.

"Say it," Desmond told him.

Fenton blinked. "Hail Satan."

"Like you mean it, dipshit!"

Fenton shook. "Hail Satan! Praise him. I love the Devil!"

Something rustled at the end of the row of registers. Desmond swiveled his head on his huge neck, his nose and mustache quivering, a dog nose testing the air. The soldiers fell in line, having heard it too. Dizzy Q pointed. He followed her finger and that's when he saw the dark silhouette of a man, tall and lean and perfectly still. He must have frozen when he realized he'd been spotted.

Desmond turned to Fenton and handed him a box cutter.

"You know what to do," he said.

~

Fenton would have gulped if his throat weren't so sore. His fingers trembled around the handle of the box cutter.

You suck cock.

He tried to shake the thought from his mind as he edged closer to the shadow man. Why hadn't the guy tried to run? Why hadn't he made a move? Fenton trembled even more to think the guy would stand his ground, that he might have to fight.

That's 'cause you're a faggot.

Fenton clenched his teeth, the salty taste of Desmond' protein shake still fresh in his mouth. An evil heat built within him, a self-hatred that rose and boiled, fueling an inevitable discharge.

Desmond sure knows how to discharge.

Fenton cursed under his breath, telling his own brain to fuck off. He wasn't a fag! He loved titties! He loved getting *his* dick sucked, not sucking someone else's! That was disgusting. He'd only done what he had to do to survive. He just hoped if he killed this guy he'd never have to suck another dick to prove himself. He liked to think he was tough enough, but if he cut this asshole's throat it would be first-degree murder. If caught, that would mean prison, and then he'd be sucking more cocks than a hair metal groupie.

You used to love that music. Remember your Nelson poster? Ha ha, queer bait!

Fenton walked faster, anger overcoming his fear and triumphing over what little good sense he had. He reared back his arm and swung with the box cutter, aiming at the shadowy man's neck. There was a tearing sound that made Fenton shut his eyes tight, but while he yearned to recoil he kept on hacking, and if his victim fought back he did not feel it, such was his rush of rage.

I'm doing it! I'm killing someone! Who's the fag now?

Something gave way and brushed against his cutting hand. His eyes opened as he stumbled into some unknown obstacle. Whatever faced him caught the light and reflected it. Perceiving it as a plunging knife, he squealed and jumped back, and that's when the display fell to the floor.

Bob Saget's decapitated head smiled up at him.

Behind Fenton, the Devil's Food crew golf clapped quietly.

"Nice job," Desmond said. "You killed a cardboard cutout of the beloved host of *America's Funniest Home Videos*."

Laila snorted. "Yeah, dickweed. I love *Full House*. You're a monster!"

The gang all laughed at him. Fenton looked at the butchered, glossy cardboard, Saget's perfect teeth mocking him in a grin that now seemed sinister.

Saget.

You know what that rhymes with, don't you, cocksucker?

~

When the girl came down the back hall, Ruby ran to her. Stephanie arrived with a bloody nose, a nasty new limp and no blouse, leaving her in a lacey bra and jeans. They embraced.

"Oh, child, are you hurt bad?"

"I'm okay," Stephanie said, "just a little bruised."

Antonio lumbered behind them and when Stephanie saw him her jaw dropped. "Oh, fuck. Dude, that's...I mean...*dude.*"

"I know," Antonio said. "But I can still fight. Where's that little shit with the Mohawk?"

"No," Ruby said. "No more fighting if we can avoid it. It's time to get out of here. I don't care if we have to bash through a wall— we're getting the hell out!"

Stephanie sniffed back blood. "I don't wanna see another grocery store as long as I live. You guys have any extra weapons?"

Antonio rubbed his chin. "Follow me."

They went down the hall to where the forklift cage was. It was locked.

"Fuck!" Antonio said. "That could be a great weapon."

"Maybe something more practical, "Ruby said.

He pointed to the swinging doors that led into the meat department. "I have a place where I hide my best knives, that way other departments won't take them and forget to give them back, eh?" He winked, his use of humor surprising Ruby, given the shape he was in. "I have a butcher knife so sharp you can cut a fly in half in midair. We get it and do like Ruby say. We find a way out, no matter what."

He reached to his breast pocket and took out a pack of Camels. Ruby patted his hand down when he went for his lighter.

"No smoking," she said. "The glow of your ciggie will give us away."

"Oh, right." He put them away. "Okay, let us go."

~

Though the fans had died out when they cut the power, the meat room remained cool. It chilled the sweat on Stephanie's flesh. The rise of goose pimples reminded her she was still able to feel, and that meant she was still alive.

And what a life.

Here she was, crouching in the shadows of a cooler while her coworker moved rolling racks stacked with trays of steaks and pork chops in search of a knife she might use on another human being. She hoped it would be Gordo. If she had her way she'd get to cut the little rapist's sack off and shove it down his throat, then snip his pecker off and use it as a hacky sack. Then they could leave. She'd feel a whole lot better making him a eunuch. Guys who don't take no for an answer don't deserve to own the tools needed when someone finally says yes.

She looked at the slabs of meat, wondering if she'd ever be able to eat it again after all she'd seen tonight. Just the sight of Antonio alone could turn someone into a vegetarian. His mutilated flesh made bile rise in the back of Stephanie's throat. It was a miracle he was still standing. He'd wrapped the wounds in cellophane.

Antonio took a butcher knife from the drawer and handed it to Stephanie. When she brought the enormous blade to her arm she was able to shave some soft peach fuzz away with it. It was that fucking sharp.

She smiled. "Radical."

~

Before they left the cooler, Antonio took one last look at the meat room, his second home for the past five years. Even if they survived and the Devil's Food goons were arrested, he doubted he'd be able to come back. Who would even want to shop here after the story broke? Freshway had become a house of horrors. That was bound to have a negative impact on business. Getting food here would be like eating brunch at the site of Sharon Tate's slaying by the Manson Family. Murder houses never sold again. Murder stores would end up closing. He'd often worried Freshway would close due to Devil's Food stealing all their business, but up until now they'd held on. Devil's Food had simply figured out another way to shut them down.

He ran his hand across the cellophane covering a tray of perfectly trimmed and tied tenderloins. He kissed his fingertips and carried the kiss down to the USDA prime steaks. Even Todd couldn't take away Antonio's pride for bringing them in, making his meat case the most popular in town. He had long come to think of the meat department as separate from the rest of the store, as if he were running his own personal butcher shop, just like his father had. Meat was in Antonio's blood, part of his heart and history, old world craftsmanship at its finest.

Prime.

It meant the best possible quality, the most important thing, or a state of great vigor and strength. *The prime of one's life*. Antonio deflated when he realized his prime had just passed. The only *prime* at this moment belonged to the killers stalking them. They were the most vicious people he'd ever encountered. If the Freshway crew were going to get through this, they'd have to be just as merciless. Fight fire with fire. Burn the motherfuckers down.

He closed the cooler door behind him.

The dream was over. Time to face his new reality.

CHAPTER TEN
TORN APART

SCOTT SWUNG HIS ACURA INTO the side entrance to Freshway. The pleasant night air blew through the open windows, whipping his long hair around. It sucked the fat one to have to go to work, but they might not have to worry about employment for long if they weren't careful.

"You see Wad's car?" he asked Gabe.

Gabe peered out the passenger window at the collection of cars in the front parking lot of the grocery store. "I don't think so, dude. We're safe."

"Cool." Scott swung the wheel to the left, making sure his head-lights never flashed beyond the side of the building where someone looking out front could see them. Did it seem darker than usual? Maybe the store lost power and the time clock was fried anyway. Regardless, he didn't want to alert anyone to his and Gabe's arrival since they were rolling in so late.

"Told you so," Gabe said. "Wad probably cleared out in about thirty seconds, that piece of shit."

True enough, back at his place, Gabe appealed to reason when they were only about ten minutes behind schedule. If they were just a little late, he speculated, they ran a much bigger risk of running into Todd, or as he and Scott dubbed the manager almost a year ago, "Wad." They'd get their asses chewed out, maybe even fired if he noted their tardiness. But if they took their time and showed up even later, Wad would already be gone and they'd avoid disciplinary action. Outta sight, outta mind.

Besides, Gabe just scored some grass called Mean Green not ten minutes before Scott pulled up to his apartment building to take them to the night shift. Gabe hadn't even had a chance to unroll the baggie yet, so he said they might as well hang out at his crib while he rolled a few joints for the long hours ahead.

While Scott waited and shared the inaugural Mean Green blunt, he'd played some Pit Fighter on Gabe's Sega Genesis. They talked about how it wasn't shit compared to Mortal Kombat, the bad-ass arcade game that showed up at Funtown a couple months ago. You could rip out a motherfucker's spine, which made it so much more hardcore than stuff like Street Fighter. They couldn't wait for the game to show up on one of the home consoles, and they discussed how it better have all of the gore. Scott only owned a Super Nintendo, but he trusted that if either console got it right, it'd be the SNES for sure.

Gabe finished the joints, but the army dude in Pit Fighter spit on Scott's guy while he was down, and he got so pissed off he refused to leave before he exacted his revenge, so there went another fifteen minutes. Good thing Scott had some Mean Green to calm him down and put his head in a pleasant space even while he drove them nearer to another wasted night breaking their backs for Wad.

He guided the Acura toward the rear of the store. The tape player blasted through the speakers, Pearl Jam's album *Ten*. Scott picked it up this summer after hearing one of the songs on an indie radio station. Work might be constant waves of shittiness drowning him thirty-five hours a week, but sweet tunes and bud made it bearable. The seismic shift toward grunge music in the last year felt like a part of Scott's core identity, something that played as a soundtrack through his senior year and the pivotal transition from bullshit high school to the real world. Come September, he'd be packing up his CDs and a shitload of flannel shirts, heading out west for school.

He envied Gabe, living on his own in a palace of empty pizza boxes with no parents bitching at him, a bong within arm's reach in all three rooms. He was a few years older than Scott, but they'd become fast friends on the job when they discovered their mutual interest in grunge music. They worked the backroom while listening to their respective Walkmans, lending each other tapes through their shifts. Scott let Gabe hear Nirvana's first album, *Bleach*. In return, Gabe gave him Soundgarden's *Badmotorfinger*. He dug Chris Cornell's near falsetto vocals. They were a lot better than that King Diamond stuff he used to listen to. How did he ever get into that shit?

Scott's buzz took a paranoid turn as they pulled around the back of Freshway. He almost expected to find Todd waiting for them with his arms crossed, but instead they found a tractor-trailer rig backed up to the loading dock, its heavy rumbling loud enough to be heard over Pearl Jam's "Once."

What the hell, did I turn in at the wrong store? Scott wondered. Though almost positive he hadn't, he started to wonder if Mean Green was some heavier shit than either of them realized.

"Dude, that's a Devil's Food truck," Gabe said.

"Yeah, but what it's doing here?"

He drove past the truck and on to the handful of parking spots beyond the driveway that looped around the other side of the store. The lights back here failed to illuminate the cab well enough for Scott to determine if anyone sat inside it. So what if someone did? They couldn't know what time he and Gabe were supposed to start. They were now late enough that it was almost the top of the hour, when it would make sense for someone to be punching in for a shift.

The car faced an open field behind the paved lot of the store. A hundred yards beyond that stretched a black ribbon of woods where Scott could hear the shrill insect songs through his open window. The trees led to a suburban neighborhood on the other side, but not for at least a mile.

Scott switched off the ignition, flipped the cassette tape, and twisted the key a little more so the battery kept playing Pearl Jam. He studied the truck in his rearview mirror. No activity going on that he could see inside the cab.

"Maybe it's some joint effort between the stores for the overnight," Scott finally said.

Gabe thumbed open a tin of Altoids, revealing the three blunts he rolled earlier. "I think we owe it to ourselves to conduct a different joint effort before we go in there."

Scott smiled and turned up the stereo. What was another five minutes? He was pretty sure no one saw them come in.

~

Desmond's radio crackled. Big Delbert said, "Hey, boss."

Desmond pressed his walkie-talkie. "Yeah, Big D."

"You know I'm back here keeping an eye on the ass-end of things. Well, we may have a couple tryin' to spoil the big orgy. I ain't sure. They might end up leavin', from the looks of it."

"I think if they saw the orgy, it's only right they get to join in, don't you?" Desmond said.

"They're not acting like they saw nothin', but if you want me to give 'em an official invitation to the fun—"

"No need. We've got escorts out front who should be properly greeting all of our guests. I'll make sure they shake their asses over there pronto."

"Copy that." Big Delbert clicked off the call.

Desmond stared at the walkie-talkie with growing rage, hearing its casing groan as he tightened his grip. What was the point of stationing guards outside if they were going to miss someone driving through the parking lot? He primarily wanted them to head off any escape attempts, but that also meant making sure no one got near on the outside.

The others watched expectantly, including Laila, Dizzy Q, Fenton, and the blockade of nine other Devil's Food employees. Desmond kept them spread out between the aisles and checkout lanes while they waited for a progress report from Marcel, Eve, and Gore. They'd been gone awhile, but maybe they were just back there poking every dead hole in the latest Freshway losers who'd reached their expiration date.

Motorcycles grumbled outside. While not nearly as loud as actually riding around on a hog, the patient thunder of the idling engine packed enough volume to obscure other sounds—like someone in a car who pulled in through the side entrance. In his assistant manager days at Freshway, he'd chased off some teenagers who parked behind the store to make out, but he thought it far more likely they had some stragglers from the night shift. That stoner Gabe was one of them, always reeking of marijuana, eyes so bloodshot it looked like every vessel had burst.

Gore emerged from an aisle to the front of the store, walking gingerly, head down. Not the look of a returning conqueror, even by that scrawny little fuck's standards. A bad feeling swirled in Desmond's gut, for which he admonished himself. Hell foretold their victory; they had no cause for fear. Satan commanded triumph.

"The hell took you so long, Gore?" he asked. "And where's Marcel and Eve? They still back there weltering in blood?"

Gore shook his head. "No, they're...they're dead." His voice dropped at the end, but Desmond heard him perfectly.

A few of the Devil's Food employees gasped.

A wave of cold washed over Desmond. "*What?*"

"I think Antonio did them."

"You 'think'? Why didn't you see it? Were you hiding away, crying like a little girl while the other two were fighting for Hell?"

"No! I was on top of Stephanie, and I was about to split her twat in two...you know, for Satan...and, uh, some asshole must have hit me from behind. Total cheap shot. When I woke up, Eve and Marcel were dead and the others were gone."

Just like that, Desmond had lost half his Inner Circle. Eve and Marcel were the ones he trusted most in the group, too, the seasoned professionals. Truly committed to the cause, and reliable workers besides.

"Lucky thing they didn't cut your head off while you were passed out, isn't it?" Desmond said.

Gore shrugged. "Yeah, they must've thought I was dead, or just too chicken shit to kill in cold blood."

Obviously parts of the tale were bullshit, but Desmond let it go for now. They needed to preserve their greater numbers. Sparing Fenton already seemed like the right move.

Gore did a double take, finally noticing the man of the hour. "Hey, what's he doing here?"

"I'm part of Devil's Food now, I'm one of you," Fenton said. When his voice nearly cracked, he added, "Praise, hail Satan!"

"What? Fuck you, you closet Christian poser! Desmond, we can't trust this sponge-throat faggot, he doesn't even like death metal!"

"Enough!" Desmond said. "He's going to prove himself, aren't you, Fenton?"

"Yes, sir."

"You've got some proving of your own to do," Desmond told Gore. "You two go find Antonio and the others, and you both better come back with some fucking heads. I don't mean Bob Saget's, either, Fenton. Dizzy, take your group and go with them. Make sure they aren't skulking around on the sales floor. The rest of you stay put."

Gore bristled but didn't have the balls to complain. He branched off with Fenton, Dizzy, and four of the others toward the back of the store.

With that out of the way, Desmond said, "Laila, what the fuck's going on here?"

Laila flinched. "What do you mean?"

He walked over to her, arms swinging, grinding his heel on Bob Saget's decapitated cardboard head. "Are you deaf, bitch? Almost half of us are dead and Big Delbert just reported intruders."

Laila backed away, making idiotic vowel sounds.

"Maybe you *are* deaf." Desmond stopped in front of her, sticking his face right up to hers. "Whuh-whuh-uh-ah…you sound like Helen Keller."

"I didn't know about any intruders!" Laila finally managed to say. His supposed satanic priestess looked awfully close to breaking down in tears. Even in the dark he could see her lip quivering like some child's. It disgusted him.

"Why?" he shouted. "Did they leave that little tidbit off the memo when you were jacking off those entrails last night?"

"They don't reveal everything!"

"So is that why you look like you're about to piss your little panties, 'cause you don't know if I'm gonna let you live through this night?"

She shook her head. "I'm sorry, Desmond."

"You've got that right. You couldn't be any sorrier than what I've seen tonight. It's pathetic. I'd cut your fucking throat right now if I didn't think you were so worthless that your soul would just float up to heaven and escape Satan's wrath."

Laila gulped.

Desmond scouldn't believe he'd stuck himself with the weakest of the Inner Circle, a girl who couldn't divine entrails for shit and a weakling who could barely stand upright with that heavy tool belt around his waist.

"You'd better be right about us vanquishing this Christ-scum," Desmond said, waving a finger in her face. "Because if we don't, I'll take you out myself before they get the chance."

With that, he slapped her cheek as a promise of harsher things to come. Then he headed for the foyer to get his men out front to take care of their intruder problem.

~

Kyle joined Booker, attaining the safety of the hallway to Todd's office after following in a crouch from register to register. The worst part was being so close to where Mila lost her life. Kyle held on to that thought tight, more aware of it than how exposed they would be if the Devil's Food scum outside looked into the foyer. Someone would have to be standing at the exit to see down the full length of this hall. It branched off from the register lanes, running parallel behind the service desk. Kyle had to run to that desk at least ten times on a regular work day, grabbing smokes for customers who acted like Marlboro or Camel put out exactly one kind of cigarette, never specifying filtered, non-filtered, menthol, 100s, or whatever until he inevitably came back with the wrong thing.

The time clock hung in this hallway too, strategically placed across from Todd's office where the little prick could keep tabs on everyone clocking in and out. He always made a show of checking his watch, verifying no one got there late or left too early. The closed door seemed to mock their plight now, a reminder of Todd's absence. It boiled Kyle's blood to think of their boss cozied up at home while they were in here fighting for their lives. All of this was almost as much Todd's fault as Desmond's. They wouldn't even be here tonight if not for him.

Booker put a hand on Kyle's shoulder. "Come on," he whispered. "Let's get up there."

Despite the sound of motorcycles out front, Kyle had heard Desmond ordering Fenton around, Fenton obliging him like the little bitch he was—*yes sir, hail Satan.* Kyle hoped he got the chance to wring that traitor's neck.

That was one more thing he wouldn't get to do if they just abandoned the store, though. Booker was right about the unfavorable odds, since Devil's Food brought the numbers and the weapons. But what if Kyle and Booker somehow made it down from the roof, got past the people outside, and managed to find some help, only to be too late anyway? It wouldn't matter, and Kyle would have lost his best chance for payback.

Booker led them past Todd's office, where the emergency exit teased them at the end.

"Be ready to run," Booker said, and Kyle tensed up, but when

Booker pushed at the door, nothing happened. The bastards blocked off this exit too.

That left the doorway with the stairwell to the upstairs storage.

"Okay," Booker said, "we have to go up." He sifted through the keys in the red light from the EXIT sign.

Kyle whirled around when laughter broke out among Desmond's group. It felt like it was meant for him, though he knew that wasn't true. Once again he found himself looking right where Mila had died. Was that the shadow of her body in the wreckage?

"Got it," Booker said. He started moving up the stairs.

A radio crackled near the registers. Kyle strained to hear it, but it sounded too warped with static.

"Kyle!" Booker whispered.

Kyle turned back to him. "Go ahead and get the door open. I wanna hear this."

Booker sighed but resumed his ascent.

The radio talk stopped after a few seconds. Kyle couldn't hear any of it. He'd hoped for some confirmation about the fates of the others.

Then Gore started talking. Kyle listened to his back and forth with Desmond. Apparently Freshway was giving these satanic freaks some hell of their own, more than they could handle.

Booker managed to feed the key in the storage door at the top of the stairs. The bolt slid out of the lock. "Kyle, come on!"

"I'm staying!" Kyle whispered up. "Go get help."

He turned away from Booker's shadow, back to the hallway and the front entrance. Where Mila fell. Even if the bastards had slaughtered the rest of Freshway, he knew he couldn't leave her like this—especially not while they still had a fighting chance.

"Kyle!" Booker tried again.

Kyle tuned him out, didn't look back. Losing Booker's strength hurt their chances, but they obviously needed help. By all means, send in the cavalry, just let Kyle get his hands on Desmond first.

He almost started drooling when Desmond ordered Gore and Fenton to take a group and go looking for Kyle's coworkers. That didn't leave very many to cover the front with Desmond. Kyle heard the Devil's Food dictator ripping Laila a new asshole. The other five left behind might not be much more formidable than her. The opportunity seemed to be getting closer and closer, almost heaven-sent.

He wasn't expecting Desmond to walk across his field of vision. He pulled his head back to the edge of the doorway. Desmond never looked his way, though. He just rubbed the bridge of his nose as if annoyed, then turned and walked toward the aisles, his five servants tagging along.

Kyle studied the filet knife, imagining all the tender places he could cut his former supervisor until Desmond was begging Kyle to stop, screaming so loud for an end to the pain that Mila might hear his pitiful cries up in heaven. It would be the equal of Kyle's own grief over her loss, a life for a life.

I'm going to punish him for you, Mila. When he comes back in here, he's a fucking dead man.

~

Scott rolled the windows up before he and Gabe started burning the joint, just in case anyone looked out the back of Freshway. Neither of them smoked cigarettes, so unless Scott could convince someone he was driving around with a fog machine in midsummer, somebody could probably figure out what they were doing in here. Plus, a lack of fumigation didn't seem like a bad thing when it came to Mean Green. Scott felt so relaxed, his seat could have swallowed him into the mouth between the cushion and backrest.

"There's this Fender Mustang at the mall," he said, passing the joint back to Gabe. "Just like Kurt Cobain's. I'm gonna get that bad boy 'fore I leave."

"I didn't know you played."

Scott shook his head. "I don't. But dude, you know how close I'll be to Seattle out there?"

"How close?"

"Like, fourteen, fifteen hours away. That's way closer than we are here, ya know?"

Gabe coughed slightly as he exhaled a swath of smoke. "Yeah. I mean, I guess it is."

"Imma start my own band out there."

"Oh, cool. You gonna take lessons?"

Scott accepted the blunt back from Gabe. "Don't need to. It's in me, ya know? The music. I've been feelin' it. I've just gotta, like, channel it. I played on that Fender for a minute at Strings, and the sales dude said it sounded like I'd been playin' my whole life. Said I could be the next Nirvana."

"Oh, rad."

"Hell yeah, man. Grunge is really goin' places. It's the new music; it isn't, like, just some passing fad for Generation X. I wanna be a rock god just like my idols. Kurt Cobain, Chris Cornell, Layne Staley, Scott Weiland—these guys will be rockin' out well into their 80s!"

Scott knew he could tap into his angst. Living under his father's thumb, still having to work all summer despite busting ass at school for so many years…that blew the big one. Scott used to be more easygoing, but he couldn't go back to that now. He saw through the fakeness of everything to the secret truth—shit really sucked. What was there to be happy about? Even this car was just a hand-me-down from his mom, who cruised around these days in a much nicer Buick Regal. Yeah, Scott had a lot of reasons to be bummed.

"You oughta probably take some lessons anyway," Gabe said.

"A lot of these guys are self-taught. You just gotta think positive."

"What can I say?" Gabe grinned. "I'm a negative creep and I'm stoned."

They laughed at the reference to the first Nirvana album as "Even Flow" ended. The tractor-trailer rig's rumbling sounded a lot louder now, but Scott forgot about that as "Alive" played through the speakers. He felt moved to wax philosophic about it, really in touch with it his place in the world.

"*Love* this song. Even though stuff just, you know, sucks, you get through it. You keep fightin' and g'tting' through life."

On cue, Eddie Vedder sang the chorus.

"Right there." Scott pointed at the stereo, where the radio clock now put them sixty-four minutes late for their shift. He started to harmonize with Eddie. "I'm still aliii—"

The chain hit the driver's side window. Glass exploded across the front seats of the car, opening tiny cuts on Scott's face. He screamed. Someone yanked open the passenger door and dragged Gabe out the other side.

"What are you—" Scott started to say, then screamed again as someone grabbed a handful of his hair and ripped him through the window. He hit the pavement in a heap. Gabe landed beside him, shoved to the ground.

Three men stood over them. Two were the sort of bruisers who must have spent a lot of time pumping iron in the gym. One wore a shirt that said OBITUARY in bloody letters over surreal artwork with a man cocooned in webbing and a red eye in the sky. Brass knuckles glinted off his fingers. The other bruiser's shirt read MALEVOLENT CREATION above a horned idol holding up two stone tablets. He offered them a sardonic grin within his Van Dyke beard. Though of a slighter build, the third man seemed just as intimidating with his face concealed by a leather mask. He sported a necklace with Jesus Christ hanging upside down on his crucifixion. Scott had listened to enough heavy metal to know this guy wasn't here to invite them to bible camp.

More ominously, the guy in leather carried heavy chains that draped around his knuckles and trailed to a pile on the pavement.

Back in the peaceful sanctuary of five seconds ago, *Ten* continued to play in the tape deck.

The man in the Malevolent Creation shirt smiled down at them crookedly. "Well, well...looks like we got ourselves a couple of Pearl Jammers."

The other goons chuckled. Scott started to push himself up and a boot from the brass knuckler mashed his face, shoving him hard against the Acura.

"Bo, do something about that shit before it gives us all AIDS, will you?" the bearded bruiser continued.

The one named Bo pressed his boot harder into Scott's face. Pain flared brightly, making him cry out. When he thought his cheekbone would collapse, the pressure finally relented.

How could this happen to them him and Gabe outside of Freshway? Its tortures had always been garden variety before, expected and endured with weary resignation. This was something far more sinister. The thundering noise he'd heard a minute ago wasn't the tractor-trailer rig. It came from motorcycles parked a few feet away. These scumbags rode in on them while they were oblivious, smoking up in the car. More chains draped over the bikes.

Bo pulled open the driver's side door, which collided with Scott's head. He flopped over, fireworks bursting across his eyes.

"Alive" cut off in mid chorus as Bo pushed the eject button on the tape deck.

"Oh, thank Satan for that," said the man who'd called them Pearl Jammers. "I'm forever by a radio saying 'what is this horrible fuckin' crap', and the answer is always Pearl Jam. Here you two lovebirds are partying down to your very own copy. "

Scott scooted closer to Gabe, away from the reach of the car door.

"Why're you doing this?" Gabe asked.

"I bet you don't even know who Suffocation is, do you?" the man continued, ignoring the question. "Hell, we'd turn you loose right now if you had a single Earache release in that car. Bo, you see any Napalm in there? Bolt Thrower?"

"I don't see no Napalm, Vince," Bo reported, tossing things around in the car. "No Bolt Thrower either. Found some Nirvana and Alice in Chains, though."

Vince laughed. "Oooh, Nirvana and Alice in Chains. You boys need a license to operate music that heavy?"

The man in the leather mask chuckled too, muffled behind the zippered mouth.

"If that truck driver sees this, he's gonna call the cops!" Scott said. He heard the whininess of his own voice, the fear, but couldn't help it. These were grown men pushing them around. He felt as weak as he did his freshman year, when the seniors seemed so much older and intimidating.

Vince put a hand to his face in mock alarm. "Oh no! I guess we'd better run away and let you guys get back to your Pearl Jamming."

Bo stepped back from the Acura and shut the door.

Scott opened his mouth to say something else, he wasn't sure what. Bo snatched him by the neck and slid a cassette into his mouth.. Bo pushed Scott's chin until his teeth clenched on the plastic. The hand dropped away, but before Scott could spit out the tape, Bo hit him in the jaw with a right hook. Scott crunched through the plastic on reflex, the shards indistinguishable in his mouth from the teeth loosened by the brass knuckles. He dropped over on the pavement again, pieces of plastic and pulp drooling from his mouth. The Pearl Jam cassette clattered under his face, brown spools unwinding.

Gabe shouted, "Motherfucker!" and pounced at the bruiser, leaping onto his back and hooking an arm across Bo's throat. He barely got the chance to tighten it to a chokehold before Bo drove his weight backward against the Acura once, twice. The guy in the leather mask rushed forward, chain scraping the asphalt, and looped a punch over Bo's shoulder that clocked Gabe in the face with metal-cinched knuckles. Gabe's head snapped back as blood burst from his nostrils. He crumpled on the pavement, gasping in pain.

"Hold this poser down!" Bo said, stalking over to the motorcycles.

Scott tried to boost himself on one elbow. His jaw throbbed from the brass knuckle blast. It felt like he'd swallowed a pint of his own blood. He had to do something, though. Gabe tried to stand up for him. Whatever they had planned for Gabe might be worse than some loose teeth.

"Jeremy, bring that other pussy over here," Vince said. "We don't want him running off to Lollapalooza."

The irony cut through the fog of Scott's pain and confusion. Of all the names their tormenters could have, he couldn't believe one of them was a *Jeremy*. Just like the sixth song on the Pearl Jam album.

The leather guy roped his chain around Scott's throat like a noose. Scott gagged instantly. He pried at the metal links, but they wrapped his skin so tight he couldn't get his fingers underneath. They pulled tauter still as Jeremy choked up on both handfuls of chain and dragged Scott across the parking lot to where Gabe lay. Black spots fluttered across Scott's vision, and just when he thought he would pass out, Jeremy eased up on the grip enough that he could breathe again. The chain remained wrapped around him, a leash for Jeremy to yank him back in line.

Gabe's eyes met Scott's across a couple feet of pavement but miles of anguish. His friend's usual heavy-lidded stoner expression here came from the verge of unconsciousness. Scott feared Gabe might be better off succumbing to it.

Vince and Jeremy stretched Gabe's arms out into cruciform, then each stood on one of his wrists and legs with their boots. Gabe strained meekly, but mounted a more animated effort when Bo's motorcycle revved up like a chainsaw. Bo drove around in a circle, riding toward the back of Freshway. His headlight revealed someone behind the wheel of the tractor-trailer rig. When the biker raised a hand toward the truck, his index and little fingers extended in a devil's horn sign, the driver returned the gesture.

Scott's stomach sank. Everyone was in on this. No one would help them.

Bo looped back in their direction, the guttural roar of his motorcycle louder in Scott's ears, the headlight harsher in his eyes. Gabe showed a greater awareness of his predicament, twisting to free himself from Vince and Jeremy's constraints. He didn't generate much momentum. His arms stayed flat. He shouted uselessly for help.

Ten yards away, Bo reared back on his bike, lifting the front wheel up. He rode inexorably toward Gabe on the rear wheel, though Scott heard his friend screaming over the throttle of the engine.

Bo's going to stop the bike inches away from Gabe's head, Scott thought. *We'll both probably piss ourselves, and these assholes will beat us up some more, but they'll go. They're not gonna kill us, there's no way.*

And Bo did lower that front wheel as he approached, but the tire landed expertly in the middle of Gabe's face rather than harmlessly on the asphalt. Scott heard the crunch as Gabe's skull and face collapsed under the heavy weight of the motorcycle. The tire dipped into the groove of the hollowed face, a gutter-wash of blood blasting up between skin and rubber. The bike caught traction and rolled across Gabe's chin and chest, bones popping like knots in a fireplace, until the back tire climbed the crown of the head to plant itself in the shattered pit of Gabe's skull. Here, Bo peeled out, the tire shredding through the grisly cavern like a sander. Flesh, bone, brain, and skull fragments blew out the back of the wheel in a crimson mud puddle as the tire slid within the excavated cranium until Bo vaulted off the body. Thousands of red droplets spattered across Scott's face and into his open screaming mouth.

Scott wasted no time, lurching to his feet and scrambling for his car, blinking away drops of Gabe's blood. He tried to shrug off the chain as he ran, but it snapped taut before he'd gone three steps. His legs flew out from under him and he struck his ass, choking again. When he turned, he found Jeremy standing on top of the other end of the chain.

Vince reached down to take hold of Scott. His red-spattered face cast a ghoulish appearance in the glow of Bo's headlight as the motorcycle circled back. Vince gave him that crooked smile again. "You wanna go for a little ride too, you grunge pussy?"

No! Scott tried to say, but he could only make a strained rattling sound.

"Get that other bike," Vince called to Jeremy. Surprisingly, he began to unwrap the chain from around Scott's throat.

Scott drank in the air gratefully, coughing and spitting. The skin of his throat burned from the abrasions, his vocal cords feeling crushed.

A few feet away from him, Gabe lay motionless. His face didn't even look real, more like a special effect. Just a stringy red trench burrowed through the bone structure, like wet earth under tire treads. Scott smelled the sharp tinge of burned rubber and voided bowels.

Bo pulled up, swinging his bike between Scott's legs as though to ram his balls. Scott launched himself backward, scuttling like a crab, and Bo braked a few inches away from his crotch, laughing. He gunned the engine, but kept the brake locked.

Scott's relief at this stay of eunuch status was short-lived as Vince knelt by his ankle and roped the chain above Scott's shoe. He offered the other end to Bo, who started securing the chain to the body of his bike.

Jeremy pulled up beside them, another chain draped off his ride. Vince began affixing that chain to Scott's other ankle.

"No!" Scott shouted. His voice singed his throat. He bent forward to free his ankles from the chains but Vince created an impressive tangle that couldn't be easily unknotted. There wasn't enough room for Scott to slide his feet through the makeshift cuffs.

Vince knelt beside him. "I get it, man, I get it. You're super-bummed you're about to die, and the last song you heard is some pansy Seattle bullshit. How do you like your chains, Alice?"

Bo did an impression Scott assumed was supposed to be Eddie Vedder, an *eyyyyyyyy* sound. Jeremy fastened the loose end of the chain around the frame of his motorcycle.

"Please," Scott croaked. "You don't...you don't have to do this."

"The fuck I don't," Vince said. "Father Satan would never suffer a weak cunt like you to go on breathing, and he'd be right to take us out if we were stupid enough to let you."

Scott shook his head. He strained to talk over the engines. "No! I don't like grunge...I hate Pearl Jam! That was Gabe's tape!" Despite his pal being way past caring, Scott felt guilty about lying to save his own skin. This might be his only shot, though. "He made me listen to it because we were smoking his weed."

"Still not a very good reason," Vince said.

"I like metal," Scott said. "I love King Diamond."

"But do you like death metal, boy, or anyone who actually believes in the devil?"

"Yes!"

"Like who?"

Scott tried to remember the bands Vince mentioned earlier, but drew a blank. Maybe the terror of the situation inhibited his memory, maybe also some of that Mean Green. He racked his brain for the fastest, evilest shit he knew about.

"Slayer!" he said. He'd seen one of their videos on MTV. He hadn't liked it, although he might have liked it even less if it had been a fast one. Speed wasn't his thing.

"You wouldn't be trying to bullshit us, now, would ya? Slayer are gods, but that's only thrash."

"No, I'm not. I need to hear more death metal for sure, but Slayer's evil and I love that."

Vince smiled. "What's your favorite Slayer album, then?"

Shit! What was that video called? If he could just remember it, he'd noted how the song and album title were the same. No, it hadn't been fast, but even the death metal albums worshiped by these psychos probably weren't fast all the way through either. It was the end of *Headbanger's Ball* on MTV, so he and Gabe had chanced upon it one Saturday night, waiting for videos by bands that were actually cool. Gabe even made a joke about the song name. What was it?

Seasons…Seasons of the Bitch! That was it. They'd laughed, maybe less because it was funny than because they were stoned. The memory didn't trigger the correct song title, but he knew it was partially right, and that was good enough.

"*Seasons,*" he said confidently.

Vince's good humor dried up. "You know, you mighta bought yourself five more minutes with *Show No Mercy, Hell Awaits,* or *Reign in Blood. Seasons in the Abyss,* though? Fuck you, Pearl Jammer. You're no Slayer fan." He stood up, looking sickened.

Scott screamed for help, his tortured voice barely able to carry above the idling motorcycles. He waited for police sirens, red-and-blue lights to flash around the corner to grant a last-minute reprieve, or someone from Freshway to rush out to intervene. He was going to college in September, he would start a band and be the next Nirvana. It couldn't end like this!

Vince walked to Bo's motorcycle. Scott couldn't hear the exchange from the ground, but Bo looked unhappy about ceding control. He finally slid off the seat, looking pissed.

"You ready, Alice?" Vince shouted.

Scott lurched to his feet. The chain shackles fastened around his ankles looked as impossibly tangled as a ball of Christmas lights. He balanced on his right foot, trying to slip the left one through the links.

"Come on!" Vince called to Jeremy. Their bikes accelerated to eardrum-shaking thunder. Each chain provided about four yards of slack before the motorcycles rolled off in tandem, stretching both lines taut. Their momentum jerked Scott's feet out from under him. He landed hard on his back and kept going, the starry night sky seeming to move above him as the bikes dragged him across the asphalt.

They went slow at first, Vince and Jeremy riding side by side, coordinating their route. Scott continued screaming, both for someone to *for Christ's sake help him*, but also from the increasing pain as they dragged him over the pavement. This always looked painless in the movies, but the reality proved far more excruciating as the back of his shirt tore away, causing his skin to scrape directly against the concrete.

Bo and Vince picked up the pace. In the illuminated pools beneath the sodium arc lights, Scott saw large smears of blood as they pulled him along like a human paintbrush. They drove in configurations of the number six three times in a row, laughing and whooping. Even Bo, the sulky onlooker, cheered up a little. At last, both bikes stopped, leaving Scott to writhe in a spreading crimson puddle.

Over the steady thrum of their engines, Vince looked over his shoulder and shouted, "Cheer up, boy! You get to die doin' what I love…tearin' up poser wimps with death fuckin' metal!"

They revved up their bikes and each launched in opposite directions, Jeremy going left, Vince to the right, both of them shouting *"SAAAAATAAAAAAAAAN!"* Scott stared in horror as the chain slack diminished and his legs spread apart. He tried to anchor them, but they jackknifed beyond his normal range of motion until he was stretched to a full cheerleader split. The chains yanked forward like snapping rubber bands as the horsepower of the motorcycles pushed past his resistance.

Scott's legs snapped at the pelvic girdle, ripping from their sockets. His responding screech could have been mistaken for the tires burning the asphalt. The force of the high-speed wishbone continued to rip through him, opening a bloody groove at crotch level that gaped wider as the bikes sped off. Blood and entrails burst out as he was wrenched apart at groin level, the groove deepening through his torso like an earthquake fissure.

Scott's pupils dilated as the headlight from Vince's bike spun back around, rushing at him like a train through the tunnel of death. Almost as a last act of defiance, Scott thought of the chorus to "Alive," wished he could have sung it as the blood spilled from his mouth.

I'm still alive…still ali—

The bike barreled into his detruncated form, blasting through anatomical sludge. By the time it shattered his sternum and hit his chest cavity hard enough to leave tire marks on the burst sac of his splattered heart, Scott's eyes saw nothing of Vince's motorcycle wheels ramping over his remains.

Or Jeremy's a moment later.

Or Bo's a minute after that.

CHAPTER ELEVEN
THE KRUSHER

GORE FELT LIKE HE WAS going to puke. Two crotch-shots from Stephanie in rapid succession had given him lingering nausea in his gut, a sickness amplified by the shocking loss of Eve and Marcel. Gore tended to treat mortality like something that happened to other, weaker people, but tonight offered a sobering perspective. One night you could be having group sex with your devil cult, lapping a dead twat while a bitch reamed your asshole with intestines, and the next you could find your friends just as lifeless as that self-same twat. Crazy.

If he needed evidence of just how badly the group dynamic had been spoiled, he only had to look at Fenton, who was supposed to be his ally now. How could Desmond bring this loser into something meant for gods among men, wolves among sheep?

As they made their sweep of the sales floor, Gore couldn't help thinking Fenton and Dizzy Q didn't exactly inspire confidence in a show of strength. Desmond should be here with them leading the charge instead of barking orders back by the registers and the *Enquirer*'s accounts of celebrities and their secret terminal diseases and gay double lives. They needed to ferret out these Freshway fuckers and snuff 'em. Gore felt good about Richard and Trey in their current group for that capacity, two heavy hitters in bad-ass Incantation and Autopsy shirts, Richard wielding a spiked ball bat and Trey a short-handled pitchfork.

Priscilla and Alex rounded out the procession, both also better options than Dizzy Q and Fenton, if a lower caliber than Trey and Richard. Priscilla wore a shirt with the classic wood etching of Vlad the Impaler and carried a claw hammer, with carpenter nails stuck through the bun of her brown hair. Alex chose a Cannibal Corpse *Eaten Back to Life* long sleeve and brought a freaking tomahawk. He kept giving Gore shitty looks because he'd shown up in the same *Dawn of Possession* shirt Gore chose, then had to go back to his car for a back-up shirt to save them the embarrassment of being twins. It was understood which of them would be subservient, with Gore in the Inner Circle, and Alex obviously didn't care for that. Maybe he should have changed his tampon, too, while he was at it.

Dizzy Q sent Alex and Priscilla to watch the doors to the back while the rest of them went aisle by aisle. They couldn't have the Freshway crew sneaking out here to hide in a section Devil's Food had marked clear, then attacking the front when Gore's team went into the back, or worse, ambushing Gore's group from behind when they went to root the cowards out. They hadn't found much of anything so far out on the sales floor but products to be stocked or discarded and a couple of price guns. Gore made a mental note to use one of those before he left. He could leave the cops a hell of a deal on Darla's dead brat.

The seven of them should be plenty to deal with Ruby and Antonio. Gore wanted Stephanie all for himself. He owed that bitch. Hopefully he'd feel like he adequately humiliating her when the time came. His aching testicles offered a dismal forecast for the rectal punishment rigors he'd concocted for ol' Steph since his prior failed attempt, but he aimed to make her swear fealty to Satan before he launched a medicine ball of dick snot into her bowels.

As they inspected an aisle with canned chili and soup, Fenton said, "Dude, wish you'd warned me about the initiation." He'd been pretending like he and Gore were still friendly acquaintances and Gore didn't hate his guts.

"What initiation?" Gore asked. "Desmond asked me to work at Devil's Food and I said yes. Didn't know he'd start hiring poser wimps back then.''

"Well, whatever you call it," Fenton said, ignoring the insult.

Something about his reedy voice suggested a confessional un-burdening of the soul. Gore had been waiting for Fenton to try to justify his prior weakness, and it sounded like the moment had arrived. He only wished he could puke right in Fenton's face, *Exorcist* style.

"Having to, you know…" Fenton's voice dropped to a dramatic whisper. "Suck him off."

"What?" If someone had popped up behind a box of baked beans with a weapon at that moment, Gore might have been a corpse. "Let me get this straight…you're saying you had to blow Desmond to join Devil's Food?"

He looked at the others trailing them, some of whom nodded their heads.

"Come on, man, stop screwing with me," Fenton said. "I know you did it too." He sounded like a patient who'd received lab results notifying him of a terminal illness. *You're just playing around, right, doc?…Right?*

Gore laughed. "You think I'd suck someone's dick just to work at a grocery store? I'd still be at Freshway if that was the deal. You fucking poser. That's about what I'd expect from someone who made fun of Immolation. Careful with that box cutter, I'd hate for you to break a nail."

He'd tried to avoid looking at Fenton since the search began—he already felt sick enough as it was—but he wanted an imprint of this humiliation in his memory to savor. They were across from the meat department now, and the lights illuminated the existential crisis and horror sculpted in Fenton's punch-worthy visage.

"Holy shit," Gore said. "Did he write that on your forehead?"

Fenton rubbed above his eyes, trying to erase the offending message. It stayed right where it was. "What is it? What does it say?"

Gore grinned. "Nothing at all… *kitten.*"

~

"I say we go!" Matt said.

Tony shook his head. "You're crazy."

"You're crazy, if you don't want to go."

The debate had carried on the past five minutes, ever since the strange transmission on Tony's walkie-talkie.

"Jamie wants to go," Matt said.

Jamie bit his lip, kept his head down and his flashlight trained on the magazine spread before him on the tree house floor. He did a convincing imitation of someone so focused that he hadn't heard a word of the discussion. It almost wasn't even an act, because he could barely pry his eyes away from this issue of *Buxxxom*.

"Whadda ya say, man?" Matt said.

Jamie sighed inwardly. Matt always volunteered him for things he didn't want to do. It earned him three trips to in-school suspension last year, but somehow only two for the shit-stirrer himself. Jamie should have known he wouldn't survive the summer without temptation.

"You want some *puhhhhsssssssay*, don't you?" Matt added, saying the word just like they sang it in a 2 Live Crew song the three boys listened to tonight. Matt had brought a portable stereo with a mix tape "borrowed" from his older brother, 2 Live Crew on one side, the Geto Boys on the other. Side A offered songs like "Me So Horny," "The Fuck Shop," "Face Down, Ass Up," and the infectious "We Want Some Pussy," which they must have rewound and played five times while laughing hysterically. Side B provided background music now, as Bushwick Bill set up an orgy with two of his bitches to reach "The Other Level." It felt wrong to listen to— Jamie's mom would probably ground him for a week if she knew he'd listened to any of this "filth"—but it was awesome and fun. It made him feel a little reckless. Matt might not have to do much arm-twisting.

Jamie nodded, knowing he wouldn't get away without acknowledging the *puhhhhssssay* question, and because it was the God's honest truth. He *did* want some *puhhhhsssay,* it was the most consuming thought in his young mind.

"Good, cuz I don't wanna miss out on g'ttin' more," Matt said.

Tony scoffed. "Bullshit."

"Man, you're just jealous that I already got some."

"*Riiiight*, your bitch at the lake last summer. The one your own brother said he never saw."

"Fuck you, dude. It happened. If I see her when we go this summer, it'll happen then, too. Maybe if you'd gotten some real pussy, you fags wouldn't be satisfied with those magazines."

Jamie didn't say anything about that either, because he loved the magazines. The three of them found the tree house out here in the woods earlier this afternoon, and more importantly the treasures within, including this stack of pornography someone stashed here. The pages were water-damaged and looked like they might have been buried out here in the woods before being dug up. The tree house had seen better days, but it still held together, and best of all appeared to have been abandoned, so it provided them an instant collection of naked women and a sanctuary to keep their newfound fortunes away from their parents and siblings.

A plan quickly took shape to schedule a sleepover at Matt's, where they could camp out in a tent in his backyard. They'd done it enough times to know his parents wouldn't check on them past ten o'clock, and they could get away with sneaking back to the tree house for a few hours to pore over their new collection. They could (and would) do that every day now, but it seemed like they should commemorate their find with a proper celebration.

Jamie had seen issues of *Playboy* in his twelve years on the planet, perused in secret when his family stayed at his uncle's house over Christmas. He thought it didn't get any better than that, but these magazines gave him cause to reconsider. *Playboy* seemed kind of tame, he now realized, the nude women rationed out between articles, interviews, and jokes. You got to see what you wanted to, but mostly tits and ass. Jamie had seen that in movies before, and it was great (his favorites were *Mischief* and *Fraternity Vacation*) but he was after the stuff they *didn't* show you in movies. He wanted to go beyond the T&A, beyond the fleeting glimpses of bush.

Buxxxom finally offered him this opportunity, along with other fine publications like *Screw*, *Juggs* and *Slut* all strewn about the tree house. These nude beauties spread themselves wide, smiling invitingly. They seemed to know a secret. Jamie wished they would tell him. They sucked dicks both real and rubber, and were penetrated by same. The pictures seemed so much rawer than *Playboy*. He thought if he licked the bush on the pages before him, he would feel fuzz on his tongue. Were it not for the presence of his friends, he'd be sorely tempted to try.

Jamie flipped a few pages to the ads in the back, seeking a diversion.

"Listen to this," he said. "'Feeling horny tonight—"

"*Yes*," Matt interjected.

"'—then call up me and my girlfriends, and listen to us slurp nasty brownholes over the phone.'"

Tony gagged. "Oh, that's so grody. Why would anyone do that?"

"Yeah," Matt said. "It's about as hard to understand as why we're sitting here in a fuckin' tree house when that guy on the walkie said *orgy* a minute ago!"

They'd brought their walkie-talkies for something to do to pass time around the neighborhood as they waited for the cover of darkness. It mostly served to build the fever pitch since half their transmissions amounted to *Dude, can't wait to check out all those titties in the tree house...over.* They took the walkies with them after they split the tent. Matt must have left his on by accident, because in the middle of Scarface's account of a "Quickie" on the tape player, they intercepted the strange transmission on the channel they always used.

"Okay, but whadda ya want us to do about it?" Tony asked.

"What do you think, dickhead? *Go to the motherfuckin' orgy!*"

"We don't know where it is."

"He said Freshway, asshole!"

"He did? Are you sure?"

"He said 'the fun at Freshway.' You heard it, didn't you, Jamie?"

Jamie shrugged. "I guess."

Tony shook his head. "That doesn't make any sense."

"'Course it does," Matt said. "Freshway's on the other side of the woods. It's the only reason we heard him on my walkie."

"I mean having an orgy at Freshway doesn't make any sense, *asshole.*"

"Oh, sorry, do you need them to do it at a fuckin' furniture store before you'll go to one?"

"Eat shit." Tony held up a hand to block the glare as Matt aimed his flashlight in Tony's face. "Stop it!"

"All right, if you missed the Freshway, did you at least hear him say anyone who saw the orgy should get invited?"

"So? Dude, we couldn't even get tickets to *Basic Instinct.* There's no way they'll let us into this."

"Maybe they will, maybe they won't, but you're both pussies if you don't at least go look."

Jamie waited for Tony to refute the insult, point out the idiocy of going. Instead Tony said, "Shit, I don't care. I'll go."

"Whadda 'bout you, Jamie?" Matt asked. "You ready to get yourself laid? Or are you gonna stay back here and whack off while Tony and I go get the real thing?"

Matt grabbed his cheek and pulled it back and forth to simulate the sounds of masturbation. Firmly in Matt's corner now, Tony turned his fist sideways and pulled it up and down over his crotch.

Jamie wondered how the porno stockpile could go from being the find of the century to a source of ridicule in a matter of hours. He did want to go check out the store, though; of course he did. The magazine women were amazing, but the thought of seeing naked flesh in person made him lightheaded. He just didn't want to get busted doing it, because as pissed off as his mom was over in-school suspension, he couldn't even imagine the kind of hell he would catch over a friggin' orgy. Still, were the people at Freshway really allowed to be doing this? Maybe the biggest risk from discovery belonged to the people at the store, and Jamie and his friends could use it to their benefit somehow. The prospect made him feel warm all over.

"I'm goin' too," he said.

Matt and Tony abandoned their jack-off pantomiming. They all high-fived.

"Awesome!" Matt said. "Now let's have group sex and do the Rambo!"

Reluctant exhilaration filled Jamie. He had no idea what the whole Rambo thing meant, but only the feeling mattered in that moment.

The "Hey, We Want Some Pussy" chant began before they'd all scaled down the tree, and carried them for much of the next frantic mile as they hurried to the store and their date with destiny.

~

Picking at his zits, Alex kept watch by the swinging doors between the bakery and seafood sections along the back of the sales floor. Farther down at the corner of the store, Priscilla stood guard by the bread and produce aisles. They were both tasked with sounding the alarm if anyone from Freshway showed their faces in the back.

It was Alex's bad luck that Gore had survived the night so far. If anyone had to ride the blade from Devil's Food, Gore would have been his choice. He hated that cocky little bastard. He looked like the sort of weakling who probably got his ass kicked at school every day and then cried at home with his face in his mother's boobs, wondering why the world was such a mean place. Alex knew Gore's type well, as he used to make the lives of such losers a living hell back in his school days. Beating them up in the locker room, ramming their heads into lockers, shaking them down for all their money if he caught them in the bathroom; he did all that and more. After he saw *Heathers* his senior year, he really enjoyed getting some-one in an arm lock and not letting them out until they offered some humiliating confession. Usually he made them say that they liked to suck big dicks, because that's what the jocks in *Heathers* forced a geek to say, and Alex wasn't very original. Had Gore been enrolled at Alex's school, he would have been weeping more days than not if Alex had anything to say about it.

Desmond liked the little twerp for some reason, though, so Alex had to deal with the indignity of showing respect for such a candy-ass. The expectation that he should have to change his shirt tonight because only Gore deserved to wear the Immolation design still burned Alex's ass up. If Gore had anything to offer, Marcel and Eve wouldn't be dead right now. Alex didn't feel good about going into battle with him, and definitely not this new recruit Fenton, who didn't need so much as an arm lock to suck a big dick, much less admit to it.

Satan represented rebellion, but more importantly strength. It meant dominating the weak, taking what you wanted, and pursuing life's pleasures at the cost of someone else's pain if need be. Alex dug the indulgences permitted by Devil's Food, the black mass or-gies and all that shit, but he'd really been looking forward to tonight, where so many of the participants were unwilling. It was much more pleasing to hammer down the law of Satan in those circum-stances. Otherwise it kind of felt like Woodstock with pentagrams, and Alex had signed up for far more twisted shit than that. He couldn't wait to storm the back and drag this store's enemies to their violent ends.

It sucked that so many Devil's Food faithful were dead, but Alex resented their weakness. He'd gotten a good look at the Freshway crew at the start, and maybe two of them seemed capable of defend-ing themselves. This should have been an effortless slaughter; he didn't like that it reflected poorly on him. He was ready to spill holy blood.

Alex checked toward the store corner nearest his side, then be-hind him in case someone from Freshway might be creeping up on him. When he turned around, he saw a face drop away from the porthole of one swinging door.

Adrenaline flooded through him. Alex raised the tomahawk, a lighter weapon than what many dragged along for the siege. He could bury it in someone's skull two or three times before they even knew what was happening.

He approached the back, craning his head to look through the windows for someone fleeing from the double doors. He was pretty sure it was a young girl who dropped out of sight. There was only one hot bitch left alive, probably the one Gore had tried and failed to take. Yeah, he should call for the others now, but Priscilla would alert them in the next few seconds when she saw him missing from his post anyway. If Gore could survive a clash with a Freshway clown, a certified bad-ass like Alex would come to no harm. A minute was all the time he would need to come back with the bitch's head. He couldn't wait to see the look on Gore's face when he found Alex parading his conquest around. He'd probably look more pained than she would.

Alex pushed both doors open and stepped back. Nobody crouched in wait for him, so when the doors swung out and in, he slipped through the gap with his tomahawk at the ready. The dim lighting offered plenty of shadows to hide in, but Alex could see well enough where no one would be able to sneak up on him without plenty of warning. He checked the hall behind him in the direction of the bakery and saw no activity. It seemed more likely the girl slipped to the right down the longer corridor. He could hear the faint rumbling of Big Delbert's rig down at the loading bay.

The baler machine provided the nearest point of interest. It stood tall against the wall on his right, a green monstrosity still powered by the generator with its safety gate open and a pile of boxes inside waiting to be crushed. A red eye glowed in the dark from a button on its controller panel. Enough light for Alex to see a hint of flesh sticking past the far edge—someone crouched in hiding.

Alex smiled. In the immortal words of Evil Chuck, *Some say she's naïve…she's a stupid bitch!*

He crept forward, intending to swing the tomahawk into her soft skin, but she was dumb enough to stick her head out first. She gasped and stood up to face him, holding a butcher knife in front of her. She staggered, wincing from some kind of pain in her leg. His dick hardened as he imagined sawing through her creamy white throat with her own blade.

Alex wanted to say something cool and intimidating, but settled for, "Are you ready to die, bitch?"

She backed up a couple steps, stumbling. "You first, crater face."

He closed in, tomahawk raised, now even with the baler. Boxes in the baler tumbled as a man popped up from inside it, wielding a knife. Alex reacted quick enough to grab the ambusher's wrist and twist it. The knife struck the floor. The man's other arm clenched around Alex's throat, pulling him up off the ground. It cut off his oxygen instantly. Alex's heels kicked the baler as he struggled.

A second woman emerged from the cover of darkness beyond the baler, a granny with her own blade. The cowards had set a trap. Alex flailed backwards with the tomahawk, but it either glanced off the top of the safety cage or the man grabbed his wrist and stopped the momentum. If he could just set his feet and flip the guy out of the baler—

He realized a better alternative, given the dangerous circumstance this man put himself in. Alex stretched for the control panel to hit the button that would activate the compressing ram. His fingers wouldn't have reached it, but the tomahawk could. The baler groaned to life, but the old bat ran over and pushed the button to stop it.

Alex tried to brace his feet on the baler to push himself off and hopefully bring the guy with him, and that's when the hot girl bent down and dragged her knife across his calves, cutting through both Achilles tendons. Alex dropped the tomahawk and tried to scream, but it came out as a strained grunt with the man's arm so tight on his throat.

The granny and the girl grabbed Alex's legs and heaved until he flopped over the lip of the baler into the boxes. The man who'd choked him stepped on Alex's back and head to boost himself out of the baler. The safety gate groaned as someone pulled it down, shutting Alex inside.

"No!" he shouted. His weight flattened several boxes and put him near the bottom. He tried to stand up, but fire burst through his severed tendons and he fell on his face again, screaming.

"You fuckin' cowards! Open this thing and fight me! I'll fuckin' kill you!"

Alex turned over on his back. The baler roared to life and the ram descended, a flat plate of metal that crushed boxes, plastic, aluminum, anything at all until enough of it formed a cube big enough to be loaded on a pallet and transported for recycling. Cardboard groaned around him as it succumbed to the pressure. Alex forced himself to one knee, then the other, bracing his hands against the ram. He pushed against it with all his strength, fully expecting

Satan to grant him the power to reverse its trajectory and spare his servant's life.

Instead it continued its descent, exerting profound pressure on his knees as his arms dropped lower and lower from overhead.

He continued ranting, as much to psych himself up as the chance they might actually listen or the others from Devil's Food would reach him in time. "Let me out, you pussies! Fight me fair! I'll fuckin' kill you! I'll fu—"

The ram bore down on Alex's head with his body braced in the position of a most yielding pillar. His arms flopped uselessly at his sides as his skull crunched, flattening the frontal and parietal bones and bursting his brain. The pressure ejected one of Alex's eyeballs. A sliver of brain matter ejected through his left earhole. His sockets collapsed and the facial bones sagged as what remained of his head wrenched backward. The cervical bones strained and shattered until the back of Alex's head rested between his shoulder blades, and the ram compressed his torso until his backbone snapped, folding Alex's broken body backward. It continued to flatten him, pulverizing his sternum in a rolling cascade of cracking bone that minced the organs within. Fully bent in half and sandwiched against the terrain of collapsed cardboard, Alex burst apart like a ketchup packet.

~

Fenton tried to scrounge up some sympathy in the produce section over the sight of Darla's mutilated body, her unborn child similarly scooped out and hacked to pieces, but it just wasn't happening. This was the worst night of his life, of anyone's life. The disgusting sight only served to remind him that he'd thrown in with some total crazies, and if he didn't uphold his oath to them, it would only get worse. He couldn't fathom how that would be possible given the humiliation he'd already endured, but Fenton wouldn't leave it to chance.

The search and destroy operation on the sales floor resulted in a lot of former and none of the latter. Antonio, Ruby, Stephanie, Booker, and Kyle must be cowering somewhere in the back where he'd left them. Their victory seemed so impossible at that time. It was hard not to second guess his decision to flee given its outcome and the wretched taste in his mouth, but Devil's Food still had them outnumbered. The tide would have turned, and he'd have been cut down like the rest of them.

Ruby and Stephanie seemed like his best bets for easy kills.

Stephanie must have gotten the best of Gore, but Fenton was a lot stronger than him. He could overpower her. He could easily overpower Gore too, for that matter. He could put a stop to all the tough talk from that skinny little bastard.

Oh, really? You going to rape his butt to show him who's boss? Or is that just the kind of guy you are now...Kitten?

No!

Fenton shook his head to repel the sickening notion. His misery had deepened since learning of his new nickname. Gore would be off limits, but it was open season on his former pals at Freshway. He could at least do what he wanted to those arrogant pieces of shit, and maybe regain some of his self-respect. All their bravado would count for nothing if they just wound up as corpses anyway.

He headed for the backroom, where he knew they'd been hiding.

CHAPTER TWELVE
INSTINCT OF SURVIVAL

BOOKER SQUEEZED THROUGH THE ROOF latch and closed it. He stopped to catch his breath. The air had cooled with the coming of night, a gentle breeze giving the illusion of a peaceful, normal evening. But the knife tucked into his belt was a grim reminder of the truth. Passing an array of vents, he went to the edge of the roof and looked out upon the front parking lot. The flaming pentagram was dying down. He could see his car, a ship to a man stranded on an island.

Well, he was this store's Skipper and he planned to get what remained of his crew home to safety. Kyle had been his Gilligan and Booker wished he'd whacked him with his hat some more. He'd been unable to get the stupid kid to go with him. He also had no idea where the rest of the Freshway crew was. His best bet now was to get help. But he'd have to get down from this fucking roof first.

He couldn't just jump. It was a two-story building. Maybe when he was younger his knees could have taken it, just as they'd endured a pounding on the football field. But he was over forty now. He'd probably break every bone in his legs and good luck running for help then. The only things at the front of the store that might break his fall were still too close to the ground and he doubted the awning would hold his weight.

A low rumbling caught his attention and he followed the sound to the rear of the store. A Devil's Food tractor-trailer idled at the loading dock. The driver's side window was down, a tattooed arm hanging out, holding a cigarette. Booker heard voices and music. He turned to see a group of bikers just dicking around, a boombox pumping out that heavy metal where the guys sang like Cookie Monster. One of the bikers wore a leather gimp mask.

Freaks.

Spread across the pavement like strawberry jam were human remains streaked with tire marks. Despite all the gore he'd seen tonight, Booker's stomach still gurgled. He breathed deep, holding back the nausea, and walked in a hunch so not to be spotted as he moved toward the truck. It wouldn't be a far drop to the top of the trailer. Maybe eight feet. Would the shadows and the music and the rumble of the truck cover his descent? If he could get to the driver soon enough he could hijack the truck and haul ass to the police station.

"Okay," he whispered to himself, a habit that got worse the older he got. "You can do this, my man. Eye of the tiger…"

He inched to the edge, crouching like Batman looking down on Gotham. He dropped, telling himself to not stiffen up and to bend his knees upon impact. When he hit the top of the trailer he laid flat just in case someone had heard him. There were no shouts. No indication he'd been noticed. He got into his hero-crouch again, feeling like Bruce Willis gearing up to kick Alan Rickman's ass. Peering over the left-hand side, he saw the driver's arm still dangling out the window and a plan—however ludicrous—formed in Booker's head.

"You must be crazy," he whispered. "Watch over your boy now, Mama."

He swung over the side and as he sailed past the driver's door he grabbed onto the trucker's arm, dislocating it.

The trucker howled. "Great Cesar's ghost!"

Booker swung from the arm like a pendulum until he heard the elbow snap. Behind him, the bikers began yelling, and though Booker didn't look over his shoulder he knew they were drawing near. He opened the driver's door, drew the filet knife from his belt, grabbed the trucker by his Dixie flag t-shirt, and slit his throat. As the redneck gargled blood, Booker pulled him from the cab and he hit the ground with a thud, his skull cracking against the pavement.

Booker sneered. "The south ain't risin' again, cracker."

He slammed the door shut and stepped on the gas, but the truck continued to idle. The bikers stopped running toward him and went back toward their motorcycles. Booker had never driven a big rig before. There were a lot more switches and pulleys and buttons, and he had no time to experiment. He had to learn real fucking fast. Where was the hell was the parking brake? He pulled a lever and heard air hiss. Air brake release, maybe? The roar of approaching motorcycles caused his mouth to go dry. Panicking, he flicked switches and pressed buttons, trying to get the damn thing to move. He must have done something right, because the rig rumbled forward. He floored the gas and turned toward the oncoming bikers in a very one-sided game of chicken. The bikers veered clear, but by turning sharply he managed to block their path with the long trailer. In the side mirror, Booker saw one of the bikers fail to stop in time. He slammed into the side of the trailer, his body flying backward as his bike sailed beneath the truck. As he scrambled to get up, Booker accelerated, and the rear wheels caught the biker and pulled him under feet-first, steamrolling his body. Pulverized, his head popped like a zit, spewing brains and other goo.

Booker pulled on the horn lever in celebration. "Eat me!"

His merriment didn't last long. Trying to maneuver the rig proved more difficult than he initially thought. The rear parking lot was significantly smaller than the front, so he had to back up again if he were going to go anywhere but into the woods. As he tried, the other motorcycle drew down on him, the remaining two bikers on it together. Riding bitch, the leather gimp swung a chain over his head like some S&M Lone Ranger. The trailer thudded and shook. Booker had backed up too far and hit a telephone pole.

There was a scream as the pole fell, wires sparking. A man in a Devil's Food uniform was strapped to the pole and when it came down he came with it. The sound when he hit the pavement was like twelve dozen eggs cracking at once. Blood burst from his mouth.

"So you're the one who fucked the lines," Booker said.

The man was crippled but moving…until the snapped wires hit him. He convulsed as electricity coursed through him, smoke rising from his flesh, his eyes bursting, his construction helmet blown from his head like a bullet.

Booker maneuvered the truck again but hit the store's trash compactor, a long, metal tunnel bolted to the concrete.

"Fuck it."

He floored the pedal, trying to demolish the compactor enough to make his turn, but the tires merely screeched as they burned into the pavement. He was stuck. His best course of action was to run. Hopping out the passenger side, he charged along the side of the building. He looked to the woods—one option. But his car was not far away—a better option, if he could get to it. He had to try. The beam of a headlight was growing, casting his shadow before him. It grew longer and longer, the roar of the motorcycle like twenty chainsaws.

Chainsaw, he suddenly thought. *Of course!*

The steps they'd built for the floral department on Valentine's Day! Todd had purchased a chainsaw for Booker to construct them. Of course Todd didn't trust his employees to not steal it from the storage room, so he'd kept it in the office, hidden on a bottom shelf. Was it still there? Damn! Why hadn't he thought of it sooner?

A lot of good it did him right now.

Running around the front of the store, Booker stumbled as a chain swung just over his head. The bikers came up beside him and Booker ran to the patio area, using the tables and chairs as obstacles to block the motorcycle. Still the bikers gave chase. Booker ran around a table, grabbed a chair, and threw it as the bikers whirred past. It landed true, knocking the gimp from his seat. He slammed into one of the trashcans sealed to the pavement. Booker pounced on him, snatching the chain away.

"My...back," the gimp said. "Help...I think I'm p-p-paralyzed."

Booker used the chain to whip the gimp's skull, then ran along the front walkway, his side pinching, legs cramping. He approached the front doors where Desmond's truck had crashed into the foyer.

The man on the bike did a U-turn. He was coming right at Booker now, cackling like some rabid jackal. There was only one way to run.

Booker ducked back into the store. The motorcycle madman tailed him into the foyer. Booker flung the chain at him but missed, and then hurled himself over the shattered pallets and the pulped carcass of poor Mila. There was no time to be deft. He winced when his shoes tromped through the red mud of her remains. The mess of the pallets were too jagged for the motorcycle to drive over, so the rider raced through the store entrance in an effort to go the long way around to get to Booker. It wouldn't take him very long.

Initially Booker opened the door to Desmond's truck in search of a potential weapon that would have more reach than the knife. But when he saw the keys dangling from the ignition, he realized he'd found the greatest weapon of all.

~

"Well, that was gross," Ruby said.

Blood oozed through the baler's grates.

"We had no choice but to ambush," Antonio said. "I know you wanted no more violence, Ruby, but we've found no way to escape out the back. We can either wait here and pick 'em off, or try our luck going through the sales floor."

They heard a commotion out back. Engines. Shouting. Something slammed.

"What the hell are they doing now?" Stephanie asked.

"Oh, shit," Antonio said. "You think they're coming in through the rear?"

Ruby frowned. "I don't want to wait and find out."

"Sales floor it is," Stephanie said.

The trio ran down the hallway of back stock, going for the doors to the bakery department. If they'd waited a moment longer, they'd have seen the tractor trailer pull out of the loading dock, leaving the door wide open for them to escape the building.

~

Staying low behind the register lanes, Kyle watched Desmond and his diabolical flunkies as they moved across the store. He cursed himself. How the fuck was he supposed to take down all six of them on his own? A filet knife was hardly the best tool for mass murder. The only way would be to pick them off one by one like a silent sniper. If only he had a gun instead of a blade meant for taking scales off fish.

Where were the others? He could really use their help here. Christ, he could only hope they were still alive. It pained him to imagine Ruby murdered the way Darla had been. Not long ago, Stephanie had been trying to fuck him in the bathroom; now she might be hanging from the rafters with no skin. It made his stomach gurgle. Then he thought of Mila again and his blood pounded at his temples.

Okay. You're outnumbered. But you've gotta Chuck Norris this shit, dude. There's got to be a way. Do it for Mila!

He crept out of the register lane, a spider in the shadows. As a child he'd wanted to be a ninja (another goal he'd missed) and had taken karate. Sure, he'd retained none of it, but the fantasy fueled him now. He felt oddly cinematic as he lurched and tiptoed. All he needed was a bitchin' mask and some Chinese stars. It was a delusion, but it gave him the balls to press on, stalking his prey.

The hunted has become the hunter!

He stifled a laugh, well aware he was losing it.

CHAPTER THIRTEEN
THIS TIME IT'S WAR

DESMOND RUBBED THE BRIDGE OF his nose. He needed an aspirin. Things were not going as smoothly as they should have. As he walked down the medicine aisle, Laila and the other employees tailed him like annoying smaller dogs.

What're we gonna do today, Spike?

He'd retained four goons along with Laila, bodies that were little more than human shields as far as he was concerned. There were Rain and Sunshine, female Siamese twins with samurai swords. They wore so much white makeup it was impossible to tell their ethnicity. Beneath those silken robes, Desmond knew they had tight bodies and tighter pussies, with tits so bitchin' they'd look right at home on the cover of *Heavy Metal* magazine.

Then there was Leroy Brown, the one black employee Desmond had. He was tall and lean and favored his mace—not pepper spray, but a spiked, steel ball connected to a handle by a length of chain. He referred to himself as "Bad, Bad, Leroy Brown" and wore a spiked collar like a junkyard dog.

And finally there was Abaddon, a man-thing so ugly he could

top that monster at the end of *Big Trouble in Little China*. He was short yet gangly, his jaundiced skin covered in curly black hairs. His nose always ran, eyes always crusted with sleep-crud. The under bite only served to make him look all the more like the demon he claimed to be. According to company policy, each store was to have one of these strange mutants, which were sent down from corporate, like some sort of hobgoblin team mascot. Desmond made it a rule to keep Abaddon in the back of house at his store. Customers would have puked at the sight of him, especially because he refused to wear clothes. His fat cock was just as long as his legs even when flaccid, and it dragged along the tile, leaving piss smears as he lumbered along.

Quite the ragtag group of goonies.

Desmond popped open a bottle of aspirin and chewed two so they'd hit him faster.

Laila came beside him. "Your lordship, I should do another reading, to foresee what shall come."

Desmond grumbled. "You couldn't predict an episode of *Matlock*."

"I mourn that I have failed you. Please, grant me the chance to make it up to you and our dark lord."

He huffed, too frustrated to debate it. Let the baby have her bottle.

"Fine," he said. "But make it snappy."

She beamed. "Yes, your excellence."

Laila got on her knees—*the one position she does the most good in*, Desmond thought—and opened her purse, spilling her ritualistic artifacts across the tile. Two tea light candles. A decayed human hand with no fingers. A blue marble. Three frog eyes. Hippie beads. The head of a Ken doll. She placed the pentagram laden tiara upon her head, lit the candles, and sang *Carmina Burana* in a low voice. Ever since they'd watched *The Doors* biopic during a "team-building" night out, she'd used the cantana whenever practicing sorcery.

"I see newcomers," she said.

Desmond's jaw shifted. "Who? Not cops, right?"

"No. They're too small to be police...they're..." Her brow furrowed, eyes pinching tight as she strained for the vision. "I think they're...*kids*."

~

"Move it, douchebag," Tony said.

Jamie was climbing up the loading dock as quickly as he could. Too many puddings had added girth that slowed him down. Getting under him, Tony pushed on Jamie's flabby ass and Matt took his hands, helping him onto the receiving bay. Jamie looked around, amazed to be inside the store. He'd never been in the backroom of a supermarket before. It made him feel naughty to be sneaking around, but that was all part of the thrill, wasn't it?

They helped Tony inside.

"Why're there hardly any lights?" Jamie asked.

"Why're you so fat?" Tony said.

"Hey, fuck you, dude."

"In your dreams, queer."

Matt shushed them. "Someone might hear us."

"I thought we were supposed to find people," Tony said. "We can't bang some bodacious babes without knowin' where they are."

"I know that, you retard. But we're still coming in uninvited."

"They said all are welcome."

"Yeah, well…"

"Well nothin'," Tony said, grabbing his crotch. "Get movin', boys. I got nine inches of danglin' fury that can't wait for that puss-puss."

Matt rolled his eyes. "Yeah, right, Tone. The only way a chick could get nine inches from you is if she fucked you four times."

Jamie laughed and Tony glared at him. Whatever. He was sick of Tony's macho bullshit. The guy was dumber than Dan Quayle. Where did he get off acting like their fearless leader?

Matt suddenly ripped a fart, a real juicy cheek-flapper, breaking not just wind but tension. The boys giggled and huddled close together, once again a team.

"All right, dudes," Matt said. "Let's go find the party."

They began singing 2 Live Crew again, but a woman's voice cut them off. "Welcome to the fun center, boys."

Jamie gasped. In the faint light, the form of a woman came toward them. As she moved under the industrial bug-zapper, the blue glow revealed her to be completely nude but for a tiara on her head. The boys fell silent, awestruck. A young woman, maybe in her elder teens. Her lithe body was smooth and hairless, a nymph with hungry eyes. She walked into the boys, causing them to circle around her. Jamie's boner pressed against his whitey-tighties, already on the verge of spurting. He'd never seen a naked girl in person, except for that time he walked in on his parents. But seeing his fat mother being log-jammed by his old man hardly counted. This was no centerfold in a sticky magazine. This was the real deal.

"Why don't you three show me what you've got?" she said, taking turns flicking at their crotches. "I'll bet you young studs have enough backed-up sperm to turn my mouth into a daycare center."

Jamie's jaw hung open. Was this one of those dreams that made his sheets stick together? *No way* this could really be happening!

"I'm Laila," the woman said. "But you can call me your little whore."

She approached Tony and started unzipping his fly. The boy's eyes grew so wide he looked like a cartoon. She took Jamie's wrist, and led his hand to her silken crotch. Its warm wetness sent shivers through him. She didn't have to tell Matt twice to cup her breasts. His clumsy hands squeezed like he was trying to get juice from an orange. The boys closed in on her, touching and being touched, lost in euphoric amazement. In truth, Jamie had only expected to be a peeping tom at this shindig. That he was gliding his digits across an actual *puhhhhsssssay* was enough to make his eyes roll in wonder. His diary was in for a treat tonight!

Quick and catlike, Laila freed Jamie's dingdong from his shorts. He looked down, seeing his own t-shirt, Alfred E. Newman smiling up at him. Below Newman's face, a girl's hand was doing to Jamie's dick what he did to it five times a day. Now all three boys had their shorts around their ankles, their wieners saluting their wanton goddess. Her hands rose to her head and Jamie grinded into the cleft of her buttocks, so focused on wedging his dick between those pink cheeks he failed to notice the twin daggers Laila was pulling from her tiara.

His belly suddenly stung, then went warm and slick. When he opened his eyes, Alfred E. Newman's face was torn in half, a waterfall of crimson raining down on Jamie's boner and Laila's shuddering buttocks.

"Holy macaroni!" he said.

A flash of a blade and Matt's dick was split like a hot dog. Tony was in the middle of coming, oblivious with his eyes shut tight, and Laila raised both daggers to his face and peeled it from his head like an apple skin. His red skull chattered and screamed.

Jamie tried to run and tripped over the shorts at his feet. He kicked out of them, leaving him nude from the waist down, and ran holding his gushing wound. He'd been sliced from his nipple to his belly button. It hurt like hell but at least he hadn't been disemboweled…yet. Who knew what this crazy bitch would do to him if she caught him? He dared to look over his shoulder and was relieved to see she was busy with Matt. Laila was straddling him, but not in a good way. She'd planted a dagger in each side of his neck like Frankenstein's bolts and was sawing through it, Matt's arms pinned beneath her legs. Jamie told himself he'd mourn his friend once he was safe enough to do so. For right now, he only ran.

When he reached the end of the hall he made out a shape in the dark, something blocking the doors to the sales floor. The stout silhouette came forward slowly. It was even shorter than Jamie was.

"You okay, kid?"

Jamie panted. "Oh, jeez, mister. You gotta help me. I—"

His words got lost in his mouth when the man stepped into the light. He was like that dwarf from *Willow*, only he had the face of a gargoyle that had been kicked in the teeth and peed on. Warts peppered his cheeks and forehead. Most revolting of all, he was naked. Jamie gaped at the little person's potbelly pig of a dong. The man smiled when he saw Jamie gaze upon the massive, hairy cock. That's right—the cock itself had hairs *growing out of its shaft!* Jamie couldn't help but vomit. It spattered at the man's feet and he walked right through it, the head of his big ol' dick dragging through chunks of bile.

Jamie turned to run, but Laila was coming down the other end of the hall. She was slathered in gore from the neck down and wore a length of intestines like a feather boa. Jamie's moment of hesitation was all the time the mutant man needed to take him out at the knees. As Jamie collapsed, the man scooped up vomit and swabbed it on Jamie's anus. As Jamie looked back in horror, the man took a second helping of puke and lathered his dick up with it, using it as lube to get erect.

Tony may not have had nine inches, but this guy did, and once he was all the way hard, he gained another four. And when that hairy head broke the seal of Jamie's virgin butthole, he got to feel every one of those inches as he was literally fucked to death.

~

They sprinted down the wide aisle between dairy and frozen foods. There were a good amount of displays in the center of it they could hide behind if need be. Ruby hoped it wouldn't be necessary. With any luck, they could get to the front doors without being spotted. Having been smashed in by that pickup truck, there would be no way for the shattered glass partitions to be blocked off.

They had to get out soon. Ruby was tired. She thought of the detectives from the dime store novels. *I'm getting to old for this* they always said. Well, Ruby wasn't getting old; she *was* old. Old and tired and scared.

Beside her, Stephanie clutched the tomahawk they'd stolen from that zit-faced goon they'd crushed. Antonio limped behind her, a butcher knife in each fist. He was a bloody wreck. Ruby glanced at the tile beneath him.

"Oh no," she said. "You're leaving a trail, Antonio."

He looked, seeing the blood that ran from the bakery doors to where he now stood. His whole body seemed to slacken in defeat. He mumbled something in Spanish. Though she didn't speak the language, she knew it was a prayer.

"You two must go," he said.

Stephanie shook her head. "No fuckin' way."

"You must leave me behind. They'll be able to track me, but that doesn't mean they should track you too."

"We can't leave you," Ruby said.

"You must. I'm too weak to run. I can only stand my ground and fight."

"C'mon," Stephanie said, taking his arm. "You're talkin' shit."

He resisted the girl. "Please. I cannot be responsible for leading these crazies right to you. Get out and call the police. I will find somewhere to hide, okay?"

But how could he hide if he left a trail of blood? A tear ran down Ruby's cheek. What hurt most was Antonio was right. She and Stephanie's best bet was to run like hell for the foyer. It was their last hope for escape.

"Stephanie," she said, taking the girl by the hand. "He's right. We have to get our butts in gear. I don't like it anymore than you do, but we've got to leave him behind."

The girl's eyes brimmed with tears. "Shut up!"

"Keep your voice down."

"I'm not going anywhere without Antonio."

"Stephanie, please. We mu—"

Laughter interrupted them, the cruel laughter of the mad. They looked up. Mohawk boy stood at the back of the aisle, his power drill in hand. There were two metal *clank* sounds behind them, and Ruby turned to see identical women with samurai swords they dragged across the floor.

The villains closed in, moving forward in a steady march of doom.

Ruby clutched her knife. She thought of the boys at Iwo Jima, Normandy, and The Alamo, thought of Uncle Sam and Annie Oakley and John Wayne and Daniel Boone and Christa McAuliffe and Magnum P.I. Most of all she thought of her husband and son, her two biggest heroes.

"All right you sons a bitches," she said with a snarl. "This is one old lady who ain't gonna take it anymore."

There was a terrible crash at the front of the store. Somewhere, someone screamed, "Holy fucking shit!" and the roar of vehicles echoed through the aisles, followed by more crashes, like a series of bombs landing.

Ruby grit her teeth.

It was D-Day.

CHAPTER FOURTEEN
SCREAM BLOODY GORE

THE TRUCK DEMOLISHED THE SLIDING doors as Booker drove into the store, running over stacks of paper towels. As he rode around the registers he wiped out the cutout of Bart Simpson, Butterfingers soaring into the air. A pentagram air freshener swayed from the rear view mirror and he tore it away.

"To hell with The Devil," he said.

As the last biker raced away through produce, Booker pursued him, cursing all the way down the front end. He spotted two Devil's Food employees; a man holding a pitchfork and a woman with a hammer. They ducked behind a wall of RC Cola twelve packs, as if Booker wouldn't drive straight through the motherfucker, which he did. The barricade detonated, creating a shower of soda as he plowed it down. Booker savored the look of pure terror on the faces of the Devil's Food jerks. The man chucked his pitchfork at the truck like it would matter. It didn't. The woman was smarter and jumped out of the way as the man was given the *Maximum Overdrive* treatment, the grill ramming into him, his body tumbling under the tires with a thud that rose the axle.

Booker laughed. Revenge was actually kind of fun. He turned on the radio—House of Pain's "Jump Around". He cranked it, doing donuts as he chased the woman, the tires throwing the wet remains of her friend. Unlike him, there was no fear in her eyes, only the lethal glare of a panther. Booker came close to clipping her with the bumper, but she leapt and sank the back of the claw hammer into the hood and clung like a deer tick. She smiled, revealing fangs— actual *fangs*.

Must have had one hell of a dental treatment, Booker thought.

She reached for the space between the hood and the wipers, holding on as she raised the hammer and bashed a hole in the windshield.

"Shit!" Booker threw the steering wheel hard to send the truck down the laundry and cleaning aisle. He'd hoped to also throw the psycho tumbling over the front of the hood, but although she slid, she held fast to both her grip and the hammer. Her screaming face filled the windshield. He craned to see around her. He didn't want to hit a load-bearing pillar and end up disabling the truck.

The aisle ahead looked free of obstacles, other than a display of Tide detergent. Booker hit it hard, soaking the girl with soapy blue liquid as bottles exploded and flipped. She shrieked her displeasure, looking like she'd been slimed in *Ghostbusters*. She pulled herself back to the windshield and swung again, bashing the side window. Booker flinched from the flying shards.

He punched the gas harder. "All right, bitch, you like to break glass?"

The truck flew through the remaining aisle, picking up speed. As they neared the end, Booker hit the brake again. The force tore her fingers off at the joint where they were curled around the hood groove. She spun off the truck and hit a lobster tank face-first in front of the seafood section like a Scud missile. Glass shattered as gallons of water exploded across the floor, lobsters tossed out with them. She rolled in an awkward ball of limbs until she hit the seafood freezer case. Incredibly, she pulled herself to her feet. She lurched forward a step, a huge sliver of glass embedded in her face, bisecting her forehead and eyeball. She looked almost like some kind of sea creature with her wide mouth of fangs, a lamprey perhaps.

Even so, she was in the wrong section, needing to be relocated with the rest of the dead meat.

Booker punched the accelerator and bulldozed her. Broken glass sprinkled from the headlights as he sandwiched her against the seafood case and the truck. She vomited blood as she flopped over, as if to seize the hood again, but her legs didn't join her this time. Booker reversed to point himself back toward the produce section. The girl's torso slid off, its innards sloughing. He flipped on the windshield wipers to clear the spritz of blood from her brief finger painting.

Booker frowned at the clear path before him. He'd lost track of the biker and there was no chance of making it through produce to pick him up again. There were too many display tables and ice chests. The truck roared through the potato chip aisle. Booker was stalking now, like the mystery driver in *Duel*. That bastard Desmond was here somewhere, and Booker intended to turn him into roadkill.

~

"What in the name of Beelzebub?" Desmond said.

The commotion was cataclysmic. He and Bad, Bad, Leroy Brown sprinted through the medicine aisle and peeked down the next aisle to see Desmond's pickup annihilating everything in its path. It was like a one-man demolition derby.

"Motherfucker!" Desmond shouted. "Don't scratch my new paint job!"

He spotted Booker at the wheel. Luckily he hadn't spotted them yet.

"Whadda we do, boss?" Leroy asked.

Desmond rubbed his chin. "Okay. I'm gonna gather the troops on the walkie-talkie. In the meantime, I want you to get that asshole outta my truck."

Leroy smirked. "Say what?"

"I need you to demobilize him 'fore he runs us all over."

"Fuck that."

Desmond grimaced. "Are you being insubordinate? I can write you up for that."

"How'n the hell am I supposed to take down a truck?"

"Mace him!"

Leroy held out his mace. "You can feel free to borrow it. Show me how it's done. I think I need managerial guidance here."

Now Desmond was getting mad. "You dare go against your superior?"

"Look, boss. I love Lucifer, but I wasn't plannin' on meetin' the motherfucka tonight. Know what I'm sayin'?"

Desmond exhaled and put out his hand. "Fine. Give me the fuckin' thing."

Leroy handed it over. Desmond grinned and swung the chain, the steel ball slamming into Leroy's face, three spikes lodging there. Leroy wobbled, stunned, blood filling his eyes.

"This is what I get for being politically correct?" Desmond said. "I hire an ethnic and my reward is to be disrespected?"

Leroy was unable to answer; a spike had pinned his lip to his nose. He shuddered, falling against the metro of cough drops. Desmond kicked him in the ribs a few times before reaching for the handle of the mace. He expunged the ball from Leroy's mutilated skull and swung it down again, spraying the man's teeth across the tile like a game of marbles. Desmond swung the medieval weapon back and forth. An eye dislodged from the socket with a wet pop, the top of Leroy's head skinned of some of its afro, his neck shredded to the point of decapitation.

Desmond dropped the mace and picked up the head. He stuck a finger in each eye socket and put his thumb in Leroy's mouth. He reeled his arm back, ready to bowl.

"Forget writing you up," Desmond said. "You're fired!"

~

A man's severed head rolled across the sales floor.

Kyle covered his mouth so not to scream. His stomach rolled but he steadied himself. The head was African-American but so mutilated he couldn't be sure if it was Booker or not.

Please…please don't be.

The store was alive with chaos, a blood-drenched pandemonium that made his head spin. He heard racing engines and loud crashes, but remained tucked behind the Cheez-It display, unable to see but not wanting to risk being seen himself. All he knew was people were actually *driving* through the store.

He also heard the sound of battle coming from the dairy department. People screaming, steel clacking against steel. He thought of the women he'd seen with the samurai swords.

Please, God. Let the others be okay.

Kyle shook his head. *No atheists in foxholes*, he thought. If only Mila could see him now, asking God for the strength to survive.

Just as the decapitated skull stopped at the end of the aisle, Kyle saw a bald man out of the corner of his eye, walking toward the bakery.

Desmond.

And he was alone.

Kyle clutched his knife. He rose, slow and silent, moving on the balls of his feet. He formed a karate stance and, thinking of Mr. Miyagi, focused on the meditative vision of a bonsai tree. It centered him, transforming this stock boy into a straight-up warrior. His brain sang Mark Safan's "Win in the End" from the movie *Teen Wolf.*

Desmond walked in a slow gait, hands on his hips. When he reached the end of the aisle he paused there and peered around the corner, watching for any attack but failing to cover his rear. Kyle licked his lips at this opportunity. He inched closer. Closer still. Adrenaline gave him the shakes.

When he was right behind the big, bald prick, Kyle raised the knife with both hands, high above his head, and stared at Desmond's fat neck, the perfect place to strike first. Holding his breath, he swung down, and in that same second Desmond spun around, laughing, and punted Kyle square in the chest. Every bit of wind exited Kyle's lungs as he was sent to the floor. He gasped, eyes wide as Desmond stepped on his arm, pinning it so he could snatch the filet knife from his hand. Kyle tried to stab, but only managed to prick Desmond's finger.

"Ouchie," Desmond said with a smirk as he got down beside him.

Rage flushed through Kyle, mad at Desmond for what he'd done to Mila and mad at himself for his failed attempt at vengeance. He'd blown his best and only chance. And now, he may have blown the rest of his life.

As if reading his mind, Desmond said, "You always were a loser, kid."

Then he started stabbing.

Desmond punched the skinny blade into Kyle's side again and again. Pain like he'd never imagined quaked through him. Had his kidney burst? Was his stomach pierced? His guts throbbed and stung within him, blood pooling around the knees of his killer. Every last morsel of strength was bled out of him, and soon he wasn't even able to thrash.

Tossing the knife, Desmond lifted Kyle from under his armpits. He started dragging him through the bakery, leaving a river of blood between tables of burger buns and croissants. Kyle's vision had blurred, but he realized he was being pulled behind the display case to the production floor. He heard something beeping and there was the green glow of a timer in the dark.

No…

Desmond hoisted him up.

Kyle was too weak to do anything but beg. "No no no…please."

Desmond threw him into the large, vertical bakery oven and slammed shut the door. When Kyle tried to get up, his legs wouldn't support him any longer. Soon his metal coffin began to glow orange like the neon sign outside the nudie bar down the street. He wished he were there now instead of locked inside this death trap. He clawed at the stained-brown glass to no avail, and when he looked up saw Desmond standing on the other side, smiling like he was waiting for his Hot Pocket to be ready.

Kyle began to cook. His skin turned pink and blistered, the tissue flaking. He tried to get up again and his head hit a burner, singeing hair from his scalp. All he could do was scream. Turning red, his belt buckle seared into his belly. His sneakers melted. As his body shriveled, his hands charred to black and as he made one final paw at the glass the fingers fell away. He coughed against the rising smoke, and then realized it was coming from him.

He was being cremated alive.

Without eyelashes or brows, he looked up for a God who was not there. The only one Kyle saw was Desmond, grinning wide, his dick in his hand, ejaculating as he watched Kyle burn to a crisp.

~

Gore salivated watching the twins go to work. They spun their blades like oscillating razors, charging Ruby and Antonio like they were straight out of *Riki-Oh: The Story of Ricky*, Gore's favorite kung fu flick.

"You can have the spic and the old bag," he'd told them. "But the slut is mine."

When it came to Stephanie, Gore had a bone to pick and a boner to plant. He stalked toward her now, his longest, thickest drill bit spinning. He was going to plant this thing so deep up her snatch it would empty out her womb. But first he was finally—*finally*—gonna get all up in that ass.

Stephanie backed away from the sword-spinning sisters as Antonio lunged at them with knives blazing. The guy was kind of a bad ass, Gore had to admit, but there was no way he was getting out of this one. Already he was bloodier than the sanitary napkins trash bin in the ladies' room at Devil's Food. Sometimes Gore snuck in there just to satisfy his taste for blood. He'd stick a piece of used Maxi pad between his cheek and gum like it was a lump of Skoal, or gnaw on a crusty tampon like jerky. Well, today there'd be no need. He was going to bite into Stephanie's titty and nurse from her bleeding nipples.

She spun around to face him, holding Alex's tomahawk. That explained what happened to that asshole. No love lost as far as Gore was concerned. He flashed Stephanie his crocodile smile and whirred the power drill. Its vibrations reminded him of the dildo he'd once found in his aunt's bedroom drawer. It had smelled like butthole, but the drill smelled of steel and oil, thrilling him as he came at the girl.

Their weapons collided like *Star Wars* lightsabers, the blade of the tomahawk making sparks against the drill bit. They pivoted and parried in this dance of death, two young lives, one destined to meet the ultimate end. She made a desperate shot at hacking into his shoulder, but he managed to shift out of reach and her momentum made her stumble. She had to let go of the tomahawk to break her fall, and it spun across the tile floor, disappearing under a shelving unit.

Gore's cock stiffened. He moved upon her in slow, ominous steps, imagining himself as Michael Myers from *Halloween 4*, his favorite of them all. But unlike in the movies, Stephanie ran off without tripping, and Gore possessed no magic ability to somehow appear in front of her. He picked up the pace, chasing her past the bakery. He saw Desmond behind the counter, jerking off at the baking oven. Any other night, Gore would have thought someone had spiked his Mello Yello with a tab of acid. But this was no normal night. This was the glorious hour of satanic slaughter. He returned his attention to his prey as she ran into the deli.

~

Stephanie jolted as she came around the deli counter.

A woman her age was standing by the rotisserie oven, wearing nothing but a coating of gore, a tiara, and a length of guts like a beauty pageant sash. The madwoman turned to look at her, and Stephanie saw the oven was on, the golden glow revealing three chickens spinning on the racks.

Was this lunatic really cooking right now?

When the chickens made a complete turn, Stephanie realized how wrong she was. She saw eyes, ears, and teeth.

Those are no chickens.

The heads of three young boys turned round and round, dripping buttery juices, their blistering flesh speckled with rosemary and black pepper.

With Gordo coming right on her tail, Stephanie had no time to scream. She grabbed the woman by the hair before she could react and slammed her face on the steel prep table. The girl's nose exploded. She collapsed onto the floor, dead at best, unconscious at the very least.

The ominous buzz of a power drill raised the little hairs on Stephanie's body. Gordo was drawing near.

Running around the prep table for cover, she spotted the block that held the deli knives and drew the thickest, longest one from its slot. She spun back to Gordo, but all she saw was a drill bit whirring just before her eyes. She dodged the attack but the bit spun into her hair, binding it and plucking strands from her scalp. Blood spilled into her ear. Gordo tried to pull the drill free but it had lodged itself there. Snarling, Stephanie slashed at Gordo, but tears clouded her vision. Gordo kicked her legs out from under her and she fell hard on her tailbone. The knife spun away just like the tomahawk had.

She grunted, aching in her effort to get up as Gordo undid his jeans. His thin pecker bobbed when it was unleashed. She pointed and chuckled.

Gordo turned pink. "What're you laughin' at, bitch?"

"Is that your cock or did you just slap some dog fur on a Popsicle stick?"

"You fuckin' bitch!"

He landed on her as if he was trying to win a wrestling match, but instead of tapping the floor he started tearing at her bra. The cups ripped free, her breasts jiggling, much to Gordo's delight. He was panting like a dog humping a leg. He twisted one of her nipples and hocked a loogie onto the other, all the while his hard-on digging at the crotch of her jeans. Gordo smiled, his rotted teeth glistening green as Christmas, and started undoing Stephanie's belt. She turned her head away in disgust.

That's when she saw her knife.

It had slid just below the table where the manual can-opener was mounted, barely out of reach. If she could just get Gordo to budge she could scoot over and snatch it.

"I'm gonna stick my dick up your ass," Gordo said. "We'll see how small you think it is then!"

Stephanie took a deep breath, then batted her eyes at him and puckered her lips, putting on the best show possible. "Yeah, baby. Give it to me good."

Gordo froze, a dumb as fuck look on his face.

"Stick it in me, baby," she said.

"Wh-wh-what?"

Clearly these were words no girl had ever said to him before. What kind of a sick bitch would want to take this rat-faced twerp to bed?

"Gimme some wiggle room," she said, "so we can get my jeans off."

She licked her lips for emphasis. Gordo's jaw fell open.

"You...want it?" he asked. "R-r-really?"

"You've shown me you're a man who takes charge. That *really* turns me on."

Stephanie slowly unzipped her fly. She moved her hips as a reminder she needed room to wiggle out of her jeans. As soon as Gordo rose up, she snagged the knife in one hand and Gordo's dick in the other. He shrieked and tried to pull back but she held tight, spraining his hard Johnston. She slashed for his stomach but he blocked it, and his arm came open in a gash of scarlet. Raging, Gordo punched her in the face. He sat on her chest and tried to grab the knife. Like an idiot he gripped the blade and Stephanie drew it back, opening his palm. His punched her with his good hand. Stephanie saw stars. By the time she blinked them away, her knife was lost and Gordo had mounted her head.

"I'm gonna fuck your mouth!" he said.

Cleary his anger was blocking what little sense he had. Stephanie held her breath so not to inhale the reek of his crotch, and opened her mouth to receive him. He thrust in and out, knocking her skull upon the tile, and she sucked until he was fully hard again. She had to time this just right. She moaned as if with pleasure, slurping and twirling her tongue, using all the skills she'd gathered over the sixty or so cocks she'd had in her mouth since she'd turned thirteen. In less than a minute, Gordo began to shake, and the moment his sour jizz smacked the back of her throat she bit down hard.

Gordo made a reverse scream, an inhalation of blinding pain. Stephanie shifted her jaw back and forth, sawing at the meat of the still spewing wiener. Gordo hit her but she refused to relent, and when he finally put his hands on her shoulders for leverage and pulled himself free, her teeth peeled away the top layer of skin from the shaft. Her mouth flooded with salty blood and saltier cum. Gordo squealed. As he tried to get over her, his balls dangled before her face like a baby's mobile, and she spat out his fluids and sank her teeth into a testicle.

His body seizing, Gordo collapsed in pain, so overcome with agony he couldn't even fight her. She ground her teeth into the hairy sack, feeling the ball give way, the cells secreting, the tiny ducts rupturing, the epididymis tube freed from its tight coil.

Gordo convulsed upon her face, then fell still.

Stephanie tried to slide out from under him but bumped into his elbow, and the movement caused her to swallow the testicular remains. She spat but it was no use. Grabbing onto the table, she pulled herself up. Shivering, she leaned on the table and burped.

The sound of an engine caused her to look up. A motorcycle raced by and she ducked, holding onto the can-opener. A big metal clamp held it to the table and you had to wedge the huge, bulk-sized can beneath the lever to pop it, and then had to turn the lever by hand to open the can. Todd would never spring for an electric one, the cheap bastard, so the deli crew was stuck with this beast.

Beside her, Gordo groaned.

She grabbed his Mohawk, dragging him up with her, then slung him over the counter, bracing him between her and the table. She pushed his head into the can-opener, raised the lever and jumped up, using all her weight to lower the blade into Gordo's temple. It dug into the bone and he shot awake, but was unable to move. Stephanie started cranking. The blade turned in a circular pattern and Gordo moved with it, trying to ease the pain by going with the flow, but instead assisting the opener in tearing into the left side of his face. The flesh separated, skull chipping, and when it reached his mouth the blade broke his nasty-ass teeth apart.

When there was no leverage to turn him any further, Stephanie stepped back to catch her breath. Gordo was stuck, half his face mutilated beyond recognition, his jeans around his ankles, blood dribbling for his demolished genitalia.

Stephanie's head ached. Something was stressing her neck. She reached up and touched the drill. In the chaos, she'd forgotten it was stuck in there. She tugged but it would not budge, so she went back to the block and drew a knife and cut her hair until it was free. She hit the trigger. The drill powered back on.

Mad with laughter, Stephanie returned to Gordo. He'd passed out again, but she knew the perfect way to wake him up. She spit onto the head of the drill bit and guided it upward between Gordo's buttocks, finding his anus.

The drill came back to life.

So did Gordo...but not for long.

CHAPTER FIFTEEN
PINNACLE OF BEDLAM

"JESUS," FENTON SAID. "WHO THE fuck is this now?"

Two headless bodies were splayed before the mop sink like rag dolls of meat. Young boys, half naked. He stepped over them. It just didn't matter anymore.

Where the fuck are the others?

He'd come back here to find the Freshway crew, but they were gone. Had they escaped?

That's when he noticed the loading dock door was wide open. A rush of relief soared through his entire body. He laughed, slapping his legs.

"Hot damn!" he said. "Un-fuckin-believable."

He sprinted toward the dock, but just before he could hop down he saw the sea of carnage in the back lot. Bodies were pulverized, road-rashed, charred, and mutilated. Gas fumes rose from a mangled motorcycle and the tractor-trailer was beat to shit.

"Fuck this," Fenton said, stepping away.

It had to be a trap. Everyone else out there had been slain. He wasn't dumb enough to be the next victim.

He ran down the hall of back stock, looking for someone to kill so to prove his devotion to Satan. Not that he believed in that sort of hocus-pocus. The Devil was about as real to him as Alf. At least he loved Alf. But he had to show Desmond he would do whatever it took to appease the dark lord (hopefully that didn't include gargling any more cum). Still tasting that load, he snagged a can of Tab to wash it away.

A foul stench hit him. It reminded Fenton of the Port-O-Potties at Lollapalooza. Around the bend he saw a third body, the most gruesome of all. Like the others, the kid was headless and had his pants down, but unlike his friends his asshole had been stretched enough that his anal canal resembled a drainage pipe. A stream of bloody feces had flowed out and the ass cheeks were spattered with custard-colored jizz.

Fenton dry heaved. "Sweet, merciful crap."

He stepped over the body but slipped when he hit the sloppy turds and fell upon the carcass, splattering a cornucopia of bodily waste about him. He bucked and brayed and slid, wishing he'd sprung for the slip-resistant safety shoes Booker had been nagging him about. He had to grab on to the dead boy's buttocks to brace himself, and they fluttered with lard as a final death fart bubbled out. Fenton was so close he had no choice but to eat the flatulence. When he heaved this time, it wasn't dry.

Whimpering, he at last stood up, dripping every bit of human waste known to man.

"Christ," he said. "I look like an abortion."

His hatred cranked, he walked to the doors leading out to the bakery, so focused on the hunt he failed to see the hairy little man crouched in the shadows, chewing on the fat boy's heart.

~

The samurai sword twins had appeared almost spectral to Antonio, with their pallid faces emerging from the shadows at the end of the aisle. He'd rushed to engage them, deeming them the bigger threats.

"You try to stay behind me, Miss Ruby," he said over his shoulder.

"The hell I will!" Ruby said, hurrying to draw even with him. "We're in this together, Antonio."

Though light-headed from blood loss and exhausted from the sustained toll of the night, Antonio smiled.

Elsewhere in the store, bedlam reigned—screams, curses, pleas, and the cacophony of something big plowing through the store, crushing and demolishing everything and everyone in its path from the sound of it.

The twins were locked in attack stances. The reach of their blades made it hard to get in close to them. His arms already dripped blood from multiple cuts. Both of the swords arced toward his face, practically in tandem. He dodged to the left and lunged. The knife would have plunged into the ribs of the twin to his left, but he had to yank his hand back as the other sister hacked at him a second time. He nearly lost his arm.

He'd tried to provide a human shield for Ruby, but she managed to slip in beside him. The sister who almost chopped off Antonio's arm howled and swiped at Ruby in a tight configuration, like someone trying to cut up a swarm of gnats. Ruby shouted, a crimson line spreading across the front of her shirt. She staggered backward. The twin moved in to stay in range.

Antonio threw himself sideways, striking the sister in the side and knocking her into the open dairy case. He turned back to the other twin just in time to see her sword slicing toward him. He ducked his head again, thinking she'd missed until warm blood streamed down his face and neck. He spotted a petal of flesh by his foot that had previously formed the upper part of his ear.

Before she drew the sword back, Antonio thrust his knives forward, down on one knee under the span of her arms. The soft skin of her abdomen parted with expert precision. He ripped both blades aside, spilling a clumpy wall of entrails through the egress. She collapsed to her knees, gurgling blood.

"Antonio, behind you!" Ruby cried, running toward him with her knife raised.

He saw rather than felt the sword appear, the blood-streaked steel emerging from a puncture in his chest until the hilt of the sword nudged his back. The other twin had regained her equilibrium much sooner than he'd expected. Fire erupted through the perforation. He twisted away from the sister who had impaled him from behind, taking the sword from her. He hit the floor on his side, barely able to take a breath, the inevitability of his mortality piercing his breast.

He had fought all night with his friends to get back to Nelly, Roberto, Bella, Emilia, and Mamá. It wasn't fair or right, but it would end here like this.

The sister vaulted out of the dairy case beside her dying twin, but not before Ruby dropped her knife and tore the woman's sword away first. Antonio would have smiled if not for the overwhelming pain. She lacked the finesse of the twins, but the sharpness of the blade required only that she aim true. Antonio thought the sister might flee altogether, but after rolling away from Ruby's initial swings and putting some distance between them, she held her ground.

Antonio tried to pull himself upright, but the sword felt like a two-ton anchor. Ruby's knife may as well have been five miles away as five feet.

The sister heaved open a freezer door, effectively blocking Ruby's strike, then cartwheeled past Ruby to where her twin had fallen. She was coming for the other sword available to her, and if she took it out of Antonio, it likely meant the end for Ruby.

She slid on the floor beside him, seeming to move in fast forward. He rolled onto his back despite the horrendous pain, so she wouldn't be able to access its handle. She kicked the flat side of the blade, cleaving open more of his chest as the sharp side nudged forward, easily parting skin and tissue. Agony brought him on the verge of passing out.

Ruby lumbered toward them from down the aisle, grimacing. The twin spotted Ruby's dropped knife started to crawl past Antonio to get it. He seized her by the hair and jerked her toward the sword in his chest. The sister shrieked as the blade tip burst her eyeball and sank into her skull. Worms of glistening ocular tissue and fluid oozed down the shaft. As shockwaves of pain rippled through him, Antonio yanked his hand back with the woman's hair still knotted around his fingers, dragging her head with him. The sword carved its way through her skull until it exited the crown of her head. The scream cut off. Brain tissue clumped around the blade, warm blood spilling over his lap as she flopped away.

Ruby knelt beside him, tears in her eyes. She took his hand. "Oh, Antonio. I'm so, so sorry."

Antonio squeezed her hand, shaking his head. He could think the words without a problem, but saying them proved far more difficult. "Is…okay, Miss…Ruby. You go…n-now. I …I go…too."

Then he was unable to think the words either.

The shadows of the aisle seemed to blanket everything at once.

~

Ruby wiped her eyes. She wanted to mourn Antonio, but what would his sacrifice be if she let one of these devil-worshipping cowards knock her off this mortal coil while she sobbed with her back turned to danger? She'd lived long enough to know mourning would wait for more convenient circumstances.

She checked both ends of the aisle, wincing at the weight of the sword. The incision burned her chest, blood soaking the front of her shirt and dripping down her pants. A couple inches deeper and it might have been fatal. While the sounds of death and anguish came from all around, no immediate threats presented themselves now. She might be able to walk right out the front door this minute with everyone else occupied.

Even if that were possible, though, she wouldn't do it. She couldn't leave without finding Stephanie. The girl had survived her first brush with Gordon, a boy who barely weighed a buck soaking wet, and Ruby thought she could do it again. She sure hoped that was the case.

They'd come so far, against insurmountable odds. It all had to be for a reason. She couldn't fathom why God wanted to take a family man like Antonio instead of a lonely woman like herself. He must have some purpose for her in all this. She would fulfill it, whatever it might be.

"Holy Antichrist, you're still alive, old lady?" a voice said.

Ruby flinched, choking up on the sword. A woman had appeared at the end of the aisle. She held a fire axe, and Ruby thanked The Lord she hadn't traded the sword for the brass-knuckled knife despite its unwieldy weight. She'd need the longer reach.

As the woman drew nearer, Ruby recognized her. She'd been a part of that initial onslaught in the backroom. That seemed like a lifetime ago, but Ruby hadn't forgotten her.

"I have to say I'm not surprised *you're* still alive, young lady," Ruby said. "Not with that yellow streak down your back."

"The name's Dizzy Q. You'd be smart to remember it, 'cause you'll be beggin' me for your life in about two seconds."

"You mean you're not gonna run the other way with your tail between your legs again? I'll give you a head start."

The woman's evil smile withered. "Fuck you, you old bag!"

Dizzy Q charged Ruby, one hand holding her axe at the base, the other sliding up to the top to bury it in Ruby's head. Heavy though it might be, the sword was probably lighter than that axe, and Dizzy Q didn't look particularly sturdy to begin with. When she got close, Ruby dropped and swung at the hateful bitch's legs. The axe whooshed overhead. Ruby missed one leg, but the sword went through the other like wet paper.

Dizzy Q lurched to the side, a fire hose spray of crimson bursting from her leg stump. Her axe clunked to the floor. She slumped against a freezer case, squalling at an ear-splitting decibel. Ruby's next swing cut the screaming off, hacking open the woman's throat and the arteries within. A bloody mist like the produce wet walls hissed from the wound. Dizzy Q tipped over, still trying to fend off the attack as Ruby advanced, holding the sword with both hands, hacking away crudely. The defending arms were soon shed across the floor in pieces, left hand, right forearm and hand, left forearm.

Her own arms burning with the effort, Ruby swung the sword into the woman a final time, hacking deep into her torso. She didn't think she could pull it back out if she wanted to.

"You should have run away again," Ruby said, gasping. She stooped over to pick up her knife, wincing at the soreness in her back.

After a couple of breaths, she started to work her way back down the aisle, where she'd last seen Stephanie.

~

Desmond sulked his way down the rear of the store, seeing body after body. In the deli, Laila was on her back, covered in blood. His minion Gore was stuck in a fucking *can-opener* for Hell's sake. The last of his inner circle were dead. How the fuck had the Freshway twerps taken them out like this? How had they survived this long?

Look on the bright side, he thought. *At least* you're *not injured.*

As long as Devil's Food had a strong leader, he could re-staff. Maybe have a job fair at the store. But would Alaric, as the regional manager, allow Desmond to run the place after this level of turnover? He certainly wasn't in competition with the Molina store now. They'd bested him in every way by taking out the Win-Dicker Grocery Mart by fire. He'd had the potential for an actual body count here, not just a decimated building, but he'd blown it, just as surely as that Fenton fuckwit had blown him.

Where was that fuckwit anyway? He was supposed to be proving himself.

Desmond needed to rally whatever was left of the troops outside. He raised the walkie-talkie.

"All units, respond."

He waited. Static. He repeated the command. Nothing.

Could it be? Could they have been taken out too? What a clusterfuck. What a goddamn Chinese fire-drill shit-storm disaster of a clusterfuck. Furious, he threw the walkie-talkie against the wall. The sound of screeching tires made him turn his head just in time to see his dented, blood-slicked pickup haul ass around the corner, heading straight for him.

Desmond dived behind the meat counter and the truck ran through it, spraying glass and steaks and chicken breasts in a confetti of choice cuts. The sound was deafening. As the truck peeled away, Desmond ran through to the meat prep room. Reaching the back room, he jumped over a decapitated kid and ran past the walk-in freezer to the cage where the forklift was parked.

When he'd quit working here, he'd thrown his manager keys right in Todd's miserable face. It was a satisfying experience. But what Todd didn't know is Desmond had made copies of all of the ones that didn't have DO NOT COPY stamped on them, because key-makers refused to do it.

One of his spares unlocked this cage. Another fit in the forklift's ignition.

He fired it up.

"Cowabunga, dude."

~

Steam rose from under the hood. The truck was still moving, but it wouldn't last long. Booker had to make the most of it while he still could. Pulling away from the demolished counter, metal brackets tore away and were dragged along like streamers.

He heard the *potato-potato-potato* of the motorcycle and spotted it in his rearview mirror. It was coming on strong, the biker swinging a chain over his head and screaming a death metal roar. Just another maniac.

Booker put the truck in reverse so to run into the nutjob, but the truck stalled out.

He turned the key repeatedly. "C'mon! C'mon!"

The motorcycle raced through the scattered ground beef and chicken thighs, heading for the driver's side door.

"C'mon, baby!" Booker said to his ride. If he tried to turn it over much more he'd flood the engine, but this was his only shot. "C'mon, you fuck—"

The engine started and the radio came back on. Bill Ray Cyrus hillbillied his way through "Achy Breaky Heart". The collisions must have changed the station. Booker gunned it and the truck charged backward, and as the biker approached Booker flung open the door.

The motorcycle crashed into it, shaking the whole truck, and the biker was propelled through the window, taking the door with him as he flew into a stack of canned peas. He slid across the back aisle, leaving a long, red smear. He struggled to get up, his chain still in hand. Booker turned the truck around. The man rose, glass shards covering his head and shoulders like a pincushion. His face was all but gone, leaving a peeled skull with staring eyeballs, and he stood perfectly still, as if they were in some spaghetti-western showdown.

Sick of the shit-kicker, Booker changed the radio station.

Right Said Fred's "I'm Too Sexy".

He bobbed his head to the catchy tune, singing along, and floored the gas pedal. The biker gave him a rictus grin and flung the chain at the windshield. The safety glass became a spider web. Booker crouched in order to see.

He shouted. "Die, you easy ridin' son of a bitch!"

The biker didn't even try to get out of the way. He just kept on smiling and threw up the devil horns salute with both hands. Even over the roar of the engine, Booker could hear the man's final words as the bumper took him.

"Hail Satan!"

And then he was blood pudding.

The truck idled. Booker sat back, letting his muscles relax. He took one deep breath before putting his hands on the wheel again, looking around the store.

No time to rest. My people are still out there.

He switched gears to back up off the corpse, not noticing the forklift until it rammed right into the passenger side of the truck. The damage to the windshield had completely blocked it from view.

The truck shuddered as the forklift pierced its side.

Booker held on tight. "Jesus Fucking Christ!"

Good thing he always buckled up for safety, otherwise he would have been thrown out the hole where the driver's door used to be. He gripped the wheel for his life and the forklift backed away, removing its deadly lifts. Booker reversed, catching a glimpse of Desmond in the driver's cage. The man was cackling, insane. Smoke billowed from the hood of the truck as Booker backed up. It had gone from gray to black. Leaning forward, he threw punches at the windshield until the sheet of safety glass folded, and knocked it out of the way. He coughed against the smoke but at least he could see again.

Desmond faced him head on. The long, steel lifts of the forklift were raised halfway, level with the truck's grill. Had the truck still been at full power, Booker would have had more confidence, but it was shuddering and farting exhaust, parts of it dragging and falling off. It would be difficult to build enough momentum to slam the forklift back or knock it over. Just revving the engine made the truck shake and clatter. The hood was bent from the crash and he could see the first flickers of fire.

He knew what he had to do.

Booker undid his seatbelt. He hit the gas, the truck shuddering as it pressed on. Desmond charged right at him. As the vehicles closed in on each other, Booker stomped on the gas pedal, rising in his seat, screaming over the wheel with the battle cry of the damned. Just as the lifts reached the grill, the flames whooshed and Booker leapt out of the truck, landing in the coffin case of frozen turkeys. He went into a ball and covered his head as the collision went off like an atomic bomb.

~

A tidal wave of heat washed over Desmond. He was bounced around inside the driver's cage as the pickup truck became a ball of fire. His palms burned on the forklift's metal door as he pushed it open, clothes igniting, his goatee singeing away. Lava-hot debris smacked him like a pimp on a slow night. Fire *ate* him. He jumped out of the forklift, rolling to put himself out, barely getting away from the blast as one gas tank went up, then the other, creating a mushroom of flame. The explosion tore the vehicles apart and the forklift rolled onto its side and skidded into the deli case, and as it burst the emergency sprinklers came on, cooling his smoldering body.

He pulled himself up. When he touched his face, one whole side of it had melted, and the skin had peeled from his bald head.

"Mother of all fuckers!"

He pawed his body for a weapon, forgetting what he even had. All he found was the stupid fillet knife. *Well that's just fucking great*, he thought, shaking his head. He held it out in front of him, a child with a magic wand. Limping to the coffin case he'd seen Booker land in, Desmond growled. Booker wasn't there. Desmond turned in every direction, the raining water obscuring his vision.

"Come out, come out, wherever you are!"

It wouldn't be fast. No, no. He was going to take his time killing Booker, using the fillet knife as it was intended, peeling him of every inch of skin. Then he'd tan the hide and make lampshades and a belt out of it. Maybe even a little hat. He'd turn the man's skull into a cereal bowl and mount his eyeballs on the dashboard of an all new pickup. Thank Satan he had good auto insurance.

Someone grunted behind him.

When Desmond turned around, Booker swung the frozen turkey, and then there was nothing but darkness.

CHAPTER SIXTEEN
NO MORE ROOM IN HELL

RUBY LIMPED THROUGH THE DOWNPOUR in search of Stephanie, weighed down by horror and depravity and the downright despair of it all. The only things she'd ever seen more apocalyptic than this night were the images of Hiroshima, August of '45, and the photos of stacked bodies in Nazi death camps. But while these atrocities were the pinnacle of horror, she'd seen them as black and white images on a TV screen.

This was no picture show.

The gore and devastation was in full color, a smorgasbord of human evisceration and dismemberment. Her limbs shook as she passed by the corpses. Spotting a mace on the floor near a headless body, she snatched it up, but the damned thing was too heavy for her to wield. She left it behind and held on to her knife.

Something was burning. When she came around the corner she saw the mangled wreckage of a truck and forklift. So that's what all that noise had been about. Black fog drifted through the deli and bakery, but she spotted a man striking another man over the head. Unable to tell who they were, she darted down the cookie aisle so not to be seen.

"Stephanie?" she whispered. "Where are you?"

But the lane was empty. Ruby crossed through the front end. More blood and tire tracks. More carcasses. She snuck past the openings of each aisle, scanning for the girl until she reached produce. Still no sight of her. When she stepped into the department she heard a voice.

"Ruby!"

Fenton—the turd.

She'd be better off alone than teaming up with this coward. Choosing to ignore him in her search for Stephanie, Ruby pressed on, but the young man was faster and came up beside her.

"I found a way out," he said. "C'mon. The receiving door's wide open."

"I can't leave."

"Why'n the fuck not?"

"Steph. She's around here somewhere. I have to find her."

Fenton smiled and took her arm. "She's at the receiving bay waiting on us! She asked me to come find you."

Ruby's brow furrowed. "She's...she's really back there?"

"Sure is. Now c'mon, let's get outta here 'fore it's too late."

He tugged her arm but she didn't budge. "Swear to me, boy."

"Huh?"

"Swear to me you're telling the truth."

He gaped. "Ruby...what a thing to say. I'm tryin' to rescue you here."

"All night you've been out to save your own ass...suddenly you care about mine?"

"I know I fucked up, and I'm sorry." He gave her the puppy dog eyes. "I'm tryin' to make it up to you. Please let me."

Doubt remained, but Ruby was desperate. Maybe Stephanie really was waiting for her back there. She had to at least go to the back room and see for herself.

"You swear?" she asked.

He held up his hand as if on the witness stand. "I solemnly swear. On my mother's grave."

Ruby exhaled. "Okay. Let's get a move one."

She stepped forward and as Fenton came in behind her she felt the tip of a blade pierce her muscle tissue.

I should have known, she thought. *Stabbed in the back.*

Once the auto war ended, Stephanie came out of her hiding spot in the deli. She was shaking with a good quarter of her hair torn out, but she was still alive.

You all thought I was just Kelly Bundy. But I'm She-Ra, assholes. I'm fucking Ripley from Aliens *and the bad ass black chick in* Conan the Destroyer!

She stepped over the girl in the tiara and out onto the sales floor. Burning wreckage and broken bodies. Enough product and structural damage to bankrupt the store. Fuck it. She didn't want to work here anymore anyway.

Stephanie gasped when she saw a man fall out of the forklift and roll on the floor, too fucked up for her to recognize. But she recognized Booker as he rose from the frozen case like Snoopy from the pumpkin patch, slow and spooky, a man on a mission. He held a Thanksgiving-worthy turkey like a football, Jerry Rice headed for the end zone.

She was about to call out to him when she saw the burning man rise. It was Desmond. Stephanie tucked back behind the cheese counter. When she realized Booker was sneaking up on him, she clutched the butcher knife tight, waiting to strike if needed. When the turkey cracked Desmond's skull, Stephanie couldn't help but cheer. Booker looked to her, then back to Desmond, who wasn't moving. He picked up the frozen turkey and bashed him over the head three more times until blood shot out.

Booker sighed. He looked to her again. "Steph?"

She ran to him and they embraced.

"Oh…" he said, seeing she was topless.

She didn't bother covering up. Let him look.

"Did we do it?" she asked. "Did we *kill 'em all*, to quote Metallica?"

He didn't seem to get her joke. Maybe it wasn't the best time for one, but she felt like celebrating.

Booker started unbuttoning his shirt. "Here, take mine…"

"Forget it. There's no time. Let's go find Ruby and get outta here."

"She's still alive then?"

"Was when I last saw her."

"Antonio?"

She shook her head. "No. I don't think so. He was bleeding to death already and I got away just as this bitch with a sword came up on him and—"

"What about Kyle?"

She only shrugged.

Booker ran his hand over his face, appearing older than she'd ever seen him. It touched her. Cleary he cared about his staff. She couldn't help but think what Todd would've done in this situation to help them—a big, fat nothing. He would've bailed out of here with a cowardice that put Fenton to shame.

Booker handed her his keys. "I'm too beat up to run. Can you make it to the office quickly?"

"Sure."

"Okay. On the bottom shelf there's a duffle bag, and in that bag is a chainsaw."

Her eyes lit like cherry bombs. "A fuckin' chainsaw?!"

"Know how to use one?"

"My brothers are into wrestling, dude. They have one they use in their amateur matches. They took the chain off, of course, but—"

"Stephanie. We're in a rush."

"Oh, right. Sorry. Yeah, I know how to use one."

"Go get it. We can't be sure how many of these freaks are still hunting us."

"Booker…why did they do all this?"

He sighed. "It's all that devil music, I think. Rots your brain."

She snickered. That was the spirit that would get them out of this. He told her to go and she sprinted down the canned goods aisle, practically skipping with excitement. It was almost over. She could just feel it. But she wasn't going anywhere without Ruby. No way.

Unlocking Todd's office, she went immediately to the bottom shelf.

The chainsaw felt so damned good in her hands.

~

Once he started, he couldn't stop.

Fenton hacked and slashed and hacked and slashed again. Then he hacked and slashed some more. The old bitch's back opened in fifty places as he sat on her. She was facedown and he grabbed her by the hair and bashed her skull against the floor, laughing his ass off.

Who knew killing could be so much fun? Had he had any idea,

he would've started murdering people a long time ago.

"You dumb cunt," he said. "My *mother's grave*, huh? That bitch ain't even dead!"

He dug into Ruby's wounds with the box cutter, then sliced her buttocks. It reminded him of using a pizza roller. The flesh stretched and tore like extra cheese, revealing the red sauce beneath. She tried to struggle against him, but was just a weak old lady. No match for a big strong man like him.

That's right! I'm a man! M-A-N! I'm not some crayon-chewin' little poofter! I'm all man and this proves it!

Killing a helpless old woman really made Fenton feel like a big shot. He was George Washington and Mr. T and the Brawny paper towel guy all rolled into one. The manliest man who ever manned. This would show Desmond and the others he was ready to join Devil's Food. Hell, he was glad to do it. More money. More pussy. More opportunities to butcher people and have this incredible feeling of power all over again. If there really was a Satan, he could have Fenton's soul. He'd long considered it worthless anyway. It was a fair trade for a life filled with excitement, especially after endless days of scrubbing customer shit stains out of toilets and, occasionally, off the floor.

As Ruby was dying she muttered something, and Fenton leaned in close to hear.

"I'm coming home, Fred...Jack...Mama's coming home, darlings...at last."

Well that wasn't very satisfying, Fenton thought.

He'd been hoping her last words would be a begging for mercy he wouldn't provide. Instead she was blowing little kisses to heaven. Well, *fuck that* and *fuck her*.

Fenton stood. He kicked Ruby onto her back. She was still breathing but they were shallow breaths. He aimed to fix that, but first he was going to cut off her saggy tits. He could bring those fried eggs to Desmond as evidence of his devotion. He tried to think of something satanic to say, the kind of thing Gore would, like an evil lyric from a death metal band, but he could only come up with one thing.

"Shout!" he said. "Shout at the Devil!"

He ripped open Ruby's blouse. Was that an actual girdle? Giggling, Fenton put his hand on her throat and placed the blade upon one droopy tit.

"Honk honk!" he said, squeezing.

She was limp as he pushed the blade in.

A motor whirred to life. A woman screamed.

When Fenton looked back he saw Stephanie. The first things he noticed were those luscious hooters. Why was she topless? Why were her jeans torn? And why was a huge chunk of her hair missing, her scalp crusted with blood. But most of all—and this was the big question—where did she get that fucking *chainsaw*?

He tried to move but was paralyzed by fear. Stephanie charged at him like it was the running of the bulls, hoisting that chainsaw above her head, a sexy Leatherface. As she got closer, panic set in. Fenton got to his feet. Once again, his shitty sneakers failed him and Ruby, though still, managed to knock him down just with her blood.

Why didn't you goddamned buy the goddamned slip resistant shoes!?

He pulled himself up on the produce steps, blubbering with fear.

"P-p-please God…" His preferred deity had sure changed quickly. "Jesus…please, save me!"

Stephanie bolted toward him like Meatloaf's bat. Her eyes, which had always seduced Fenton, now filled him with abject dread. He sobbed as his bladder released. Stephanie was upon him and the saw whirred, the stainless steel teeth tearing into his leg like the mouth of a Great White shark. He gripped the wooden case with both hands, his jaw locked from pain. A leg severed just above the knee and tumbled down the steps. Fenton tried to scream but choked on his own bile. The saw roared again, chewing through his remaining leg, closer to the hip this time. When it separated from him it spun into the air, a hairy champagne cork.

Stephanie stepped off him, as if admiring her handwork. Fenton began to crawl up the steps, even thought they led to nowhere—just more pineapples and crotons. The chainsaw revved, then rumbled, revved, then rumbled. She was toying with him.

What kinda bitch toys with a man's life?!

She stepped onto his back, pinning him as metal teeth ate through his shoulder, gnawing the bone like a wolf. The arm tumbled down.

"One more to go!" Stephanie said.

A final dismemberment. His last limb was gone. She kicked him down the stairs and he fell upon two of his discarded body parts, his own fingers poking him in the eyes. He sobbed. He pissed his pants. He whinnied, wept, and wailed. But there was no mercy in Stephanie's eyes.

"Pup-pup-please…" he said.

She placed the tip of the chainsaw just before his nose, dripping with blood.

"You're the janitor, Fenton," she said. "But you always did a shitty job. So I'll tell you what. This time…I'll be the one to *take out the trash.*"

The chainsaw growled, the smoke filling his nostrils, and Fenton chose to spend his last moment doing what he loved. He had one more second to admire Stephanie's sweet, sweet titties before his head was split, right down the center.

~

An angel.

Blonde hair. Nude from the waist up. Lovely eyes, wet with tears.

Of joy? Ruby wondered. *She must be happy to welcome me to heaven.*

The angel was saying something, but Ruby couldn't hear. That was okay. And it was okay when white light blinded her, for though the angel disappeared from view, her husband and son stepped toward her, each placing a hand in hers. Her heart swelled.

The dream she'd had so many nights had come true.

Ruby now understood why they called it "rest in peace".

THE FINAL CHAPTER
THE END COMPLETE

BOOKER HAD TO SUPPORT HIMSELF by leaning on the shelving, but made it down the soda aisle. He stopped and twisted open a Pepsi. All it needed was some Jack Daniel's. A hell of a lot of Jack Daniel's.

When he reached the end of the aisle he turned his face up, letting the water wash him. The fire alarm hadn't sounded. Maybe that asshole on the telephone pole had found a way to deactivate it. But Booker still held out hope the sprinklers turning on was an indication that a signal had been sent to the fire department. He didn't give a fuck if Freshway burned to cinders. He just wanted this night to be over. For the first time in his life, cops would be a welcome sight.

At first he thought the girl who walked past was Stephanie. He called out to her. But as he got closer he saw the dark hair and streams of blood still being washed away. The girl's nose was bashed in but he still recognized her as his former employee Laila. She was naked and dazed. A tiara sat crooked upon her head.

"Booker?" she said. She stumbled forward. "Booker...what

happened?"

"You know damned well what."

He would never forget her part in Darla's forced abortion and evisceration. That a girl this small could be capable of an evil that large was nearly inconceivable. Only the most loathsome and disturbed minds could dream up something like that.

"Booker...I'm scared."

"*You're* scared? You've got one hell of a nerve. You come in here with your army of devil-lovin' maniacs and butcher my staff, and now you say *you're* scared? Well tough titty, you little snake."

She sniffled, her mascara running. "Please...they brainwashed me. Desmond hired me, and then...then he had me gang-raped and fed me lots of drugs. I'm not sure what they did to me after that...I can't remember..."

He scowled. "Bullshit."

But her tears seemed genuine. Maybe her nose being bashed in had brought her back to her senses. Maybe she really had been brainwashed, like a satanic Patty Hearst or one of those Manson family ladies. It was easier to accept than a teen girl being purely and simply evil.

"All right," he said. "I'm not gonna hurt you, but I am turning you in to the authorities. You've murdered people here tonight, Laila."

She shook her head and put her face in her hands. "No...no..."

"Hopefully you can get the help you need, but first you have to explain yourself to the cops."

Laila whimpered. "Okay."

Cautiously, Booker put out his hand. The girl took baby steps to him and placed her hand in his; so tiny and delicate, and yet the hand of a psycho killer. She looked up at him with eyes like a new-born doe's.

A chainsaw thundered and suddenly Stephanie was charging at them. She was speckled with blood and chunks of torn flesh, screaming like a banshee.

"Booker!" she said over the roar of the saw. "Get away from her!"

"Steph! It's okay, Laila is—"

A quick flash. Something pointy removed from the tiara. He let go of the Laila's hand but she pounced on him, legs around his waist, arm around his neck, and stabbed him in the shoulder with her hidden dagger.

"Say you love Satan!" she said. "And tell me I'm pretty!"

Booker punched her in the ribs but she held tight, a cowgirl on a mechanical bull. He slammed her back into a shelving unit of refried beans and the cans fell upon them in a tin hailstorm. The dagger pierced his shoulder again, right in the same spot, and Booker cried out as Laila twisted the blade.

Jumping up and backward, Booker dropped them to the floor, landing on Laila with all his weight. Something in her crunched—perhaps many things. He got off the girl and kicked her knife away. She rolled onto her side, gasping for air.

"You're crazier than a shithouse rat," he said.

The girl got on her hands and knees just as Stephanie ran up with the chainsaw. From the look of her, Booker knew Stephanie wasn't about to let Laila get off easy by surrendering to the police.

"Steph!" he said. "Wait!"

But she ignored him. With Laila down on all fours, Stephanie swung the saw low, between the girl's legs, and brought it up right between her vaginal lips. Slivers of labia tore free as the saw ripped through her taint and into the cleft of her tiny buttocks. Laila's crotch exploded, hot gore spraying Stephanie like a hydrant, the splash-back hitting Booker's face, making him literally eat pussy. He spat and tried to raise his arms to block the spray, but the wound in his shoulder made one useless.

Laila fell to the floor but Stephanie was in a rage, the stress having snapped her. She continued sawing. Guts popped out through the dead girl's back. Stephanie followed the spine, splitting Laila—all the while screaming and screaming, calling Laila every dirty name Booker knew and then some more. And when she reached the skull the saw struggled against it, so she went for the neck. Laila's severed head spun away. Stephanie punted it into the air. The head landed in the discount bin with the holiday merchandise that had failed to sell. Laila was now *half off*.

The saw rumbled in Stephanie's hands as she stood over the corpse. Booker watched her, waiting for her to come back down to earth. He could only hope her rampage was temporary insanity and she hadn't become just as crazy as the people they'd been fighting all night.

Stephanie turned off the chainsaw and let it swing from one hand. She looked at him with blank eyes. When he hugged her, she hugged back.

"We're the last ones left," she said.

"It's over, Steph. It's over. Let's go home."

"And never come back!"

"You got that right."

They took one last look at the store from the front end. Fresh-way was now *Flesh*way. All was carnage and destruction. Black smoke rolled down the aisles like fog in a John Carpenter movie.

Arm in arm, they leaned on one another for support as they walked through the register lanes to the front of the store, Stephanie dragging the chainsaw with her. Booker wondered if she'd ever feel safe enough to let it go. Through the vestibule, he saw the first pale blue glow of dawn splitting the horizon. Better yet, he heard sirens.

"Everything's gonna be all right Steph."

She put her head on his shoulder. "I'm coming to your house."

"What?"

They stopped. Stephanie put her back to the register and gazed into his eyes. Even slathered in gore, she was beautiful.

"I don't wanna be alone," she said. "I wanna come with you."

Booker took a deep breath. So many times he'd had female employees flirt with him. He'd always stayed professional, not wanting to risk his job for a piece of ass, no matter how young and tender. Well, corporate could take their company policies and shove 'em where the sun don't shine.

He pulled Stephanie to him, her soft body squishing against his. They kissed. The passion was unlike anything he'd ever felt, because both of them were supercharged with the simple thrill of being alive, something you never appreciated until it was almost gone. Their tongues danced and her hands touched his cheeks, pulling him in for more. He moved upon her and they accidentally turned on the register's conveyer belt. They giggled, noses pressed into each other, so overwhelmed by relief they failed to notice the man with the cracked-open skull until he was right on top of them.

~

Desmond flung Booker into the wall.

Framed liquor licenses and national food safety certificates fell to the floor and shattered. Booker pawed for a shard of glass to use as a weapon, but Desmond stomped on his hand and punched the bastard in the face.

"No fraternizing with the staff!" Desmond said. "No matter

how nice them titties!"

Desmond laughed. Booker had opened his skull. Time to return the favor.

When Desmond had come back to his senses, he'd felt the back of his head where the worst of the pain was. His skull was cracked. He was able to put his index finger in there up to the second knuckle, the shards of bone giving way like an eggshell. For all he knew his brain was probably exposed. His lungs were raw with smoke, flesh crispy as bacon, and he limped when he walked. But he still had fire in him—the glorious fire of hell. If nothing else, he was going to see these two die.

He just needed a weapon. Booker had used a goddamned frozen turkey to great effect. Surely there was something Desmond could...

A chainsaw came to life. Desmond gulped. He hadn't realized the blonde bimbo had one. From the position they'd been standing, it had been blocked from his view. The girl stood before him now with a death stare, her bloody breasts jiggling from the vibrations of the saw. The buttons of her jeans were undone and they hung tight to her hips, the slightest bit of yellow pubic hair curling from the top of her low-cut panties. Covered in the gore of multiple people, she looked even hotter to Desmond than ever before.

"Drop the saw, sweet cheeks," he said. "Let's you and me have a little fun. Maybe I can *smooth up in ya.*"

She shook her head. "No dice."

"C'mon...I'll throw your little ass up on this register and give you a ride."

"In your dreams you Freddy Krueger-lookin' motherfucker."

"What's wrong, baby?" he asked, smirking. "No sympathy for the devil?"

Stephanie grimaced. "Pick out any dead body in this place and I'd rather fuck it than you."

Booker lunged for Desmond legs, holding them together. "Now!"

Stephanie swung the saw. Though he tried, Desmond was too weak to break free of Booker's hold, and the steel teeth chewed through the remains of his shirt and into the half-melted flesh beneath. He tore open, pain bursting as his lower intestines were sliced through, one rubbery tube dangling out of his belly like a second dick.

191

Falling away, Desmond braced himself on the register, his torso pressing onto the running conveyer belt.

There was a sudden pinch.

The dangling length of intestine was pulled under the belt.

Desmond stood up straight, trying to get away, but the conveyer was unspooling his guts like a garden hose from a revolving holder. He put both hands on the register, but when he tried to pull away the innards just came out all the faster. Slick guts folded over and under the conveyer belt again and again until it looked to be made entirely of intestines, and when his abdomen was hollowed out his other organs fell into its pit. His stomach and bladder oozed and his blackened lungs fell upon them, starting an all-out avalanche of disembowelment, and when blood filled his eyes Desmond found he was glad to go blind so he didn't have to look at this fucking world any longer.

Fine, he thought. *Hell awaits.*

~

The sirens were getting closer when Todd walked in.

Booker blinked in disbelief, then realized it must be time for the morning shift. He stood beside Stephanie, holding the fatigued girl close as he watched his boss take in his surroundings. Todd's jaw was slack with shock as saw the blood and wreckage, and he winced with disgust when he spotted the pulverized Mila, the gutted Desmond, and Laila's decapitated head in the bargain bin.

But what really made him pale was the sight of the store itself. Demolished displays, damaged goods, tire marks, shattered doors, broken glass, and various assortments of ruin. He looked upon *his store*, his baby, as if he wanted to cry.

He held out his hands, gesturing to the devastation. "What…what the hell, Booker?"

A cold rush went through Booker's blood. He said nothing.

"I leave you alone for one night," Todd said, "and this is what happens? Jesus…is that a fire in the meat department? Look at all these damages! Our repairs are gonna be through the roof! And just imagine the inventory loss. We're never gonna recover from these shrink numbers!"

Stephanie trembled with rage. Booker tried to contain her, but she stepped forward.

"You prick," she said, pointing at Todd. "You miserable little excuse for a man."

Todd scowled but still checked out her bare breasts. "Excuse me, young lady? Remember who you're talking to. I'm the boss!"

She came closer. "You lousy, rotten, shit-eating, dog-fucking, heartless, maggot-headed, midget fuckwad!"

Todd flushed. "That's it, Steph. You're fired!"

"Yeah? Good luck with staffing. Booker and I are the only ones left, little man. They killed *everybody*!"

"Everybody?"

"Yeah, and then we killed them. It was the Freshway grocery store massacre!"

Todd huffed. "And that just adds insult to injury! You know the kind of PR we're gonna need to get anybody to feel safe shopping here after this? Sales will plummet. Dear God, my store will never be the same." He put his hands on his hips and glowered at Booker. "For Christ's sakes, man, what were you thinking when you let all this happen?"

Booker's bones shook. Rage forged from years of his supervisor's disrespect, inconsideration, and downright stupidity all surged into one concentrated jewel of the brightest hatred.

"Well?" Todd asked. "What do you have to say for yourself?"

Booker lunged.

Grabbing Todd around the throat, he began crushing his larynx. Todd's eyes bulged.

"You miserable shit!" Booker said. "Your employees have been torn apart and all you can do is bitch about sales?"

Anger overpowered his exhaustion and he slammed Todd into a wall display of S. Pellegrino, dragging him through it face-first, the bottles exploding as they hit the tile. He flung his boss across the shattered glass like a Frisbee.

Todd trembled. "B-B-Booker…"

"What? Worried about getting the bottle deposits back?"

He kicked Todd in the ribs. Stephanie applauded and cheered him on. When Todd rolled over, Booker stomped his face, breaking his nose. A warm rush of bliss came over Booker then, the pure delight of a just revenge brought to fruition.

He sneered. "You're no manger, Todd. You don't wanna guide people or develop them. You just wanna have power over people so you can feel bigger. Well, you're nothin' but a bully, Todd, using a piddley grocery store job to pretend you're some kind of king." Another kick to the ribs. "But all you really are is a pathetic bully."

"B-B-Booker…"

"That's right. Say my name!" *Stomp*. "This is for taking off every holiday, and making me work them!" *Kick*. "This is for giving yourself a set schedule, but mine changes week by week!" *Punch*. "This is for never thinking of anyone but yourself!" *Crack*. "For never being satisfied with anything we do!" *Crunch*. "For diligently bringing down morale for no good reason!"

A flurry of kicks shot blood and teeth from Todd's face. Booker got on top of him, grabbed Todd's hair, and started bashing his skull into the tile. Stephanie was an ecstatic cheerleader, hopping up and down, looking like a bloody stripper on a trampoline.

"You tell him, Booker!" she said. "Whoop his ass!"

Booker punched Todd with his one good arm, his knuckles crunching against the man's jaw. "This is for Ruby and Mila and Darla and Antonio," he said as he pounded away, "and everybody else who died tonight, all 'cause you wanted this place to look like opening day every day, even though we don't have the staff or the tools!"

As he slammed Todd's face into the floor again and again, Booker gorged on the sweet nectar of payback, a flavor more delicious than any product they sold. Of all the people he'd killed tonight, Todd would be the most deserving. At least the Devil's Food crew was open about how evil they were. Todd was the kind of villain who brutalized anyone in his employ but was chipper and delightful around customers and especially his regional superiors. He was Adolf Hitler in Mr. Rogers' clothing.

"Die, you piece of fly-eaten shit!" Stephanie said, clapping as Booker beat their boss to death.

As Todd's last breaths wheezed through his broken mouth, Booker leaned in close to the fucker, whispering what he'd always wanted to say to him.

"It's just a grocery store, Todd. It's *just a fuckin' grocery store.*"

~

Fire trucks and police cruisers entered the Freshway parking lot, their wails and flickering lights as elating as a carnival. Stephanie held hands with Booker as they came into the foyer. The giant hole left by Desmond's truck was like a portal back to her normal life, away from satanic, rapist, cannibal lunatics; away from the whiny customers, low pay, and shitty hours that came with working at this goddamned store.

She couldn't do retail anymore. No fucking way. She would buckle down and pursue her dream of attending beauty school. Then she would open a salon—run her own business and make her own policies. The hours would be reasonable for everyone. No clopens. All employees would get the holidays off. Best of all, she could do what she loved—tease hair, master the art of makeup, and play Whitesnake all day.

But first she was going to Booker's place to fuck his brains out.

As they stepped out into the cold light of morning, Booker took the chainsaw from her and removed his shirt so she could cover herself up. The last thing Stephanie wanted was some pig seeing her topless. There was no lowlier profession than police officer—except maybe grocery store manager. Todd had been the worst of them all, but she and Booker agreed to weep for him for the cops and the press, telling them Desmond had killed him before they were able to take him down. Oh, how they wished they'd gotten to him a moment sooner. Maybe their beloved store leader would still be with them.

"You know," she said. "You could be the boss now."

Booker laughed. "Fuck that. I'm taking early retirement."

As they stepped across the walkway, she noticed another corpse. Whoever it was wore a leather gimp mask, their body twisted like licorice around the metal garbage can. The flaming pentagram in the lot had mostly died out, but it had caught a car on fire. It blazed against the sky like a roman candle. Stephanie smiled when she realized it was Fenton's. He sure as shit wouldn't be needing it.

Also on fire was the roof of the store. The flames of the collision must have reached the break room upstairs, which didn't have safety sprinklers like the sales floor below. The building was quite the sight, the shattered windows streaked with blood and Mila's remains visible from outside. Booker told her there were more bodies out back too. The arriving lawmen would have seen some of them on the way in.

Two cops hopped out of a cruiser, guns drawn.

"Let go of the girl!" one of them shouted.

Booker and Stephanie looked at one another. Her clothes were bloody and torn, and she had to cover one exposed breast with her hand. Beside her, Booker was shirtless and covered in blood, holding a dripping-red chainsaw. What exactly did these stupid pigs think?

The other cop barked too. "Step away from her and put your hands on your head!"

Booker blinked. "You talkin' to me?"

The cop inched forward, his fat belly as repulsive as his buzz cut. "I'm not gonna tell you again!"

"Hey!" Stephanie said. "Don't—"

"Just relax, little girl. We're here to rescue you."

"But he didn't—"

"Jesus Christ!" Booker said, outraged. "I'm the assistant manager here! You think just 'cause I'm black I killed all these white people?"

"Hands on your head!"

"I can't put my hands on my head, asshole! Look at my—"

Booker gestured to his bad shoulder, too quickly for the officers. When he stepped forward, Stephanie pulled him back...just in time. A single shot went off and when Booker collapsed to the ground, Stephanie thought he'd been hit, but the bullet shattered the glass storefront instead, having just missed him. Stephanie fell on her knees and covered Booker like a blanket.

"You wanna kill him?" she said. "Then you gotta kill a pretty white girl too! See how the press likes *that*!"

One of the policemen stood over them. He lowered his pistol. "Sorry...we just thought..."

"Eat shit!" Stephanie said. "He's the hero here, fuckbrain—not *you*!"

"What were we supposed to think? I mean...he had a chainsaw and...I mean..."

Stephanie and Booker got their feet. The policemen looked at her exposed breast. She eyed the chainsaw and when Booker noticed he steered her away, having read her mind. After what these pigs had almost done, Stephanie wanted nothing more than to carve up some pork chops!

"This girl needs an ambulance," Booker told the cops. "Can you boys handle getting her to one without killing innocent people?"

The officers turned red.

Paramedics arrived and one of the cops placed a consoling hand on Stephanie's shoulder. She shoved it away as if batting a mosquito. The cop flinched but said nothing, and as the paramedics moved in he shrugged and walked away, the look on his face saying: "Kids. What can ya do? They're all nuts."

Stephanie didn't want to let go of Booker's hand. "Don't leave me."

"It's okay. I'll see you at the hospital."

Additional ambulances pulled into the lot. Booker leaned in and kissed her and she went at him passionately, knowing the cops were looking on with slack jaws. When the gurney rolled toward her, Stephanie and Booker looked into each other's eyes and smiled.

"You're pretty tough," he said.

She winked. "And I like it rough."

Stephanie lay back on the gurney, letting the paramedics tend to her. Some wounds she hadn't even noticed until now; little cuts all over her body, bruises, and pieces of glass wedged in her skin. Tears rolled down her cheeks, washing some the blood away, but never the memories of what had put it all there. Above her she saw only sky, all the radiant colors of a new day, her long dark night in Hell having passed. As they rolled her into the ambulance, she turned her head away from the site of the burning wreckage of her former workplace and saw the pristine Devil's Food grocery store just across the street. The image of their little devil mascot winked at her, his pitchfork in one hand and the band of his diaper in the other.

Stephanie gave him the finger. "Get thee behind me, Satan."

EPILOGUE
AN INCARNATION'S DREAM

FROM WITHIN THE HOLE IN the wall, he watched the firemen sift through the remains. The flames were out now, and the lovely little bodies had all been hauled away on stretchers. Corporate people with Freshway pins on their blazers walked through the wreckage with clipboards and cameras, talking about insurance and public relations damage control.

However bad things get, capitalism goes on. What mattered to these soulless corporate swine was getting the store back together, even if it meant a complete overhaul.

Men in suits debated whether they could recoup their losses here or if they should build a new location on the other side of town, away from the scene of the biggest mass murder in state history.

From what Abaddon was hearing, it would be too expensive for them to relocate. Despite the apocalyptic carnage, there was still much to be salvaged.

They could rebuild. They could remarket. They would go on.

Abaddon rubbed his belly and quietly burped, the taste of the dead boy's heart still at the back of his throat. He had to admit,

Freshway had some damn good food.

He dug deeper into the hidden crevice where he'd stored the fat boy's lower body. This would be a good spot to hibernate while the black sperm he'd planted in the corpse's ass could germinate, birthing a new batch of demons like himself, another spawning in the glorious name of Satan.

Abaddon smiled.

He was gonna like it here.

CLOSING TIME

AN AFTERMATH BY RYAN HARDING

Thank you, shoppers, for hanging in there with Freshway through our overnight renovations and the associated "complications." For those of you who have gutted it out, you might be wondering about our soundtrack choices (if not our sanity). Kris addressed it some in the intro, and I'd like to elaborate.

My death metal fascination hadn't begun by 1992. My first encounter would have been in 1994 with Napalm Death's *Death by Manipulation,* listening to a borrowed cassette in a haze following wisdom tooth surgery (and an eventual dry socket—would not recommend). No lyric sheet or real map to understanding what was going on, but it seemed all-too-appropriate given the circumstances. Later that year I picked up Cannibal Corpse's *The Bleeding* after a friend told me I might appreciate its horror/gore attributes. He was correct. I followed along with the lyric sheet to not-so-radio-friendly hits like "The Pickaxe Murders" and "Fucked with a Knife." In time I acquired their first three albums, gradually adjusting to the heaviness, speed, and of course those vocals which alienate so many. I discovered Obituary too, and a friend started loaning me tapes every week, getting me into bands like Macabre, Carcass, Dismember, Suffocation, Terrorizer, Bolt Thrower, Malevolent Creation, Morbid Angel, etc.

In 1995, the beginning of my senior year, I worked in a grocery store, and it was as miserable as Kris said. My primary motivation was to earn money so I could order bootleg horror videos. I was rabid for Italian movies and other Euro horror, which often didn't make it to the USA uncut. One day after school I received several of those movies in the mail from an order…and I couldn't watch any of them because I had to go to work. I probably gave my notice that week, not coincidentally, and I didn't enter the work force again until the following summer. However, I lasted long enough to have experienced the nightmare of Thanksgiving in grocery land. It was preferable to a Devil's Food siege, but just barely.

You've probably seen internet articles about the lasting impact of the music you embrace in formative high school years. There's a lot to be said for that, though death and black metal still resonate for me as much as they did in the mid/late 1990s, beyond the gateway albums. Not to the exclusion of all other music as it was for me back then, but something I continue to follow "religiously," still discovering gems I missed from their time and the continuing exploits.

Kris and I named the chapters in this book after death metal song titles, most of which came from albums released prior to summer of 1992:

"Revocate the Agitator" – Deicide: *Legion* (1991)
"Hating Life" – Grave: *Into the Grave* (1991)
"Revel in Flesh" – Entombed: *Left Hand Path* (1990)
"For They Shall Be Slain" – Unleashed: *Where No Life Dwells* (1991)
"Bleed for the Devil" – Morbid Angel: *Altars of Madness* (1989)
"Butchered at Birth" – Cannibal Corpse: *Butchered at Birth* (1991)
"Sick Bizarre Defaced Creation" – Pungent Stench: *Been Caught Buttering* (1991)
"Blind Bleeding the Blind" – Carcass: *Heartwork* (1993)
"No Forgiveness (Without Bloodshed)" – Immolation: *Dawn of Possession* (1991)
"Prime Evil" – Venom: *Prime Evil* (1989)
"Torn Apart" – Carnage: *Dark Recollections* (1990)
"The Krusher" – Asphyx: *Crush the Cenotaph* and *Last One on Earth*

(1992)
"Instinct of Survival" – Napalm Death: *Scum* (1987)
"This Time It's War" – Bolt Thrower: *The IVth Crusade* (1992)
"Scream Bloody Gore" – Death: *Scream Bloody Gore* (1987)
"Pinnacle of Bedlam" – Suffocation: *Pinnacle of Bedlam* (2013)
"No More Room in Hell" – Possessed: *Revelations of Oblivion* (2019)
"An Incarnation's Dream" – Atheist: *Unquestionable Presence* (1992)

The bands we mentioned recorded other seminal works we didn't always get to refer to by name, and even adding more names from the wardrobes (and fractured psyches) of the Devil's Food faithful, it doesn't scratch the surface of the many death and grind bands active or with legacies already cemented by that era. This underground phenomenon played out globally, not only in places like the US (Repulsion, Brutal Truth, Cynic, Exhumed), England (Unseen Terror, Paradise Lost, Benediction, My Dying Bride) and Sweden (Carbonized, Hypocrisy, Regurgitate, Seance, Merciless, Defleshed), but Canada (Blasphemy, Kataklysm), Brazil (Sarcofago, Krisiun), Finland (Demilich, Amorphis, Disgrace, Xysma), Norway (Darkthrone, Cadaver), Germany (Dead, Eternal Dirge), Italy (Electrocution, Necrodeath), Japan (SOB, Transgressor), Poland (Vader, Lost Soul), Mexico (Cenotaph, Shub Niggurath), France (Agressor, Massacra, Loudblast), the Netherlands (Sinister, Pestilence, Gorefest, God Dethroned), Singapore (Impiety, Death Squad), Australia (Sadistik Exckution, Blood Duster), and many more bands throughout North and South America, Europe, Asia, and Australia. According to Metal Archives, there were over four thousand DM bands from the 1980s through 1992, which only accounts for bands with at least an actual demo or EP. It's an even vaster underground now, with over *forty thousand* bands playing the metal of death since the 1980s.

A few years after I became immersed in the extreme side of metal, I found the extreme side of horror. Dave Barnett's Necro Publications was of profound importance in this regard. Dave published chapbooks and novels by Edward Lee like *Header* and *The Bighead,* Lee's collaborations with John Pelan (*Goon* and *Splatterspunk: The Micah Hays Stories),* and the seminal 3-way novella collab *Inside the Works,* featuring Lee's infamous *The Pig* along with stories from Gerard Houarner and Tom Piccirilli. This was the foundation of the subgenre of extreme horror, from which *The Night Stockers* was born over twenty years later. Kris and I were both saddened to learn of Dave's passing a month before this novel's publication, and consider ourselves lucky to have worked with him. We hope our book keeps the Necro spirit alive…which would be pretty death metal unto itself.

On a lighter note (though involving detuned, heavier notes), I am pleased we received the endorsement of the deranged Jeremy Wagner, guitarist of Broken Hope and author of *The Armageddon Chord* and *Rabid Heart*. It was a pleasure meeting him at KillerCon 2019 after listening to his band for over twenty years, and talking with him about his lyrical classicks from the likes of *The Bowels of Repugnance, Repulsive Conception,* and *Loathing.* Hopefully it goes without saying that Jeremy is the antithesis of the maniacs we've depicted in *The Night Stockers,* as are most with metallic warlust.

As we come to closing time, Kris and I once again wish to thank you for your patronage. If any of you want to grab a mop and pitch in on the clean-up effort, though, we wouldn't say no. As you can see, we're a little short-staffed after our night shift.

Ryan Harding
February 2021

World Downfall, Retribution, Slowly We Rot, Symphonies of Sickness, From Enslavement to Obliteration, Tomb of the Mutilated, Deicide, Blessed are the Sick, Effigy of the Forgotten, Mental Funeral, Realm of Chaos, Leprosy, Like an Everflowing Stream, The Rack, Piece of Time, Onward to Golgotha, just to name a few of many.

For this new edition, Kristopher would like to acknowledge:

Thanks so much to everyone who has read and enjoyed this book in its initial run, helping to make it the winner of the Splatterpunk Award for Best Novel in 2022. Thanks to K Trap Jones for giving this grocery store massacre its first happy home with The Evil Cookie Publishing. Also, appreciations to my good pals along the trail—Aron Beauregard, Daniel J. Volpe, Josh Doherty, Brian Keene, Gregg Kirby, C.V. Hunt, Bryan Smith, Kristopher Rufty, Mona Kabbani, Wile E. Young, Marc Ciccarone, and of course, Ryan Harding. Additional thanks to Edward Lee and Jeremy Wagner.

Thanks to the following bands for warping my young mind: Carcass, Morbid Angel, Deicide, Napalm Death, Cannibal Corpse, Pungent Stench, and obviously, Slayer.

Big thanks to Bear (rest well, my precious baby) and belly rubs to Shadow.

Extra big thanks to the lovely Chandra Claypool.

And special thanks to Tom Mumme—always.

Ryan STILL raises the devil horns to…

Lucas Mangum, Edward Lee, Chandler Morrison, Bryan Smith, Brian Keene, John Wayne Comunale, Jeremy Wagner, Jason Taverner, Christine Morgan, Jeff Burk, Doug Dobbs, Jonathan Butcher, Christina Pfeiffer, C.V. Hunt, Aron Beauregard, Daniel J. Volpe, and Sam Bowling, plus all the headbangers who slaughtered posers in the name of this book, or at least voted for it in the Splatterpunk Awards. Extra hails to Kelly Robinson, Trips, Truman, and the Pawsitivity Crew, and all the sick, blasting death metal that has possessed me in the past 30 years!

A special thank you to Kristopher Triana for sharing all the slicers, dicers, blades, crushers, hooks, etc., with me on this journey of total death. Deluxe 666 membership to K Trap Jones, purveyor of the original Devil's Food (even if he calls it The Evil Cookie) chain release of *The Night Stockers*.

In memory of the late, great Dave Barnett of Necro Publications—writer, publisher, and friend.

KRISTOPHER TRIANA is the multiple Splatterpunk Award-winning author of *Gone to See the River Man, Full Brutal, The Thirteenth Koyote, They All Died Screaming,* and many other terrifying books. His work has been published in six languages and has appeared in many anthologies and magazines, drawing praise from Rue Morgue Magazine, Cemetery Dance, Scream Magazine, and many more. He also writes articles for *Backwoods Survival Guide* and *Prepper Survival Guide.*

He lives in New England.

Get signed books at: TRIANAHORROR.COM

Visit him at: Kristophertriana.com and on Substack, Instagram, Facebook, and TikTok.

RYAN HARDING is the four-time Splatterpunk Award-winning author of books like *Transcendental Mutilation, Genital Grinder,* and collaborations with Jason Taverner (the Agent Orange slasher novels *Reincarange* and *Reincursion*), Kristopher Triana (*The Night Stockers*), Lucas Mangum (*Pandemonium*), and Edward Lee (*Header 3*). His contributed the novella *The Profile* to the anthology *Call Me Hoop* and his short stories have appeared in anthologies such as *Brewtality, The Distended Table, The Big Book of Blasphemy, The New Flesh: A Literary Tribute to David Cronenberg, Splatterpunk Forever, Past Indiscretions, Into Painfreak,* and *The Year's Best Hardcore Horror Vol. 3.* His work has also been published in German, Italian, and Polish. Upcoming projects include a novel with Bryan Smith and the third book in the Agent Orange series.